A Creature in the Moonlight

A sudden flash of white to his right startled Julian from his thoughts. He jumped and raised the lantern higher. Reason dictated it was no ghost but a human trespasser. When he peered around the edge, he was somehow unsurprised to find the scared, pale face of Esmerelda Fortune.

She was, of course, clad in nothing but her nightgown and wrapper. She looked as if she'd just come from her bed, and the image of her lying against rumpled sheets reawakened unwanted feelings in him.

"M-m-my lord." She stumbled over the words but didn't lose her composure. "I can ex-explain."

The heat began below and rose to consume his chest, neck, and cheeks. Her unbound hair fell around her face in a riot of corkscrew curls, making her look like a wild creature caught in the light of the moon. Her pale face flushed a bright pink, and the color lent an attractive sparkle to her eyes. Her mouth, slightly open, caused Julian to swallow as a sudden, fierce desire to claim her lips poured through him. Damn her eyes! And damn him for a fool for this insane attraction. . . .

S0-AGI-735

SIGNET

REGENCY ROMANCE
COMING IN AUGUST 2005

Lady Whilton's Wedding and
An Enchanted Affair
by Barbara Metzger
Two novels of intrigue and romance from "the queen
if the Regency romp" (*Romance Reviews Today*)
together for the first time in one volume.

0-451-21618-0

The Abducted Bride
by Dorothy Mack
All Amy wants is some freedom, but her chaperon
won't leave her side. When she finally escapes, Amy
runs into a man who believes she is his beloved
Desiree. The next thing Amy knows, she is at his
estate, waking from a drugged sleep—and falling for
this enigmatic stranger.

0-451-21619-9

Twin Peril
by Susannah Carleton
The Duke of Fairfax is looking for a wife who will love
him—not his money. Lady Deborah fits the descrip-
tion, but her twin has some tricks to keep the lovers
apart—and keep the Duke for herself.

0-451-21588-5

Available wherever books are sold or at
penguin.com

Her Perfect Earl

Bethany Brooks

A SIGNET BOOK

SIGNET
Published by New American Library, a division of
Penguin Group (USA) Inc., 375 Hudson Street,
New York, New York 10014, USA
Penguin Group (Canada), 10 Alcorn Avenue, Toronto,
Ontario M4V 3B2, Canada (a division of Pearson Penguin Canada Inc.)
Penguin Books Ltd., 80 Strand, London WC2R 0RL, England
Penguin Ireland, 25 St. Stephen's Green, Dublin 2,
Ireland (a division of Penguin Books Ltd.)
Penguin Group (Australia), 250 Camberwell Road, Camberwell, Victoria 3124,
Australia (a division of Pearson Australia Group Pty. Ltd.)
Penguin Books India Pvt. Ltd., 11 Community Centre, Panchsheel Park,
New Delhi - 110 017, India
Penguin Group (NZ), cnr Airborne and Rosedale Roads, Albany,
Auckland 1310, New Zealand (a division of Pearson New Zealand Ltd.)
Penguin Books (South Africa) (Pty.) Ltd., 24 Sturdee Avenue,
Rosebank, Johannesburg 2196, South Africa

Penguin Books Ltd., Registered Offices:
80 Strand, London WC2R 0RL, England

First published by Signet, an imprint of New American Library,
a division of Penguin Group (USA) Inc.

First Printing, July 2005
10 9 8 7 6 5 4 3 2 1

Copyright © Beth Pattillo, 2005
All rights reserved

 REGISTERED TRADEMARK—MARCA REGISTRADA

Printed in the United States of America

Without limiting the rights under copyright reserved above, no part of this
publication may be reproduced, stored in or introduced into a retrieval sys-
tem, or transmitted, in any form, or by any means (electronic, mechanical,
photocopying, recording, or otherwise), without the prior written permission
of both the copyright owner and the above publisher of this book.

PUBLISHER'S NOTE
This is a work of fiction. Names, characters, places, and incidents either are
the product of the author's imagination or are used fictitiously, and any resemblance to actual persons, living or dead, business establishments, events, or
locales is entirely coincidental.

If you purchased this book without a cover you should be aware that this
book is stolen property. It was reported as "unsold and destroyed" to the
publisher and neither the author nor the publisher has received any payment
for this "stripped book."

The scanning, uploading, and distribution of this book via the Internet or via
any other means without the permission of the publisher is illegal and punish-
able by law. Please purchase only authorized electronic editions, and do not
participate in or encourage electronic piracy of copyrighted materials. Your
support of the author's rights is appreciated.

*For my friends
from the Oxford Experience,
with thanks*

Chapter One

England, 1822

"Women. A great lot of trouble and not worth 'alf the bother!"

The coachman's roar threatened his perch atop the carriage, but Esmerelda Fortune ignored his thunderous objections. She could not come so close to the manor house—*her* manor house—without stopping. A man would desire to see his property if he passed through the neighborhood where it was situated. She was no different simply because she was female.

With a growl, the Earl of Ashforth's coachman turned the carriage off the main road and down the rough lane. Ignoring decorum, Esmie half hung out the window, eager to take in the smallest details. The verdant shades of June shimmered in the unkempt hedgerows. Spikes of ragwort and prickly thistles flourished amongst the gravel of the short drive, but the slender, silver beech trees along the lane stood guard as vigilantly as ever. Esmie waited, breath held, until the house came into view. A lump rose in her throat.

To anyone else's eyes, the modest manor house covered in ivy and soot might appear a poor dowager whose jointure had long run out. To Esmie, the damp, crumbling house was everything. Here, tucked away across the River Isis from the spires of Oxford, lay the means for establishing her own school.

The coachman pulled the horses to a stop in the overgrown drive, and Esmie scrambled from the carriage.

"Five minutes," he barked. "The earl don't tolerate tardiness."

Esmie flung open the door and jumped to the ground. The Earl of Ashforth could wait another quarter hour for his carriage, especially when she had waited months for this moment.

Her steps slowed as she approached the house, and a fierce sense of possession spread through her, thick as honey. Here she was at last. Home.

The ancient oaken door of the manor house had been placed askew in the façade, flanked on either side by irregular, mullioned windows that gave the house a topsy-turvy appearance. To Esmie, though, it was as good as a palace. With trembling fingers, she fished the key from her reticule. She had worn the metal surface dull from much handling, and it almost slipped from her fingers. Often, at night, she rubbed it for luck and dreamed of her future in this place, when she might escape her life of service and call her days her own.

The rusty lock proved a bit of a challenge, but Esmie would not be denied. After some impatient jiggling, she coaxed the door open and stepped into the cool air of the foyer.

Relief flooded her, and her heart returned to its normal rhythm as her eyes traveled over every feature. Nothing had changed, save that the faded green wallpaper showed even darker streaks from the damp and mold. Almost forgetting to breathe, she crossed the tiled floor and opened the drawing room door. Here, the bits of furniture her mother had not sold out from under her had grown more faded under the strong effects of sun through the curtainless windows. For the first time her spirits drooped at the visible price of neglect. Time was growing short. The house could not stand inattention much longer and be restored to its former state.

One by one, Esmie moved through the familiar rooms, as if by stepping foot in each of them she could assure herself they still waited for her to make this her permanent home. Drawing room, morning room, dining room—all lay empty, the plaster moldings and mantelpieces covered in dust. Upstairs, the six bedrooms remained undisturbed except for the scratching of mice within the walls.

Esmie leaned against a door frame and allowed herself to indulge her fancy. She pictured the bedchambers filled with serious young students who would sleep soundly after a day of vigorous study. The drawing room would serve as a schoolroom. In the evenings, in the oak-paneled dining room, they would eat their simple fare, for that would be all she could afford. But someday. . . . She had heard tales of the sumptuous dinners served in the halls of the Oxford colleges. One day her students, too, would feast on beef and turtle soup with as much enthusiasm as they feasted on Greek, Latin, and logic.

She trailed her fingers along the rickety banister as she returned to the ground floor. At the rear of the house, the medieval kitchen showed the worst signs of neglect, but beyond the door, the overgrown foxgloves still bloomed, and a few hardy asparagus pushed up through the tangle of the kitchen garden. Esmie stepped outside into the little haven before her and walked to the quince tree that grew in the corner beside the dissolute stone wall. Honeysuckle spilled over the top, filling the air with thick perfume. In the quince tree, the buds of the hard fruit hung thick on the branches. By fall, there would be a good harvest and a great quantity of jelly to be made.

Anxiety clogged her throat. Would she be here in the autumn to collect the fruit? To establish a credible school, two things were necessary: money and a reputation as a scholar. Unfortunately, she had neither, but she did have a plan to procure both. Then the young women in her mind's eye would no longer be figments of her imagination but flesh and blood students, books in hand, ink stained and hardworking and happy. She, Esmie Fortune, would be headmistress of a school for girls, but not a frivolous seminary that eschewed the mind and taught only drawing, dancing, and the pianoforte. No, in her school, there would not be an embroidery hoop to be found. The netting of purses would be banned, and no bonnets would be retrimmed. Instead, Homer, Ovid, and Plato would carry the day, and her students would be as proficient in the classics as any young man in the kingdom.

Esmie closed her eyes. No small wonder she'd never dared to mention a word of her dream to anyone, just as she seldom spoke of her own knowledge of the classics and ancient languages. Social disparagement occurred with sufficient abundance in her life that she had no need to cultivate it. Only her stepfather had known, for he had been her teacher. Her quick mind had amused him, and their quiet hours in his library had meant everything to her. Esmie had basked in the novelty of his attention. Knowing her dream, he had left her this house, but as a result of her mother's expensive habits, he had been unable to leave her the necessary funds for its upkeep.

With a sigh, Esmie sank down onto the little bench carved into the wall and let the warm sun wash over her. A breeze stirred the honeysuckle. A plaintive mewing caused Esmie to open her eyes. Not two feet from her, a stray cat emerged through a fissure in the wall. With its torn ear and mangy fur, the animal looked as piteous as the house. Esmie felt an instant affinity with the creature.

"Good day, cat," she called, pleased to have a bit of company more congenial than the earl's coachman.

The cat jumped at the sound of her voice, but didn't bolt. Instead, it strolled toward her and paused to sniff the hem of her skirt. Esmie reached out to stroke the patchy fur and the prominent ribs. The cat meowed again, hungrily.

"I'm afraid the cupboard here is bare." However, she'd left the remains of her luncheon from the inn at Reading wrapped in a napkin in the carriage. Perhaps that would suffice. "No cook here to slip you the odd bit, hmm?" She reached down and scratched the cat behind its ears. The creature emitted a loud purr of satisfaction.

"Like that, do you?" She could hardly leave the animal here to starve. Surely the Earl of Ashforth's stables could use another mouser. "Come along and I'll feed you." She scooped the cat up in her arms.

With a last fond glance at the garden, she made her

way through the house. Reluctantly, she locked the front door and returned the key to her reticule. John Coachman lurked by the carriage, scowling.

"'Twas more than five minutes," he growled. Esmie turned a deaf ear and instead waited for him to assist her into the carriage. The coachman frowned and made no move to open the door. "No cat, miss. Absolutely not."

"I only thought to give him a bite to eat."

"No cats in the earl's carriage." He opened the door but made no move to hand her in.

"Why ever not?"

"Because the earl wishes it."

And the Earl of Ashforth, that paragon of perfection, was always granted whatever he wished. Esmie had little doubt of that.

The horses stirred forward several paces. When the coachman turned to reassure his team, Esmie seized the opportunity to climb into the carriage, cat and all. She stuffed the poor animal into her bandbox, where it might easily find the bread and cheese. The cat cried out, but then, discovering the food, fell silent.

The coachman returned and looked suspiciously into the carriage, searching for the cat. Esmie pasted an innocent look on her features; seeing no sign of the contraband, the coachman growled, spun on his heel, and climbed to his perch. Esmie smiled with satisfaction at thwarting the man. He had tyrannized her since he'd collected her in London and was due his comeuppance. She doubted the earl himself would exhibit half the condescension and contempt his servant displayed. Whatever the earl's feelings might be about cats, she could hardly leave the poor animal to its fate here at . . . She faltered. The house's true name was Cortland Manor, but in her dreams she called it Athena Hall. Named for the goddess of wisdom, of course. The first school of its kind, or it would be, as soon as she won the prize of the Classics Society. And used the prize money to put the house to rights and hire tutors. And found students. And . . .

Well, first things first. Today, she must travel to Ashforth Abbey to serve as governess to the earl's children.

While she was there, it should be a simple matter to discover if the paragon earl did indeed possess the *Life of Corinna,* a rare manuscript she needed to complete her compendium on noble Greek and Roman women. She had only two weeks before she must submit her work to the Society for its prestigious competition, and any new information about the celebrated ancient Greek poetess would only add to the importance of her scholarship. Once she submitted her work, the Society could not help but honor what she had achieved. Satisfaction filled Esmie. It had taken three years of late nights, cramped fingers, and tired, bleary eyes, but now her efforts would receive their due.

Esmie settled back into the plush squabs of the Earl of Ashforth's carriage. The earl himself, the man who had spurned her every effort at scholarship, was to be the means of her triumph, a fact that suited her sense of irony. She enjoyed a particular warmth whenever she imagined the earl's reputedly handsome face, stunned at the depth of her learning. There would be a gleam of respect in his eye, and no more of those vile, patronizing letters.

An hour later, Ashforth Abbey appeared at the end of a much longer drive than the one that led to her little manor house. Once more, Esmie leaned out the window for a better view, and what she saw robbed her of breath.

Ashforth Abbey nestled in a bowl of green, surrounded by woodlands, lakes, and vistas in a panorama of nature too perfect not to have been sculpted by human hands. The house itself was not an abbey at all, though a priory had been pulled down to make way for the current structure. No, instead of the Gothic arches, pitched roof, and layers of dirt found on her medieval manor, golden Cotswold stone rose three stories high in plain Palladian fashion, the center pediment above the main door supported by six massive columns. She knew from her reading that each story of Ashforth Abbey bore the stamp of one of the three classical orders— Doric below, Ionic in the middle, and Corinthian at the top. An Italianate balustrade ran across the highest story from which, fittingly, busts of several Roman emperors scowled down. Esmie swallowed hard, certain they directed their displeasure entirely at her, an imperfect interloper in this carefully cultivated paradise of perfection.

What ever had possessed her to think she might outwit the earl in his impeccable lair? The doubts and fears she'd suppressed in pursuit of her goal broke free. She could hear her mother's voice admonishing her to stand straighter, to sparkle more brightly. Esmie knew she had no claims to beauty or birth. Intelligence was her one asset. Would it be enough to achieve her goal?

The carriage rolled to a stop on the gravel drive where not a weed could be seen, and Esmie clutched her bandbox until a footman appeared. She prayed the cat would keep its peace long enough for her to smuggle him to the stables. The footman offered no greeting, but merely opened the door of the coach and handed her down.

She had never been so overwhelmed in her life, faced with the wide marble steps that led to the Abbey's massive double doors. She glanced about for some sign that her arrival had been marked, but the footman disappeared with her trunk, and no one else appeared to welcome her. In truth, the house lay oddly quiet.

Esmie mounted the steps as if approaching a holy shrine. An ominous teakwood door stood partially open. Heart aquiver in her breast, she gave it a gentle push and slipped inside.

To her surprise, the great hall was as empty as the yard. She steeled her jaw to prevent it from going slack with wonder at the majestic proportions of the room. Overcome, she twirled on her heel as she took in the massive medieval tapestry, the burnished, oak-paneled walls and the vast fireplace. She crossed the parquet floor, her steps echoing up to the elegant fan vaults of the ceiling. She had seen cathedrals that paled in comparison to this.

For several long moments she lingered awkwardly in the midst of the hall, but still no one appeared. A door at the far end of the room opened onto a corridor lined with French windows that overlooked a central courtyard. And there, at last, Esmie saw servants—in fact, she saw a great many servants, all clustered in the middle of the courtyard and looking toward heaven as if they expected a god to descend from Mount Olympus. Esmie's discomfort faded and she moved forward, intrigued by the curious sight.

One of the French windows had been left ajar, and so Esmie slipped through it and onto the neatly manicured path that wound its way through the courtyard. She looked up, curious to see what so captivated everyone—and gasped in horror when she saw a girl of five or so perched on the flat edge of the roof high above. Her little half-boots slapped against the warm stone as she contemplated the anxious knot of people below.

"Lady Caroline," a man's voice cajoled. "Pray come down, Lady Caroline."

The little girl pouted, not just with her lips but with her slumped shoulders and tangled blond curls as well. "No."

The staff groaned in one accord, and Esmie, her panic receding, guessed it was not the first time Lady Caroline had taken up this perch. She wondered where the other children could be, for the employment agent had particularly stressed the earl had *five* very difficult offspring. No doubt the other children were accustomed to such displays, and hadn't bothered to emerge for the drama. Esmie could not fault them. After hearing that the earl's children had run off three governesses since Christmas, she herself would never have agreed to come within ten miles of Ashforth Abbey if it had not been for the lure of the *Corinna* manuscript.

An older woman, the large ring of keys dangling from her waist identifying her as the housekeeper, stepped forward from the group and raised a bony finger toward the child. "I will summon your father, my lady, if you do not come down this instant."

Esmie rolled her eyes at the thought of the perfect earl called to such a scene. She had no doubt he would lift his quizzing glass, survey the situation through its superfluous lens, and give the child the cut direct.

A faint mewing from her bandbox inspired her. Unfastening the lid, she pulled out the mangy cat and lifted it against her shoulder, cradling it as a mother would an infant. The cat hissed in protest and its sharp claws dug into Esmie's traveling gown, but the ham-handed weaving of the garment protected her.

"Meow!" the cat protested loudly.

"Cat!" shrieked the little girl, and Esmie looked up to see a whirl of skirts as Lady Caroline scrambled back from the edge of the roof. "Cat!" the child trilled in delight, and then disappeared from sight.

"Cat!" screeched the housekeeper as she hurried toward Esmie, her eyes wide with horror, and her keys jangling with each step.

"Cat!" screamed the girl a moment later when she reappeared. She ran headlong through the open French window and skidded to a stop in front of Esmie. The little girl glowed with triumph. "My cat!"

Esmie stroked the cat. "Do you like him?" Gaining the upper hand with this one would require only the liberal application of a bundle of questionable fur.

"No cats. Absolutely no cats." The housekeeper jangled to a stop in front of Esmie, her thin cheeks pinched and hollow. "The creature must be gotten rid of. Immediately!"

Lady Caroline shrieked in protest.

"Gotten rid of?" Esmie rounded her mouth into a little "O" of shock. She would not surrender such an advantage to her new charge so easily. "Not my precious . . . my precious . . ." She'd have to invent a name. Surely the cat wouldn't know the difference. "Not my precious . . . Plutarch!"

"Plutarch!" This exclamation came from a new quarter. Esmie turned to see a dark-haired boy of about twelve striding across the courtyard. He was perfectly turned out in coat and cravat. No doubt this was the paragon earl's heir.

The boy curled his lip in a most unattractive fashion as he regarded the cat. "Only a woman would so debase the name of a great historian. And that is the most worthless beast I've ever seen."

Esmie tried to summon the appropriate indignation, but it proved difficult when she quite agreed with the unpleasant boy.

"Plutarch, like his namesake, has qualities of which the majority of the world remains unaware." Esmie sniffed and met the boy's contemptuous gaze. So he fancied himself a scholar of the classics? He would find her a worthy opponent, and her intuition told her that was exactly what he sought.

"What would you know of Plutarch?" the boy sneered. "*If* you have read him at all, I would wager 'twas only in translation."

Esmie bristled at the affront to her intelligence. "Dryden's translation is quite fine and will, I wager, be the definitive one for many years to come."

"Hah!" The boy's dark eyes gleamed with triumph. "Then you have not read him in the Greek? But, of course, you are only a *female*."

Even the five-year-old hellion understood her brother's insult to womankind. Lady Caroline darted forward and kicked him in the shin. The boy jumped back, yowling in pain; the sound so scared the cat that it leapt from Esmie's arms and darted into the house through the open French window.

"Cat!" shrieked the housekeeper.

"My cat!" shrieked Lady Caroline, and took to her heels after the beast. The tangle of servants moved as one, streaming into the house after the little girl. Even the boy followed, keen to witness what would be a prodigious chase. In the pandemonium, Esmie didn't notice the Earl of Ashforth enter the courtyard until he spoke.

"Who in the name of Jupiter are you?"

Esmie whirled. Her heart leapt to her throat, and pure physical attraction crashed over her as if the very stones of the house had tumbled in. For there *he* stood, as perfect, as proud, and as distressingly handsome as she'd expected.

He stood tall, of course, but not too tall. His dark, wavy hair might have belonged to the very Brutus of antiquity, from whom its arrangement derived its name. His nose, likewise, reflected the shape one might find embossed upon an ancient Roman coin. The only parts of his appearance that prevented him from being taken for a Caesar were the well-tailored coat of Bath superfine, buff-colored pantaloons, and shiny top boots that glistened like mahogany in the sunlight. His high, starched shirt points remained crisp despite the warm June sun.

Now her charade must begin in earnest. Never in her life had she been more aware of her physical imperfections. She could all but feel every frizzy curl, every lack of feminine curve, every irregularity of her features. Esmie swallowed the lump in her throat, straightened her spine, and looked the earl in the eye. "I am the new governess, my lord."

Chapter Two

*J*ulian Armstong, Lord Ashforth, stifled a groan. Governess, indeed! But who else could such a creature be? He raised his quizzing glass and surveyed her more closely. Skin and bones, flyaway hair the color of a dormouse, a sour expression upon her pinched features. Her one redeeming quality lay in a pair of fine gray eyes.

"So? Who in the name of the gods are you?" The harsh repetition of his question didn't cow the chit. Her chin rose, but fell just short of actual defiance. He was accustomed to servants quaking under his regard, but this upstart of a girl showed no sign of knocking knees or a trembling lower lip.

She smiled with forced pleasantness. "I believe you demanded to know who I was in the name of Jupiter. Perhaps, my lord, you should determine which deity you mean to invoke, and do so consistently."

Her manner insured he could only stare at her in return. To make matters worse, the girl stared right back with her clear, gray eyes until he dropped his gaze. He! The Earl of Ashforth! It was not to be borne. But bear it he must, for he had no choice. He must have a governess.

"Mrs. Hazelwood says you come well recommended, ma'am."

"You are known for your standard of perfection, my lord. I will not disappoint." The girl's plain speaking startled him, and even she appeared uneasy for a moment at her boldness. The earl lifted one dark eyebrow. She must be fully acquainted with his children's reputation, or perhaps Mrs. Hazelwood had forced her into coming. But the girl would not escape so easily. Someone must take the children in hand, for they held the power to ruin the delicate negotiations ahead. The Earl of Ashforth was to acquire a new countess—one whose dowry would keep this temple of perfection standing for another generation. He had no intention of allowing this poor excuse for a governess—or his gaggle of children— to keep him from his duty.

He dropped his quizzing glass, and it swung harmlessly from its ribbon. "You are called by what name?"

She blushed. "Miss Fortune, my lord. Miss Esmerelda Fortune."

The earl prevented himself from rubbing his temples with thumb and forefinger. His fingers closed around his quizzing glass instead, but his reply, which he did not mean to speak aloud, slipped from his lips. "How appropriate."

Her blush faded, and something like hurt crept into her eyes. The girl straightened her spine and looked him in the eye. "I will not relinquish my cat, my lord."

Ah, so she had introduced the creature into his household. "Miss Fortune—" He paused to swallow an ironic laugh. "I shall make you a bargain." Indeed he would, for he excelled at bargains. Heaven knew he had made enough of them with his late wife. He cleared his throat. "Since Christmas, no governess has managed to retain this post for more than two months. If you can manage to outlast that mark—let us say three months?—I shall reward you quite handsomely. One thousand pounds for each month of service." A veritable fortune, enough to insure the problematic Miss Fortune's independence, but it would be money well spent. Within that space of time, the marriage contract would be drawn up and his new bride wedded and bedded. Then the new countess could attend to the problem of keeping a governess.

Miss Fortune, it seemed, was his last hope. How fitting. "Do you agree to my terms?"

"Oh, yes." The triumphant light that shone in her eyes fed a niggle of doubt, but he ignored the feeling, just as he ignored most of his feelings.

"Your duties begin immediately. You may start by

locating your cat. I have a particular abhorrence for cats, and if I find him first, I will have him drowned in the river." He never would, of course, but she couldn't know that. To own the truth, he rather liked cats, with their imperious natures, but they must be admired from a distance. Their dander caused him to gasp and hack in a most undignified manner.

The governess looked at him to verify the truth of his words, and he refused to move so much as an eyelash. An undercurrent of rebellion flowed through his newest employee, but he should have no trouble keeping it in check. After all, he was master here, and the more quickly she could be brought to heel, the easier the next three months would be for both of them. Three thousand pounds should buy him the docility of a saint.

"Agreed, then, my lord." Without another word, the girl spun on her heel and returned to the house, leaving him to wonder whether he'd just made a good bargain for himself . . . or sold his soul to a gaunt, gray-eyed chit who might very well be more than she seemed.

Well, little could be done now. In for a penny, in for a pound—or three thousand pounds, in this instance. He turned on his own heel and crossed the courtyard to enter the house by another door, intent on placing himself as far from the cat, his children, and Miss Fortune as he possibly could.

Esmie's shoulders slumped with relief as she wandered a long hallway lined with grim portraits of the Earl of Ashforth's ancestors. Her knees quaked beneath her traveling costume as she bit her lower lip to keep it from trembling. She had seen the perfect earl and had held her own. Her name had meant nothing to him, of course, and he had not connected her with the scholarly essays he so easily repudiated. But she had stood before him, near enough to reach out and lay a hand upon his sleeve, and though he found her sorely lacking, she could no more have prevented her heart pounding in her chest than she could have burned her copy of Plutarch. He was arrogant and proud and far above her touch, but her body had leapt to life in his presence, drat the man.

Esmie sighed and sat down on the bottom step of the

nearest staircase. How odd to be attracted to a man she
despised. Better not to think of it. Best to go about her
duties and ignore the earl. She would not be one of those
ridiculous women who fell prey to attraction any more
than she would paint a pair of table screens or net a purse.

Almost as shocking as her response to him had been his
offer. Three thousand pounds. Once she won the prize and
her identity was revealed, he would not want her to remain
at Ashforth Abbey, but honor would dictate he meet the
terms of their agreement if he dismissed her. Three thousand pounds would do a great deal of good at Athena Hall.
She would think of the money and of the rare manuscript
somewhere beneath this magnificent roof, and not give another moment of her thoughts to the earl.

The long corridor beneath her feet boasted an expensive carpet, in stark contrast to her worn half-boots that
rested against it. So far she had seen no sign of the cat,
and she had lost her way as well. And then she saw
herself in the tall mirror that hung opposite where she
sat. If she were more inclined to weep, the sight would
be enough to induce sorrow. Not loud, obvious weeping,
but slow, silent tears. She tried to look at her reflection
dispassionately, to see herself as the earl had just seen
her. It was not an encouraging exercise. Why, oh why,
couldn't she possess even one small claim to beauty, so
men would look at her with respect instead of contempt?
A jabbing pain knotted her midsection.

She would never be lovely, she knew that. She turned
her head first one way, then the other, exposing the
sharp line of her jaw. At her best, with the help of her
mother's maid during the London season, she had been
only presentable. She was too thin, and had no bosom
to speak of. Indeed, she resembled the sharp edge of a
knife, and was about as comely as one.

A few tears did make their way to her eyes then and
down, where they dotted the dark cloth of her cheap
traveling costume. There, lost in the long hallways of
Ashforth Abbey, disturbed to the depth of her soul by
the earl's disapprobation, the despair she held at bay
with Homer and Aristophanes and Virgil escaped its
containment. It had all been too much. The coachman.
The cat. The earl. The prospect of managing five unruly

children, finding the *Corinna,* and completing her own scholarship as well. Esmie laid her head against the banister and indulged her lower nature.

"Sh! She's crying, you oaf. Don't disturb her."

The childish voice pulled Esmie from her dismals, and she looked up to find two pair of bright blue eyes regarding her with curiosity. The eyes belonged to a boy and a girl of about eight years old, the two faces mirror images beneath their identical shocks of bright red hair.

The boy reached into his pocket, pulled out a dirt-streaked handkerchief and thrust it at Esmie. "Here, miss."

Esmie looked at the handkerchief and then at the boy.

"Take it," the boy insisted. "I have others." He tucked the handkerchief into her hand. Esmie regarded the crumpled square of linen dubiously.

The little girl wrinkled her nose, and the freckles that dusted it danced. "Now, miss, don't take on. We're not such a bad lot. If we like you, we can be quite helpful. 'Twas only that we didn't care for the way we were treated before."

"Before?" Esmie echoed, confused.

"By the last three governesses," the child answered patiently, as if she were the adult and Esmie her charge.

Esmie sat up and started to wipe her eyes with the disreputable handkerchief before she caught herself and dropped her hands to her lap. "And you are?"

"Phillip and Phoebe, miss," they answered in unison.

Twins, of course. She hadn't known there were twins. "Well, Phillip and Phoebe, I am Miss Fortune."

"Sorry?" The boy looked puzzled, and stuck a finger in his ear, as if to clear it.

"You heard correctly. I am Miss Esmerelda Fortune, and given my rather unfortunate surname, I give you leave to call me Miss Esmie."

The twins' indistinguishable looks of astonishment were a wonder of nature. Amazing that despite the difference in their gender, two individuals could appear so similar.

"Call you Miss Esmie? Really?" Phillip looked both appalled and intrigued at the suggested liberty. And then, after a moment's hesitation, "The earl won't like it."

The earl? His children referred to him as "the earl"?

"His lordship will no doubt agree that given the harsh realities of my name, Miss Esmie is best for all concerned."

The twins looked skeptical.

Esmie rose from the steps. The moment for self-pity had passed, and as she had learned so many times before, she must play the hand she'd been dealt.

"Have you by any chance seen my cat?" she asked the twins, and both their heads snapped up.

"Cat?" they repeated with enthusiastic, questioning smiles.

"Yes, my cat. Plutarch. He's run off, and I've been searching for him. Perhaps you might assist me?"

"Cat!" they shrieked as one, and with a sharp whirl, they raced off down the hall as they screamed with delight. "Cat!"

Esmie watched them flee in search of the misbegotten creature as she clutched the filthy, if kindly meant, handkerchief. Her heart still ached, but perhaps not quite so much as before.

In the great hall, Esmie found the housekeeper, whose keys still jingled with each step as she paced before the empty fireplace. The older woman's head snapped round, and her fierce, dark eyes fixed on Esmie.

"There you are. Have you not found that godforsaken creature?"

Esmie bristled. "No. But he will emerge presently, when his stomach begins to growl. I expect you'd best warn the cook to be on the lookout in the kitchens."

The housekeeper sniffed. "Warn that Frenchman? I think not. The man screams like a fishwife if I so much as step foot in his domain. No, I will let him discover the intruder for himself. Perhaps he will put him in a fricassee."

Esmie decided that the wisest course was to hold her tongue. The housekeeper recovered herself and fixed her eyes upon Esmie once more.

"I will show you to your room in the nursery. You must be within easy reach of the children."

Esmie stifled a groan. She would much rather be at

the opposite end of the house. The manuscript likely lay somewhere nearer to the earl's apartments than in the vicinity of the nursery.

"I'm sure it will suit me very well," Esmie lied.

She followed the housekeeper up several flights of steps and down three hallways—none of which looked familiar, even after her ramble through the house in search of the cat. Belatedly, she wished she'd saved the breadcrumbs she'd fed to the beast. She could have used a trail to follow when it came time to reverse her course.

The suite of rooms designated for the nursery was situated on the top floor, overlooking the courtyard. It must be from here that little Lady Caroline had found her way to the roof. The open doorway led into a large schoolroom that contained several low tables and chairs, as well as a prodigious amount of charts, maps, and precious, wonderful books. The sight of such riches helped restore some of Esmie's sangfroid. An abacus and a large atlas lay on the window seat. Strangely, Esmie saw no toys. Perhaps the children kept them in their bedchambers, which the housekeeper indicated opened off the schoolroom. The portly woman paused at the last door and opened it as she motioned for Esmie to enter.

"This will be yours."

Spartan would have been too kind a word for the little cell the housekeeper revealed. A narrow bed. A small table with a basin and pitcher. A lantern. Some pegs along the wall. But no chair, no wardrobe, no concession to comfort could be found anywhere, certainly not a small fireplace or even a brazier. The low ceiling slanted toward a window so tiny even sunshine was denied entrance to the room.

Her trunk had been tucked into a corner. The housekeeper gestured towards it. "You'll want to unpack. The children have their tea at five o'clock. You will supervise them."

Supervise? Tea? Why should five children need any help consuming their share of toast and jam?

The housekeeper waved a dismissive hand. "I shall leave you to unpack."

The woman departed in a swish of bombazine. With a sigh, Esmie lowered herself to the floor beside her trunk and fished the key from her reticule. She opened the lid and removed the meager contents. Two serviceable brown day dresses and a morose gray sarcenet, should she ever be called downstairs in the evening. "The requisite gowns for a governess," her mother had said as she removed Esmie's other clothing from the wardrobe. The prettier dresses that had seen Esmie through two London seasons, modest as they were, had been sold to help shore up the household ledger. Esmie's throat tightened at the thought of the small amount of muslin and satin that had once been hers.

No point, however, in regrets. Esmie hung her gowns and pelisse on the pegs and placed her comb and hairbrush beside the basin. There was no place for her books, so she left them in the trunk and lowered the lid.

A noise from the doorway startled her, and she turned to see a girl of ten or so standing there. She had dark hair and eyes and a smooth, olive complexion. Esmie wondered what the earl's wife had looked like, for the children seemed to possess different sets of physical characteristics.

"Hello," Esmie offered. Something about the tight set of the girl's lips made her wary.

"You should return those things to your trunk." The girl said the words in a matter of fact tone that belied their rudeness. "You're not wanted."

Esmie rose to her feet. "Your father thinks I am needed."

The girl leaned against the door frame and rolled her eyes. "No one here wants you."

Esmie had not expected open hostility, but perhaps such feelings reflected the rapid succession of governesses the children had experienced. Or perhaps it was the other way around, and the hostility was the reason for the quick departure of Esmie's predecessors.

"Since I am in the earl's employ, not yours, I believe I shall let his wishes be my guide."

With a snort, the girl rolled her eyes. "Is it just the money, then? I shall pay you to go away."

"Pay me?" The chit's boldness astonished her. "I see. What sum of money would you be offering, then?"

"Five pounds."

Esmie almost laughed. "Yes, well, while that is an interesting proposition, I am in your father's employ."

"He's not my father!" The girl's cheeks reddened. "Don't say that again!"

Esmie frowned. Perhaps this girl was a poor relation. The thought roused a fair measure of sympathy in Esmie's breast. "I'm sorry. I thought you were one of the earl's children."

The girl's lower lip quivered before she bit down on it, hard. Esmie winced in sympathy.

"I have no father." The girl's eyes glittered. "I'm an orphan." At that moment, the older boy, the heir who had insulted Esmie's intelligence, appeared in the doorway.

"Sophie!" the boy scolded. "The earl warned you not to spread such Banbury tales." He looked at Esmie. "Ignore her, miss. This is my sister, Sophia, and the Earl of Ashforth is indeed her father, just as he is mine." He bowed formally, apparently all the apology she would receive for his earlier rudeness. "I am Viscount Stanleigh."

The girl's face fell and she stomped her foot. "He's not my father, James. He's not!" She whirled and raced past him through the schoolroom.

Esmie was too disconcerted to offer any comment. The young Viscount Stanleigh dismissed his sister with an imperious wave of the hand he no doubt copied from the earl.

"Pay no attention to Sophie's flights of fancy. She is just being disagreeable." He paused, his eyes troubled. "The twins say you have given them leave to call you Miss Esmie."

Esmie nodded.

The boy looked as grave as if he attended a funeral service. "My sympathies, miss, on your unfortunate . . ." He blushed. "On your name." With that, he turned on his heel and left Esmie standing in the middle of her barren chamber, fully aware why the last three governesses had fled. She, however, could not afford the luxury of a hasty departure. Jaw set, she followed the boy into the schoolroom to supervise the tea and cakes that would soon arrive.

Chapter Three

*T*hat evening, Esmie sat alone in her bedchamber. The lantern burned softly and Plutarch's *Lives of the Noble Greeks and Romans* lay heavily in her lap. She had played the coward and retreated to her room after supervising the bedlam of nursery tea. The old nurse had seen the children to bed an hour earlier. Quiet blanketed the most perfect home in England, but the dead silence did not soothe Esmie's anxiety or stem her thoughts of the earl.

She caressed the spine of the volume in her lap as she recalled their meeting in the courtyard. A mixture of shame and anger lodged in her throat. Why must the very sight of him cause her whole body to tremble with awareness? His conceit should detract from his allure. His condescension ought to set her nerves on edge, but one glimpse of the earl had sent her stomach into spasms. Golden warmth had spread from her knotted midsection outward into every corner of her being. Her wayward imagination, drat its imprudence, needed no prompting to conjure the daydream of the earl sweeping her into his arms. Well, perhaps not sweeping, exactly. The close fit of his coat would probably not allow for much sweeping. But somehow she would find herself near enough that he would lean down and place his lips tenderly, perfectly upon hers.

Here, the daydream ended with a snap. She cast the Plutarch aside on the table. How could she conjure such vivid imaginings about a man she truly despised? But imagine she did, though one chaste kiss was as far as she would allow her fancies to go. Truth be told, she had little idea what should happen next between a man and a woman. She had heard things of course—things that intrigued her, but sounded quite improbable, really. No, she didn't know what to imagine. Only that his kiss would most likely be perfect, as flawless—and as unobtainable—as the earl himself.

Agitated, Esmie rose from the chair. She would take a turn about the schoolroom and stretch her legs. Perhaps that would cure her restlessness. She opened the door to check that no stray children had wandered from their beds, but the room lay quiet. Yet even as she carefully measured her paces around the perimeter of the larger room, she could not impose a similar order to her wayward thoughts.

In the silence, the clock on the mantelpiece chimed nine. Too restless to remain in the nursery, she squared her shoulders and picked up the lantern from the table. Perhaps a nighttime prowl would soothe her. In fact, she could begin her search for the manuscript this very night.

She slipped from the schoolroom, but hesitated when a faint light from the far side of the staircase caught her eye. The housekeeper, Mrs. Robbins, had told her that all the servants occupied rooms on the opposite side of the house. Only the governess and the children slept in this wing of the Abbey. The mysterious light that peeked out from under the closed door sent a faint tremor over Esmie's skin. She crept forward, lantern aloft.

With caution, she pressed her fingers against the cool wood of the door. It opened on quiet hinges. She peered inside, keeping behind the heavy walnut for protection. A house as richly furnished as the Abbey was a tempting morsel for robbers, although it seemed improbable a thief would climb up here in search of treasure when far more opulent rooms lay below.

Esmie slipped inside the room and inhaled sharply. To her surprise, she found not a bedchamber but a library. This library, though, was not an aristocrat's showpiece but a room designed for the needs of a scholar. Sparks of excitement traveled up her spine. She might even now be within arm's reach of the *Corinna*.

Tucked beneath the eaves of the house, the sloping ceilings of the room provided a canopy for row upon row of bookshelves. Every available space overflowed with thick volumes and hand-bound manuscripts. Esmie hardly dared breathe. How often had she dreamed of a room like this—a place where one might hide from a world that saw only one's inadequacies? She stepped to the nearest set of shelves and trailed her fingers along the spines of the precious volumes.

Marcus Aurelius. Herodotus. Plato. This must be the earl's private collection. Esmie grew warm, her breathing deep, as content as if she'd stumbled upon a group of her closest friends. She worked her way from shelf to shelf as she examined the collection; as she moved, her pulse increased in proportion to the treasures she found.

Expensive folio editions gave way to piles of ancient, handwritten manuscripts, many of them crumbling at the edges. Annotated editions of Greek and Roman classics. Essays and critical studies from the last two hundred years. The import of her discovery pressed against her chest, and she found it difficult to breathe. Esmie turned away from the shelves and toward the long table that occupied the center of the room. On it sat a glowing lantern identical to the one she carried. Piles of manuscripts, a sheaf of paper, and a blotter covered the top of the table. Pen and ink stood at the ready. She spared a cross thought for the careless servant who had left a flame unattended in the midst of so much dry paper. The room smelled strongly of leather and more faintly of tobacco. And brandy. Esmie recognized the heady scent, for the Italian count her mother had recently wed imbibed at least a bottle a day.

A rustling from the shadows sent a shiver dancing along her skin. The lantern had not been left unattended after all.

"You're not wanted," the gruff, masculine voice barked from a dark corner. Esmie jumped. In the dimness she could just make out a wing chair half turned toward a dormered window. She clutched her lantern, acutely aware of the much-turned hem of her dress and the dreadful state of her hair, for she had no doubt who the man was.

"I'll not repeat myself, Mrs. Robbins," the earl threatened without turning. "Leave me, if you value your position." He slurred the words of the last command.

Astonished, she searched for her voice and finally found it. "It is not Mrs. Robbins, my lord. It is Miss Fortune."

He did turn then, and Esmie would have fled if some inexplicable fascination had not rooted her to the spot. For a moment he said nothing, but she felt his eyes upon her as he assessed her imperfections and measured every defect. Finally, he unfolded his tall frame from the chair and came forward into the light.

Even in his cups, his cravat still fell in exquisite folds. He had exchanged his tight-fitting coat for a dressing gown, and the draped effect of the silk only added to the air of the Caesar about him. His hand trembled as he reached for his brandy glass on the low table, but he concealed that small betrayal by lifting the glass to his lips. He downed a healthy swallow without flinching and then set the glass on the table with a snap.

"You are trespassing, Miss Fortune." What could possibly drive such a man to solitary drunkenness? And then she remembered the unruly brood she'd encountered today and decided anyone saddled with such a tribe of heathens had a right to his brandy. Only the earl was not saddled with the tribe—she was.

"I saw the light and decided to investigate." She studied him as dispassionately as she could while her pulse pounded in her ears. She did not want to provoke him into dismissing her. Of course, it might well be that he would remember none of their conversation in the morning. The Italian count rarely recalled anything past teatime, once the brandy had been decanted.

"Investigate?" He eyed her as if she were a mere mortal who had dared set foot on the slopes of Mount Olympus. "There is no one here but me. Return to the nursery."

She stiffened at his rudeness. "Can you be trusted to put out the light? 'Tis not a room where so much as a cinder should be left burning."

The earl's gaze sharpened, despite his condition. "You would have such care for musty books and paper?"

His arrogance pierced her desire not to antagonize

him. "The bound volumes are costly enough, but there are a number of fine manuscripts as well." She gestured toward the shelves. "Such works are rare outside a university library. I have only heard of one or two in private collections."

The earl froze, and she experienced a particular satisfaction at spiking his guns. Still, from the way he bristled, she could see he found her knowledge of his library provoking. Drat! If she were wise, she would make her excuses and exit the room before she antagonized him any further.

Julian grasped the edge of the wing chair for support. Why must it be this disaster of a governess? The library spun slowly beneath his slippers. No one entered this room, except for Mrs. Robbins when the children's behavior had been especially . . . He frowned, searching for the word. What was it? Children. Behavior. Especially . . . egregious. Yes, that was it. Egregious.

The gray-eyed girl looked at him with an expression akin to pity. Julian gripped the chair more tightly. He was the object of no one's pity, least of all this miserable pretense of a governess. And yet she knew the strength of his library. That fact penetrated the haze that enveloped his brain. Perhaps she would not be useless after all. The last woman Mrs. Hazelwood sent had thought embroidery and watercolor were sufficient accomplishments for his daughters, and James could have given her lessons in geography and mathematics.

All this thinking made his head spin even more. Miss Fortune held herself stiff as a poker, her pride flung about her shoulders like a mantle. So she fancied herself a student of the classics? The earl reached for his glass again, but stopped when he remembered he'd just emptied it. God spare him from would-be scholars. He suffered enough of those fools when he lectured at All Souls, and his audience there was comprised of the brightest men in the kingdom. Not to mention the appalling monographs and essays sent by the bushel to the Classics Society. The men were bad enough. Even worse were thin-faced women with delusions of scholarship.

"In time," he snapped, "my collection will be given

into university hands. For now it remains here. In my
private library."

By the way her eyes brightened, he could see she took
his meaning. Her shoulders fell, but he hardened himself.
He could not allow an amateur to poke about in the
midst of such treasures, and he certainly had no intention of allowing a woman to invade his sanctuary.

"Is it true, then, that you possess the *Life of Corinna*?" Her words were almost a whisper, but they
brought him to his senses like a slap in the face.

"The *Life of Corinna*? What do you know of that?"

She blushed, and the color took the sallowness from
her skin. "Some say it does not exist, and if it does, the
authorship is unknown," she answered, as if reciting for
a schoolmaster. "It is purported to be an account of her
life, of which very little is known. I have heard there is
a copy in England in a private library. I thought
perhaps . . ."

Julian swore under his breath. She was not quite as
amateurish as he thought if she knew of that particular •
manuscript. Indeed, most scholars did believe it a legend,
and he had been careful to keep its presence in his home
a secret, though rumors would travel about. Someday he
would give the beautifully illuminated volume to All
Souls, but not until he had provided the definitive translation and won the prize of the Classics Society. The
translation would be his greatest scholarly achievement.
He had not recused himself from the judging committee
this year for anything less.

"I do not have the *Corinna*." The lie tumbled from
his lips.

"Oh." Her face crumpled, but he could not allow himself to feel the smallest prickle of sympathy. What could
this woman possibly want with such a valuable manuscript, anyway?

"If that is all . . ." He reached to pluck a volume from
his worktable. "I prefer my solitude, Miss Fortune."

She glanced around the room as if it were the royal
treasury of King Midas, but he would not allow her admiration to sway him. His solitude was the only refuge
he had left. His title, his house, his position in society,
his fellowship at All Souls—all required he appear with-

out fault. He was, after all, the Earl of Ashforth, not some common classics scholar who could appear ink-stained, disheveled, and flushed with the glow of new discovery.

The governess did not heed his dismissal.

"My lord, I did wonder if you would have any particular expectations for my three months' tenure."

Not easily cowed, this one. Her unfortunate looks must be compensated for by an annoying amount of determination and, he hoped, steadiness of character. He needed her to last the full three months.

"Expectations for my children?" He barked with laughter. "Madam, if you can remain in the household through the summer and keep my brood occupied, I shall be more than pleased."

Her tight lips revealed her disappointment at his answer. "You have no demands with regard to mathematics or history or French?"

"My only expectation is that you and the children keep out of my sight," he snapped. Her unwitting questions had pierced the vulnerable spot in his armor. Drat the girl. He came to his library to escape thoughts of his children, though in a moment of weakness he had located the room just steps from the nursery. He needed no one to assist him in his own torment; he could manage that very well for himself.

"Do your children always refer to you as 'the earl'?"

The question hit him like a blow to the midsection. Why did she persist? He must put her in her place once and for all.

"Miss Fortune, my relationship with my children is none of your affair. You are to supervise them, see to their studies, and keep them out of my way for the next three months. Beyond that, you need not concern yourself."

Her squared, thin shoulders radiated determination. "Then it is true. They call their own father by his title."

He longed for the brandy decanter but made no move toward it. To pour another drink in front of her would be a sign of weakness. "You are dismissed, Miss Fortune." He wanted her to go, and to go now. Another brandy would dull the pain that seized his heart whenever he thought of his children. Yet another would vanquish the hurt altogether.

"Dismissed? From my position?" she asked, her intriguing eyes alight with concern.

He snorted. "No, madam. From my library. Do not enter it again."

She eyed him with a depth of consideration that almost caused him to turn away, but after a long moment, she bid him good night and turned to go, her ill-fitting dress and blowsy hair his last sight of her before she slipped through the door and closed it behind her.

And suddenly, from some long-dormant place inside, he felt a pang of longing for the human contact she had offered—and he had spurned. With a shrug, he picked up the decanter, and with a shaking hand, he poured himself another measure.

"She's returning!" Phillip hissed from his post by the door of James's bedchamber. Phoebe and Caroline were curled together at the foot of the bed, while James paced the carpet in fair imitation of his father. Sophie had refused to attend this impromptu meeting, just as she refused to participate in most of their activities. Phillip closed the door, and the four children sat in silence as they listened to Miss Esmie pass through the schoolroom. The soft click of the latch on her bedchamber door indicated that she had retired for the night.

At length, James nodded, giving them permission to speak. Even so, their voices were little more than whispers. The Earl of Ashforth's children were skilled at clandestine meetings.

"Miss Lambton will arrive tomorrow," James said, rather unnecessarily, for all four of them were uncomfortably aware of the fact. They had never met Miss Lambton, but they knew of their father's intention to betroth himself to her.

"Perhaps she will be beautiful and kind," little Caroline whispered, a dreamy look in her eyes. "Like a princess in a storybook."

Phillip groaned. "More likely she's as disagreeable and selfish as Sophie."

"Phillip!" James snapped. The cutting sound of his name

was enough, for Phillip worshipped his older brother. "Let Sophie alone," James added more gently.

Phoebe bristled at the reprimand of her twin. "You always protect her, James, but it's her choice not to be one of us."

James gave her a silencing glance, and Phoebe subsided. "Miss Lambton is most likely looking for a titled husband," James continued. "All society misses do so. The question is, what kind of mother will she make?" His words hung in the air, for this was their gravest point of consideration.

"The earl isn't in love with her," Phoebe said, still irritated with James. "One can tell when a man is besotted."

Phillip snorted. " 'Tis true. John Coachman is besotted with a barmaid in the village, and he has that odd look about him."

"What odd look?" Caroline asked.

"As if he's just seen a whole table full of cakes and sweets," Phillip answered, "and would like to dive into them face-first."

James looked at them all with a considering air. "Yes, that is the look, isn't it? I wonder if the earl will look at Miss Lambton that way?"

Phoebe sighed. "That's how we'll know, isn't it?"

James nodded. "Yes, but that's not enough. She must look at him as if he is an entire wardrobe of silk dresses. And she must look at us with as much longing as if we were the most fashionable bonnets in London." He smiled, pleased with his comparison.

"And if he doesn't?" Caroline asked. "What if he decides to marry her anyway?"

"Then we shall stop him," Phillip said with grave seriousness. "We shan't let him marry anyone until he looks at her like that."

"Cakes and sweets," declared James.

"Dresses and bonnets," added Phoebe.

"Maybe she'll bring a cat," Caroline said dreamily.

"Too bad the new governess is such a fright," Phillip said, sinking down onto the bed and resting his chin in his hand. "She might be all right, once she cheers up a bit."

"And she has a cat," Caroline added.

James frowned. "The earl would never marry a governess."

The four sat quietly for a bit longer as they considered the arrival of Miss Lambton on the morrow. Then, one by one, they slipped from the room to make their way to their beds.

Esmie returned to her room chilled to the bone with mortification at the earl's dismissal. She snatched her shawl from its peg and wrapped it around her, but despite its warmth, shivers racked her body. Desperate, she pulled the coverlet from the bed and added it over the shawl. Cold, wintry hurt blanketed her as thoroughly as the shawl and the coverlet. His dismissal of her interest in his library shouldn't sting. His rejection was as inevitable as the rising of the sun in the morning, and yet still she felt the pain of it. The certainty of his disregard made it no less dreadful.

She shouldn't care two pins for his opinion. Esmie had long ago accepted herself for who she was—a rather unattractive young woman with an odd taste for scholarship. She could never change, and yet the very thing she loved most—the classical ideals of beauty and perfection—made her keenly aware how far short of the mark she fell.

The earl recognized her deficiencies with a depth few others would comprehend. He had achieved that glorious state of *arete,* of excellence and perfection the scholars and poets of ancient Greece had described. Of course he would give no quarter for her faults. His high standards were the very reason she longed for his approval.

There. She had admitted it. She was in danger of developing feelings for a man who despised her, and she despised herself for that weakness. And now she must decide. Was three months of his soul-shrinking disapproval worth the treasures that lay just down the hall? For despite his order never to enter the room again, she could contrive to gain access to his library somehow. She could avail herself of treasures beyond her wildest imaginings. She could finish the work that would establish her as a scholar and launch Athena Hall.

Shivers crawled across her body again. Esmie crept onto the narrow bed and curled into a ball. If she had any strength left, she would reach into her trunk and find a familiar volume. Sophocles, perhaps. Or her dog-eared copy of Aristophanes. But tonight, books would not answer, and the ancients seemed a very long way from the spartan governess's room at Ashforth Abbey. Tonight, tears seemed a much greater consolation.

Chapter Four

*B*y the next morning, Esmie had gained control of herself once more, and now she stood by the window seat in the schoolroom as she surveyed her five pupils. James already worked on some unknown task, his dark head bent over his exercise book. Sophie slumped in her chair and twisted a long, dark curl between her fingers. The twins looked at Esmie as if pearls of wisdom might drop from her lips, and Caroline sat primly for the moment, her feet dangling.

How to begin? Esmie regretted the full breakfast she'd shared with Mrs. Robbins in the servants' hall. Her stomach churned, so she clasped her hands in front of her.

"Perhaps you should tell me where you are in your studies."

James barely looked up from the exercise book. His ink-stained fingers flew across the page, and when Esmie strained to see, she could just make out the Greek letters of the text he was translating. He had no need of her instruction.

She turned to Sophie, but the girl's sullen expression warned Esmie off. Instead, she nodded to Phillip and Phoebe. "Have you begun any languages? Or literature?"

The twins blanched. "We practiced our penmanship with Miss Dalrymple. She was keen on penmanship," said Phillip.

"What of geography and history?" She remembered the atlas she'd seen lying on the window seat the night of her arrival. "Do you know the major rivers and mountain ranges of Europe?"

The twins looked at her with identical blank expressions.

Thankfully, Caroline interrupted. "Miss Esmie, do you think you could teach me the letters? Miss Dalrymple said I was too little to hold a pencil properly, but if you showed me, I'm sure I could hold it as well as anything."

Esmie stood bewildered as a strange ache replaced the knots in her midsection. She shouldn't be surprised that the children wanted to learn. Most children did. She could only wonder at the stupidity of her predecessors.

But James had learned somewhere. Her eyes returned to the oldest boy. He still had not looked up from his translation. The boy didn't welcome her presence in the schoolroom either.

With a yawn, Sophie laid her head on her desk.

"Very well. I can see we have a great deal of work to do." Esmie stepped to the closest bookshelf and selected a primer. After opening it to the first page, she placed the book in front of Caroline. "These are the letters. All twenty-six of them." She scanned the room, noticing the damp that still clung to the lower windowpanes. That ought to offer an alternative to the pencil. "Here, Lady Caroline. In the window seat." The girl looked puzzled but complied quickly enough, and Esmie showed her how to trace the letters in the moisture that clung to the window. Caroline's chubby finger formed the steeple and crossbar of the "A." She looked up at Esmie and smiled.

"Which one is that?" the girl asked, and an unexpected knot caught in Esmie's throat.

"That is the letter 'A.'" Of its own accord, her hand reached out and patted the girl on the shoulder. "And a very nice one, too. Perhaps you could make several more to keep that one company." Caroline happily complied.

Esmie set the twins to work with the atlas as they copied a map of Europe in their exercise books and labeled rivers and mountains. Though Sophie still feigned sleep, Esmie could feel the girl's surreptitious glances follow her every move as she bent over the twins' bright red heads, pointing out the Alps and the

Pyrenees. Esmie delayed as long as she could, but soon enough the twins were happy with their task and she could no longer avoid the sulking Sophie. She was about to approach the girl when she saw James eye her meaningfully. Esmie followed his dark gaze as it went to the bookshelf by the door. With a barely perceptible nod, Esmie moved toward the cache of books. Most were titles far too advanced for a schoolroom, but as she ran her eyes along the spines of the books on the lower shelves, she understood what James was getting at. Collections of fairy stories, folk tales and myths abounded. Here lay familiar ground. Esmie selected an illustrated volume of Greek myths and turned toward Sophie.

"Perhaps we could begin with these." She placed the book on the desk in front of the girl, who read the title of the volume and then went quite still.

"I know these stories," Sophie snapped. "Rubbish, all of them."

The look of longing in Sophie's eyes belied the defensive note in her voice. Esmie had once sat, in a manner of speaking, in the same chair where Sophie now perched, ramrod straight. Esmie, too, had carefully concealed that decidedly unfeminine thirst for knowledge from adults she did not trust.

She sank down beside Sophie until they were eye to eye. Though she and the girl were nothing alike physically, looking into Sophie's face was very like seeing a younger version of herself. The hidden, hungry longing. The shame. The defenses like the walls of Troy holding the Greeks at bay.

"Do you know the story of Persephone?" Esmie ventured.

Sophie nodded but held herself stiffly.

Esmie kept her eyes locked on the girl's. "I have always wondered how she must have felt—half her life in the mortal realm and the other in Hades. Have you ever wondered that?"

Sophie nodded.

"Your assignment, then," Esmie continued, "is to compose a story about Persephone's life after the myth ends."

Sophie's eyes widened, her mouth formed a little "O."

At that moment, the schoolroom door banged open and the dour figure of Mrs. Robbins appeared in the doorway.

"Miss Lambton and her father have arrived," the housekeeper announced. "The children are wanted downstairs in the salon."

Five pairs of eyes darted from the housekeeper to Esmie, and her stomach dove when she saw the anxiety in each expression. She remembered the day she had met her first stepfather, and her heart twisted in sympathy. A difficult business to meet a prospective parent for the first time.

"That will be all for now, children." She pinned a bright smile upon her face. "James, wash the ink from your fingers. Sophie, will you straighten Caroline's ribbon? Phillip, Phoebe, put the atlas aside." She turned to Mrs. Robbins. "I shall relinquish them to your care, ma'am."

"My care?" Her eyebrows peaked in horror. "I think not, Miss Fortune. The earl specifically directed that you bring the children to the salon. They are, after all, your charges."

A horror of her own flashed through Esmie. She had no wish to see the earl so soon after last night's encounter, and she had even less desire to watch him gaze with approbation on the reputedly perfect form of Miss Lambton. But Esmie was the governess, at least for now, and Mrs. Robbins was correct. The children were in her charge. And she knew better than anyone how long the walk from the schoolroom to the grand salon could be when a new parent waited at the end of the journey.

"Thank you, Mrs. Robbins." The introductions would be swift, and she and the children would make a quick escape. Surely that would suit everyone. "We shall be along in a moment." She turned to find the children huddled around James, who whispered to them. She heard the words *cakes* and *bonnets,* which seemed odd. She would have loved to hear the complete content of his instructions, but when he saw her looking, he straightened and motioned to his brother and sisters to fall in line behind him.

"We are ready, Miss Esmie," he announced. They looked as solemn as one of Hannibal's regiments preparing to cross the Alps. Even little Caroline stood with her shoulders back and her head erect.

"Very well, then." Like James, her fingers were stained with ink from where she'd assisted the twins with their maps. Her skirt had gathered a line of dust when she'd knelt next to Sophie, and she'd wiped the damp on her fingers from the windowpane on her sleeve. Despair, that old friend, flooded her chest. What was the point in tidying herself, for even without these evidences of the schoolroom, she would never be cut from the same cloth as Miss Lambton. Besides, she must procure a manuscript, not the earl's notice.

Like a mother duck leading a parade of ducklings, Esmie set off toward the stairs. She stopped on the landing to ask James directions to the grand salon. It was one of the longest walks of Esmie's life, and she was keenly aware of the children's eyes fixed upon her back as they marched down to the great Elizabethan hall and then along a corridor until they reached the door of the grand salon.

Esmie hesitated. Should she lead them in or send the children first? The cowardly part of her wanted to turn to James and let him take the helm, but self-respect raised its head and demanded she raise her own. "Courage," she murmured under her breath, more loudly than she'd supposed, for she heard the children echo "Courage!" as she opened the door.

The grand salon was aptly named. Gilt and ivory silk adorned every available surface. Exquisite moldings, imposing portraits, and an enormous carpet framed groupings of elegant little chairs and tables. A banquette ran along one wall, and as if by rote, the children marched to stand in front of it in their military column, perfectly arranged by height and age.

Esmie lingered by the door, keenly aware of the earl and his guests gathered at the far end of the room. The murmur of conversation ceased, and the earl's voice rang out. "Miss Fortune! Please bring the children to me."

She blushed, and then embarrassment turned to anger. How dare he use that imperious tone? He dared, of course, because she was a mere servant and he the employer. Mortified, Esmie nodded to James, and together they led the rest of the children to the opposite end of the room.

The earl stood beside the fireplace, his hands clasped behind his back and a slight frown on his face. He would have looked like a disapproving schoolmaster if his expensive coat and pristine cravat had not proclaimed him a gentleman.

Miss Lambton appeared perfectly at ease in the opulent room, her blond hair and creamy skin nature's version of the salon's gilt trimmings and ivory silks. Mr. Lambton, the girl's father, was younger than Esmie had expected, barely into the middle years of life. His daughter came by her looks honestly, for her father had the same light hair and fair skin. Esmie curled her fingers into a ball and straightened them again. She would not betray how inadequate she felt in the midst of this company.

The earl spoke first. "Thank you, Miss Fortune, for bringing the children so promptly." He exhibited no warmth in his voice or expression, merely cold propriety. "Mr. Lambton, Miss Lambton, may I present my children?" Without waiting for a reply, he continued. "My elder son, Viscount Stanleigh." As if on cue, James stepped forward and sketched a stiff bow. Then, one by one, the children took their turns as their father introduced them. Sophie curtsied with unexpected aplomb and looked at Miss Lambton with admiring eyes. Esmie was dismayed to see a flicker of distaste cross the woman's features. Thankfully, Sophie appeared not to notice.

The twins stepped forward together, and then it was Caroline's turn. For a moment she forgot to curtsy, and instead scuffed her slipper into the carpet. Her father's sharp "Ahem!" prompted her to remember her manners.

"And this," the earl continued, "is our new governess, Miss Esmerelda Fortune."

Esmie curtsied, and Miss Lambton nodded politely, but she could not disguise the satisfaction that settled over her features when she dismissed Esmie as a threat to her interests.

Mr. Lambton proved far more polite. He crossed the carpet and took Esmie's hand, bowing over it and giving her a warm smile. "You have a prodigious responsibility,

Miss Fortune, if you are charged with looking after all five children at once."

The earl looked surprised at Mr. Lambton's familiarity, and then cross, and finally disapproving. Some spark of independence within Esmie flamed to life at Mr. Lambton's civility.

"They are a pleasure, sir. Quite eager to learn." She met his smiling eyes with her own and was astonished, and a bit disconcerted, to see a spark of attraction and interest.

"Father," Miss Lambton said as she rose from her place on the settee and came to stand beside him, "we mustn't keep the children from their lessons. I am sure Miss Fortune has a prodigious amount of learning to drum into their heads."

"To be sure," Mr. Lambton concurred, still in possession of Esmie's hand, "but that should not preclude her from joining us for dinner." He turned to the earl. "We need a fourth, do we not, my lord? Otherwise I shall pass a lonely meal while you and my daughter are tête-à-tête."

The corners of the earl's mouth went tight, and Esmie's brief moment of satisfaction turned nightmarish. "That is kind of you indeed, Mr. Lambton, but I would not dream of intruding on the earl and his guests. Besides, I am needed to supervise the nursery tea."

Mr. Lambton dropped her hand, but not the subject. He turned to the earl. "Come, come, my lord. A woman who spends her days with five children deserves the pleasure of some adult conversation. What say you, Ashforth?"

Esmie would have loved to sink through the floor. The children watched the unfolding scene with fascination, and Miss Lambton looked as if she would like to smack her father. Esmie took her bit of pleasure in the earl's dilemma. Her presence at dinner would occupy Mr. Lambton, and it would certainly clear the way for the earl to proceed with his courtship of Miss Lambton. And, yet, for whatever reason—pride, propriety, or simple distaste—she knew he would prefer it if she remained away from his guests, abovestairs in the nursery.

The familiar pain of her imperfections had actually

begun to lessen. In fact, she could feel anger growing within her at the injustice of the situation. She had not asked to be included at table. Nursery tea was by far preferable to the assessing and dismissive eyes of the earl and Miss Lambton. The events of the last few days had moved her from resignation to anger, and now she acknowledged something new and wholly unrecognized growing within her. Rebellion. Powerful and oddly liberating. She was tired of being found wanting, and weary of the earl's easy dismissal of her person and her sensibilities. She remembered the letter. The horrible, demeaning letter he'd written in response to her last submission to the Classics Society.

Before she could stop herself, she spoke. "You are kindness indeed, Mr. Lambton, and I should be happy to accept your invitation." She cast a defiant glance at the earl, who looked as if he might be experiencing a touch of apoplexy. "I know his lordship's sense of hospitality would never allow him to leave a guest without a dinner partner."

She was only tormenting herself, but Esmie no longer cared. Even the *Corinna* manuscript was not worth the humiliation. She had some pride left, and if the earl dismissed her for her presumption, then she would take her notes and books and find another position. Her work would suffer, but some semblance of esteem would be preserved. Pride had suddenly become of paramount importance, even with her ink-stained fingers and deplorable gown. Or perhaps because of them.

"Very well, then." The earl conceded with a modicum of grace. "You shall join us for dinner, Miss Fortune. We begin with sherry in the small salon at seven o'clock."

"Yes, my lord." Not sure whether she had won or lost this battle, Esmie gathered up the children and ushered them toward the far end of the room. As they moved away from the earl and his guests, she heard Miss Lambton say, "The very idea, Father, of including her at dinner. I shall be quite put off my food if I look at her odd little face overmuch."

The earl snapped some reply that Esmie did not hear because the pounding of her pulse in her own ears drowned out everything else. She moved blindly toward the door and hoped the children would follow, for at the moment she could hardly account for herself, much less her charges. And then warm fingers slipped through her own. She glanced down to see Phoebe looking up at her with sympathy. Esmie squeezed the girl's hand. James opened the door when they reached the far end of the room, and the children gathered around her and swept her from the salon like a wave carrying driftwood out to sea.

Julian watched the governess leave the room with his children surrounding her like a military escort. He kept his hands clasped, otherwise he might wring Mr. Lambton's neck. The last place he wanted that gray-eyed baggage was at his dinner table. She had seen him at his weakest, and he did not care for the feeling of vulnerability her knowledge of his imperfection generated in his midsection. Even more, he did not care for the odd sense of longing he experienced in her presence. Miss Lambton, perfect in form and face, should be the one to spark his interest. But the vapidity of her conversation made comparisons to Esmie Fortune's obvious intellect inevitable. If only he could fuse the two women into one. Perhaps that would answer. But no. Better the vacuous, undemanding Miss Lambton than a would-be scholar and termagant.

Miss Lambton also watched the small party retreat from the salon. "The very idea, Father, of including her at dinner. I shall be quite put off my food if I look at her odd little face overmuch."

Julian saw the governess's shoulders tighten at the catty remark and before he thought, he snapped, "Then perhaps you should fix your eyes upon your plate, Miss Lambton."

The girl's eyes flickered with anger, which she quickly masked. "I did not mean to be unkind, my lord. Merely practical."

And, ironically enough, Julian could see that she believed her own words. To Miss Lambton, a governess was a mere piece of household furniture, to be treated accordingly. Julian opened his mouth to give the girl the setdown she deserved, but the words did not spill out.

Instead, he saw in his mind's eye flashes of his own behavior toward Miss Fortune over the last two days. He
had no moral ground on which to stand in judgment
of Miss Lambton. He had not treated Esmie Fortune
any better.

"I'm sure you meant no harm," he answered mildly,
instead of barking the reprimand that had been on the
tip of his tongue. "And, as your father says, if Miss Fortune will be his partner in conversation, you and I shall
have more leisure to become acquainted."

This pacified the young beauty, and she smiled at him.
At one time, he might have been moved by such an
expression of affection from her. Now her obvious interest only made the room seem overly warm. He glanced
around at the beautiful salon and swallowed his discomfort. He would be a fool if he thought the calculated
interest of a beautiful woman was too great a price to
pay to maintain the splendor of the Ashforth name. And
the Earl of Ashforth was never foolish.

Chapter Five

*L*ate-afternoon sun slanted through the schoolroom windows, but in the perfection of Ashforth Abbey, no stray dust motes swam about in the light. For the first time since the morning's fiasco in the gilt salon, Esmie found herself alone. The earl had taken James for a ride about the estate. Father and son appeared grim rather than joyous at the prospect of a long gallop. Sophie had disappeared to some bolt-hole. The twins announced their intention of visiting the kitchens to see what might be expected for tea, and Caroline lay asleep on her bed, no doubt dreaming of the new letters she'd learned to write.

Esmie sank onto the window seat and ran her fingers idly over the cover of the large atlas. Dread filled her at the thought of the evening to come. Why had she so foolishly accepted Mr. Lambton's invitation? She had not taken three steps beyond the grand salon before a sharp pang of loss hit her. The *Corinna* manuscript. The earl must have hidden it in his library, and if she antagonized him into dismissing her, she would never get a glimpse of it, much less the opportunity to translate it for incorporation into her own work.

An image of the earl in all his blinding perfection rose in her mind's eye, and warmth flooded through her, culminating in a bright red stain on each cheek. If only she had Miss Lambton's blue eyes and guinea-gold curls. If only she, Esmie, could appear as at home in the grand salon, her skin and hair in perfect concert with the ivory and gilt. The only time her keen awareness of her imperfections fell away was when she lost herself within her studies, all thoughts of her inadequacies swept away by the stroke of her pen. Plutarch had recounted the lives of the noble heroes from the classic age, but what of the heroines? Esmie could not believe that half of the ancient population had not held some sway in matters of state, in philosophy and the arts, in the rise and fall of empires. So she had set out, several years before, to recount the life of women like Agrippina, mother, sister, and wife of Roman emperors. She wanted the world to know of Leontion, who in the years following Aristotle's death rivaled her male counterpart as the leading philosopher of Athens. Or Hortensia, the great Roman orator who defeated a measure to levy a tax on the women of the Roman Empire.

To Esmie's chagrin, sources were few, and mentioned the women in the most peripheral ways. In her first stepfather's ducal library, she had been ecstatic to discover a few unknown manuscripts that contributed additional details. But they were nothing to what a true copy of the *Life of Corinna* would be worth to her work. Just down the hall, on the other side of the stairs, might lay the difference between being considered a dilettante and being accorded the standing of a true scholar. And a true scholar could always find students.

But even if she proved herself a scholar, the earl would never look upon her with approbation. Nor should she want him to, she chided herself, even though she began to doubt whether the earl's appearance of perfection could bear close scrutiny. Someday she might find the man who would value her dream of a proper school for young women and her passion for scholarship. But she would find no such man at Ashforth Abbey.

She rose from the window seat and walked to the door. The corridor lay empty. It was the work of a moment to steal along to the earl's library and slip inside. The paragon and James should be gone for another hour. Plenty of time to search.

Esmie closed the library door and leaned against it, safe for the moment. Shaking, she crossed the carpet. The long table in the center of the room had been cleared of its pile of books, manuscripts, and paper. No evidence remained of her midnight encounter with the earl, except that she could still feel traces of his presence in the room.

Knees almost knocking, Esmie walked to the farthest part of the room and pulled books and manuscripts from the shelves. She lingered over one or two, and then checked for hidden compartments behind the enormous volumes. The room was silent, except for the occasional bump of a book or her intake of breath when she discovered a particularly fine first edition. She worked her way around the room until she had examined every scrap of paper in the library, but her efforts failed to turn up the elusive prize. In despair, she sank into the wing chair the earl had occupied the night before. She let her eyes survey the room again. Her gaze settled on the long oak table and her heartbeat quickened. In a flash, she leapt from the chair. Dropping to her hands and knees, she peered underneath the table. And there it was. A sheaf of papers peered out from the side of a little wooden shelf tucked up underneath the tabletop.

Esmie's insides flapped and trembled as if she'd swallowed a small bird. Fingers quivering, she reached up and tugged the packet from its hiding place. In one swift movement, she came up from under the table, set her newfound prize on the gleaming surface, and sank into the straight chair beside her. Barely able to breathe, she turned back the tooled leather cover to find a beautifully illuminated medieval manuscript. The Greek letters flowed across the page, and Esmie's throat went as tight as if someone strangled her.

The *Life of Corinna*. Tears sprang to her eyes and in a matter of moments flowed freely down her cheeks. She felt like Odysseus beholding Penelope after his years of journeying. The ink had faded with time, of course, and some words were dimmed beyond human sight. But it could be translated. Esmie knew that at once. Somehow, someway, this manuscript had been kept safe, protected from the mold and damp that took their toll on most medieval libraries. Somewhere, centuries ago, an unknown monk had copied each letter of the original Greek with his quill and ink so that the words of an ancient, unnamed writer might come alive for Esmie at this very moment.

Delicately, Esmie thumbed through the pages of the manuscript, pausing to read bits and pieces. Too soon, the rays of the sun grew longer, and Esmie heard the sound of hoofbeats outside. The earl and James had returned.

Hastily she closed the manuscript, but when she ducked beneath the table to restore it to its hiding place, she couldn't fit the volume into its secret slot. Afraid to push too firmly, Esmie turned the manuscript one way, then the other. Nothing worked. Her heart pounded as she listened for sounds in the corridor.

Jumping to her feet, she concealed the volume behind her back and made for the door. She would hide it. Once the earl was safely gone to his rooms to dress for dinner, she would try again to return it to its hiding place. The thump of booted feet as they ascended the stairs sent Esmie scurrying down the hallway, through the school-room, and into the privacy of her little cell. She glanced around with despair. She refused to slip it under the bed and expose it to mice or damp. The small table had no drawer she might use. That left only her trunk. She flung open the lid and, pushing several of her own books aside, laid the precious manuscript on the bottom. She stacked several volumes on top, and snapped the lid closed.

A fine sweat beaded her brow. Esmie stepped to the small table and poured water from the pitcher into the basin. She bent over and splashed her face with the tepid water, then reached for a piece of toweling. Beyond her closed door, she heard James enter the nursery, and the sound of his chamber door as it snapped shut. Esmie sighed with relief.

Now she just needed to determine the earl's where-abouts. Once he was in the hands of his valet, she would sneak back to the library and return the manuscript. Swallowing her anxiety, Esmie smoothed her hair and went in search of the earl.

The Earl of Ashforth marched from the stables as he swiped at the sleeves of his coat with his handkerchief.

Somehow, the wretched cat Miss Fortune had introduced into his household had managed to shed on his riding coat in the few moments that he'd shucked it to groom Pegasus, his prize stallion. Now, his eyes itched, and a sneeze welled in his nose. "Ha . . . ha . . . *choo*!" He changed course with the handkerchief and vigorously wiped his nose. Instantly his vision blurred, and he could have sworn his eyes crossed of their own accord. A series of six sneezes rang out like church bells.

"Are you unwell, my lord?"

Julian stuffed the handkerchief in his pocket and looked up to find the ghastly governess in his path.

"Miss Fortune." He nodded and swallowed another sneeze. This indignity was her fault. And he was still unhappy with her acceptance of Mr. Lambton's invitation to join them for dinner. Not that the notion didn't have practical value, but somehow her very presence seemed to irritate Julian as much as the cat hair. He moved to step around her, but she moved as well, still blocking his course.

"A moment, my lord." Her gray eyes looked troubled, as if a storm brewed behind them. Julian bit back a curse. He'd hoped to change for dinner and have a few precious minutes with the manuscript. For all his wealth and position, time for his own interests was a rare commodity.

"I'm afraid I have no time at the moment, ma'am. Perhaps it is something we could discuss at table tonight?"

She flushed, and he saw that she felt the impertinence of her dining with her betters as keenly as he did. Miss Lambton's words in the grand salon might have been rude, but they had expressed what all were thinking.

"Tonight? I'm afraid not." Her fingers plucked at her skirts, and her eyes did not quite meet his. That avoidance piqued Julian's interest. Was the mousy little governess up to something?

"What is it, then?" He wished he still had his riding crop in hand so that he might tap it impatiently against his boot. That might hurry her along.

"It's the children, sir."

He swallowed a groan. "The children are your responsibility, Miss Fortune, and I charge you to make decisions accordingly."

"Yes, but—"

"We have an agreement, do we not?"

"Yes, my lord."

"Well, then?"

Her eyes darted to the left, then to the right. "Can you tell me about their mother, sir? It might help me understand them better."

The breath leapt from his lungs in one great whoosh. No one at Ashforth Abbey *ever* referred to his late wife. His cold demeanor at the mention of her name had cured even the children of introducing the subject.

"Their mother was their mother, madam. There is nothing more to know."

"How long has she been deceased, my lord?"

He had believed the memories of Lillian no longer had the power to cause him pain, but Miss Esmerelda Fortune was proving that old wounds never heal. "She died at Caroline's birth, madam." The mention of Lillian still turned him white-hot with anger. "Five years ago."

"Oh."

He could read her thoughts in her clear gray eyes. She thought him grief-stricken over his loss. She assumed, as most people did, that he still harbored a *tendre* for his lost love. Even Miss Lambton had alluded to his late wife in glowing terms, as if by honoring the first countess she might advance her goal of becoming the next one.

"Is that all?" He stepped forward again; she retreated a few paces, but still did not move from his path. Blast, but he would never make it to the library before dinner if she did not let him alone. Appearing the paragon was a time-consuming process—time he would rather have spent in his library at work on the *Corinna*. He was scheduled to deliver a lecture at All Souls College in Oxford in a week's time, and he had hoped to present at least a preliminary version of his translation then, a preview to his triumph when he won the Society for Classical Studies annual prize. He smiled at the stir it would cause among the fellows of the college.

"No, my lord. I have other questions as well."

But did she? She looked almost desperate, and from the tiny lines that framed her mouth, he guessed she was well acquainted with desperation. What woman wouldn't bear such telltale signs if she was forced to labor for her bread, even in the relatively privileged position of governess?

And yet, something about Esmerelda Fortune made her different from other women. Perhaps her distinction lay in the set of her jaw or the sharpness of her gaze. Little about her could be deemed soft or feminine. Except for those eyes. They really were extraordinarily expressive. At the moment, they revealed a great deal more than her words. She had some purpose, but it had nothing to do with the questions she posed. For a moment, when she had asked about Lillian, he had been afraid she'd learned the truth about his late wife. But no. She wasn't after information at all. She was stalling. She did not want him to enter the house. No doubt the children had pulled yet another prank and she was covering for their misdeed.

"If that is all, Miss Fortune, I should like to dress for dinner." He paused to rake her from head to foot with his gaze, taking in the gray sarcenet that fit her like a sack. "As do you."

Her fine eyes clouded almost to black. "I am dressed for dinner, sir."

"Oh." He'd not meant to hurt her, and he mentally reprimanded himself for his abruptness. Termagant disposition or no, Miss Fortune was his only prospect for a governess to see him through the next several weeks. It would behoove him to take some care with her feelings. He assumed she did have some feelings.

"Well, then, you will allow me the liberty of returning to the house to follow your example. Anything else you might have to say can wait until this evening, madam."

He stepped around her and wondered if she would stop him. The thought of her hand on his sleeve disconcerted him.

"My lord . . ." She trailed along beside him now, and he wondered that she did not pluck at his sleeve. Was a quarter hour alone with his treasure too great a thing to ask? He was the earl, after all.

"Not now, Miss Fortune." They reached the side door of the Abbey and he marched through, intending to leave her in his wake, but she matched him step for step.

"What, madam? Are you volunteering your services as a valet as well as a governess? Will you accompany me as far as my bedchamber?"

She blushed red as fire, and the color did nothing for her appearance. For the first time since he'd encountered her in the Abbey courtyard, he'd rendered the sharp-tongued governess speechless.

Lacking words to express herself, however, did not render her immobile. She continued to trail him up two flights of the grand staircase; then, when he turned down the corridor to his own rooms, she fell away.

Her sudden acquiescence roused his suspicions. She did not mind if he went to his rooms to dress for dinner after all. So what was she keeping from him?

The answer hit him like a hammer, and he wondered at his own obtuseness. He pivoted on his heel and marched after her.

"Miss Fortune!"

She turned, guilt scrawled on every inch of her features. "Yes, my lord?"

"Have you been in my library, Miss Fortune?"

She paled.

In two strides, he passed her and mounted the staircase. He pounded up the steps, not bothering to glance back and see if she followed. He never locked his library, for no one in the house would have dared to trespass on his private sanctuary.

He flung open the door, and it banged against the wall. He crossed to the table and sank down on one knee, and his hands searched the underside of the wood. But he already knew what he would find. The hiding place was empty.

She made a noise from the doorway, and he slowly turned his head. Her face flamed once more. "My lord, I can explain."

"Explain?" He felt as if his head might explode. How dare she? Was he not entitled to even the smallest modicum of privacy? He spent his days performing his duties and honoring his position, but he must have one little corner of his life for himself. And *she* had violated what little sanctity he had carved out in this temple of perfection.

"Where is it?"

To her credit, she didn't deny what she'd done. "I meant to put it back, but it wouldn't fit properly, and then I heard someone on the stairs."

He had never been so cold and so hot at the same time. "Where is my manuscript?"

She swallowed. "In my room, my lord. I shall retrieve it."

"Not without me, you won't." He followed her down the hallway and into the schoolroom. She walked calmly, shoulders back and head held high. He imagined her long, graceful neck positioned on the chopping block at the Tower of London. Regretfully, it was the nineteenth century, not the sixteenth, and aristocratic privilege was not what it had once been.

She opened the door to her room, and he followed her inside. Its austerity took him aback. His natural tastes ran to simplicity, but this was a bit much even for him.

Miss Fortune opened her trunk and shuffled through the contents. He stood in the doorway and drummed his fingers against the wood of the door frame. He watched her as she moved objects about inside the trunk, wondering that it should take her so long to retrieve the manuscript.

And then his errant gaze noticed the rather shapely outline of her derriere as she bent over. The jolt of pure masculine interest that coursed through him caught him by surprise, and he pushed the thought, and the feeling, aside.

"Well?" He had been angry over the manuscript, but now he was furious over his own inability to control his baser nature. Lusting over the governess, indeed! No Earl of Ashforth had ever sunk to those depths.

She turned, but her hands were empty, spread before her in supplication. Her cheeks were ashen. "It's not here, my lord."

It took a moment for the words to register. "Not

there?" he echoed. "Did you or did you not take my manuscript?"

"Yes, I took it, and I put it here, at the bottom of my trunk not a quarter hour ago. 'Tis gone."

"How can it possibly be gone?"

She must be tricking him. She had claimed to know the value of the manuscript, and he had dismissed her knowledge because she was a woman. Now he saw he had been presumptuous and arrogant. She had indeed known its value, and wished to deceive him into thinking it missing.

Over his shoulder, the clock in the schoolroom sounded the hour. Little time remained to dress for dinner.

"Until tomorrow morning, madam." The words fell from his lips like clumps of ice. "You have until tomorrow morning to return my manuscript or I shall turn you over to the magistrate."

Her eyes grew more enormous. "M-m-magistrate? But, my lord, upon my honor, I put the manuscript here. Someone else must have taken it."

"Then I suggest you find it before I rise from the breakfast table tomorrow. Otherwise you will find yourself living in considerably more unpleasant quarters than this."

He wouldn't press charges, of course. He couldn't afford the scandal. But she didn't know that, didn't know that he was, in fact, the magistrate, and fear might be his only leverage in forcing her to return the *Corinna*.

"But my lord . . ."

He whirled and stalked across the schoolroom, closing his ears to her protests. Damn her eyes, and damn him for not locking the library. As he descended the stairs to his own rooms, he cursed himself for ten kinds of a fool. But he cursed himself even more for the unspeakable attraction he felt for the deceitful, difficult woman and her confounded gray eyes.

Chapter Six

*T*hat evening, Esmie delayed joining the party in the grand salon until the last moment. She trailed her fingertips along the banister as she descended the first set of stairs. An enormous ache settled in her chest when she recalled the earl's expression just before he'd stormed from her bedroom. He had eyed her as if she were the most revolting sort of insect, then he had turned without a word and stalked away. Not that she cared for his opinion. He was haughty, arrogant and . . . perfect. Irritatingly, coldly perfect.

With a sigh, she paused at a mirror hung opposite the bottom of the stairs. It was the same mirror, in fact, in which she'd seen herself reflected on the day of her arrival. Well, her image was a bit improved. She had scraped her hair into severe respectability. Her sarcenet was somewhat more presentable than her traveling costume, though both were dowdy. Her trepidation at seeing the earl lent sparkle to her eyes and a flush to her cheeks. She looked like a well-manicured boxwood, she decided. Neither pretty nor ugly. Simply there, a part of the landscape.

Esmie's shoulders slumped. Would she ever be more than a part of the scenery?

She had spent the rest of the afternoon searching for the manuscript, to no avail. She couldn't imagine who else knew of its existence, or who would have taken it. One of the servants, perhaps. Or Mrs. Robbins—for hadn't the earl mistaken Esmie for the housekeeper when she'd first invaded his library? But Esmie could hardly imagine the dour, pinched woman harboring a secret desire for the *Life of Corinna*. The children were far too afraid of their father to risk incurring his wrath by taking something so precious, if they even knew it existed. In any event, the manuscript was nowhere to be found in the unused rooms along the nursery corridor.

Esmie forced herself down the last flight of stairs, and approached the small salon. A footman in a powdered wig and livery waited in the hall to admit her. He solemnly opened the door, and Esmie forced herself across the threshold as if she were headed for a public stoning.

The moment she entered the room, the earl's eyes fixed upon her. Her pulse picked up its pace. Why did she have to be so aware of him? His shoulders were drawn up tight beneath the close fit of his dark coat. He handed Miss Lambton a glass of sherry, and his eyes met Esmie's over the other woman's shoulder. The hairs on her neck stood on end.

"Good evening, Miss Fortune." He pronounced her name in his usual dry tones.

Mr. Lambton rose from his seat beside his daughter and came toward Esmie. "Good evening, madam. You look lovely."

The simple compliment alleviated some of Esmie's discomfort. At least she would have one ally this evening.

"Thank you, sir." Mr. Lambton bowed over her hand as was proper, but his touch did not cause the shiver that ran down her spine. No, that shiver resulted from the disapproving glare of the paragon earl. "You are most kind."

The inane words somehow underscored the absurdity of the situation. Every part of her had come alive, tense with awareness under the earl's scrutiny. She had made a mistake, true, but she had not intended to commit a crime. She had only wanted to see the manuscript, to touch it, to allow herself the pleasure of a few moments in its company. . . . Much the same thing she wanted from the earl. Her cheeks flamed.

Miss Lambton ignored her entirely, for which Esmie was grateful. She would not antagonize the earl's future bride, for she looked the type to take out her displeasure on the nearest servant—or child. What sort of mother would Miss Lambton make? The answer that formed in her mind gave her no pleasure.

The door to the salon opened and the butler appeared. "My lord, ladies, sir," he intoned, "dinner is served."

The earl helped Miss Lambton to her feet and tucked her hand in the crook of his arm. Esmie had known he would not see her into dinner, but still she knew the sting of disappointment and despised herself for it.

"Miss Fortune." Mr. Lambton offered her his arm. She gladly took it and smiled at the man, the one bright spot in the current tangle of her life. They processed with all due grandeur from the small salon into the family dining room, which proved far less imposing than the state dining room. Still, Esmie's breath caught at the sight of the ornamental ceiling and the incredible curved sideboard fitted into the niche formed by the bay window. Intricate white molding, the work of Robert Adams, most likely, accented the pale green walls. Portraits of Ashworth ancestors marched in a line around the room, and a large scene of Venus rising from the sea hung above the marble mantelpiece.

Esmie swallowed her trepidation. The earl would sit at the head of the table, of course. With great ceremony, he placed Miss Lambton at his left. He nodded to indicate that her father should take the place at his right, which left Esmie on the other side of Mr. Lambton. He seated Esmie courteously before he took his seat. Footmen in livery and wigs removed the silver covers and poured the wine.

"How do you find Oxfordshire, Miss Lambton?" The earl's eyes were fixed on the other young woman. If Esmie hadn't known better, she would have thought him absorbed in Miss Lambton's conversation. But Esmie knew his lack of eye contact stemmed not from snobbery but from pure anger. And though she knew circumstances must make her appear guilty, it hurt that he would not give her the benefit of the doubt.

Miss Lambton appeared to consider the earl's question for a long moment. The other woman's troubled china blue eyes revealed her dilemma. Was the earl seeking a compliment of his home, or was he testing her taste?

"Oxfordshire seems tolerable, sir." Miss Lambton had decided he was testing her, rather than fishing for compliments.

The earl swallowed a bite of stewed partridge, but the sudden tension in his jaw showed that Miss Lambton had chosen the wrong course. "Merely tolerable, ma'am?"

"More than tolerable, actually," Miss Lambton twittered. "Quite pleasant, now that I think on it. Very beautiful, actually."

The earl's tense jaw relaxed, and the smallest hint of irony curved his lips. "Your opinion seems to improve with each passing moment, Miss Lambton."

Esmie almost choked on the earl's very fine wine. Miss Lambton missed the sarcasm entirely, and Esmie covered her amusement by the expediency of bringing her napkin to her lips. For a moment, she felt sorry for Miss Lambton.

Mr. Lambton jumped into the breach. "And you, Miss Fortune, how do you find Oxfordshire?"

Miss Lambton slumped in relief, and the earl's gaze swung for the first time toward Esmie. She could not keep the flush from her cheeks, but she kept her spine straight and her eyes on Mr. Lambton as she answered. "I have not yet seen enough of the place to hold an informed opinion, sir."

"Ah, very diplomatic, ma'am." Mr. Lambton winked at her as if they were fellow conspirators. "For myself, I have always found it best to withhold forming an opinion until one is in command of all the facts. I see you are of the same mind."

Esmie wished a blush did not stain her cheeks. "Although it is not the fashion, sir, I do try to reserve judgment until all evidence has been presented." She could not help but look sidelong at the earl, for the conversation had taken an unexpectedly pertinent turn.

The earl's jaw went tight again. Unfortunately for Esmie's peace of mind, the tension only made the strong planes of his face more attractive. "How magnanimous of you, Miss Fortune. But I have never found it to take long to assess one's surroundings—or a damning situation."

Esmie curled her fingers around her fork. "True, sir. But there have been occasions when haste has led me to improper judgments. Perhaps you might, on occasion, fall victim to the same error."

He smiled with triumph. "I doubt it, madam. I always know when I am in error."

Mr. Lambton frowned, and Miss Lambton looked lovely in her confusion. Neither father nor daughter grasped the deeper meaning of the conversation.

Miss Lambton giggled. "All these cryptic remarks! And merely from a question of how I find the countryside." She fluttered her eyelashes at the earl. "The lawns and hedgerows are green, the houses fine, the laborers industrious—what more does one ask from the country?"

The earl lifted one eyebrow. "The country is more than picturesque, ma'am. It is the backbone of England. Crops, herds, tenants. All we enjoy flows from the fields and meadows."

Esmie failed to hide her surprise at the earl's remarks. So his holdings were more than a means to finance perfection. She had not considered before what sort of landlord he might be. She assumed he demanded all his cows give the same generous quantity of milk each day and his fields to replicate their bushels per hectare year after year. He was, after all, a man of inviolable standards.

Miss Lambton still looked baffled. She covered her confusion by sipping her wine. Her father frowned at her across the table, but she refused to catch his eye. Esmie lowered her own eyes to her plate. The earl, however, did not choose to leave her in peace. "Come, Miss Fortune, do not be coy. Tell the truth. How do you find Oxfordshire?"

"I find it remarkably lacking in cats, my lord."

Esmie could have bitten her tongue the moment the sharp retort leapt from it. Miss Lambton's eyes went round with shock at Esmie's faux pas, and Mr. Lambton coughed so violently that a footman stepped forward to pound him on the back. The earl looked surprised, and then Esmie could have sworn she saw a smile flicker across his face. But perhaps it was a trick of the candle-light, because a sober expression replaced any trace of amusement.

"Lacking in cats, indeed. I find it that way myself, ma'am, which is well to my liking."

"So I have heard, my lord."

The footmen stepped forward to remove the plates and serve the next course. Mr. Lambton seized the opportunity to turn the earl's attention to his daughter, and Esmie enjoyed several moments of blessed relief from the earl's scrutiny. Miss Lambton held forth on the glories of her London season, and the earl concealed his boredom fairly well. A tendril of jealousy curled in Esmie's stomach as she watched the elegant pair converse. An image rose in her mind—a fantasy of herself seated at the far end of the table opposite the earl, where his wife would sit when they entertained. She captivated everyone as she held forth on Cleopatra's younger sister, Arsinoë Auletes, who had been banished to Cyprus so as not to rival the famous Egyptian ruler. For once, Esmie's hair curled attractively around her face, and she wore a gown not unlike Miss Lambton's fashionable ivory satin.

"Do you not agree, Miss Fortune?"

Mr. Lambton's question snapped her from her dream. "Sir?"

"Do you not agree that criminals should be punished to the full extent of the law? I fear the earl, as magistrate, has a reputation for administering justice in his domain in such a manner that restitution is emphasized, rather than punishment. I have counseled him to reconsider his principles."

The earl had gone still, his glass of wine a mere inch from his lips.

"You have a reputation for mercy as *magistrate,* my lord?" She raised her eyes to his. Her determination could not waver, or she would appear guiltier than she was. "I find that surprising."

"I have a reputation for principles, madam. Logic and reason should be applied in such situations—not emotion."

His eyes held hers. They were both thinking of the highly charged way he had responded to the loss of the manuscript. His gaze didn't waver; neither did hers. And yet she could sense a change in him. At least a bit of softening. By the way his eyes darkened, she understood that he knew she had observed the change in him. A sudden shock of intimacy, unexpected and cold as sea spray, brought her to her senses. She dropped her gaze and fumbled for her fork.

Mr. Lambton would not be deterred. "Using logic and reason to dictate punishment is the only means to insure that civilization does not fall. One has only to look to France to see the dangers inherent in bypassing the application of justice."

Miss Lambton again looked prettily puzzled at the serious turn in the conversation. "One would not want mobs rioting. It would quite ruin the shopping in London, I'm sure."

The earl's fork paused halfway to his lips. He looked as if he might speak, then shook his head.

"Truly, Ashforth," Mr. Lambton insisted. "Mercy might have its heavenly rewards, but it causes a great many problems in the earthly realm. Surely if someone took something that belonged to you, you would not find yourself so lenient."

Esmie almost choked on the minted peas. She refused to look at the earl again, but a guilty blush stained her cheeks.

"If someone took something that belonged to me, it would be returned," the earl said quietly.

"Returned? Just like that?" Mr. Lambton pushed back from the table and reached for his wine. "You are a man of ideals, Ashforth, but I had not thought you so impractical."

"Not impractical, sir. In fact, I am quite sensible. No one who knows me would dare take what is mine."

Esmie wished she might slide beneath the table and disappear from the room. The earl's contempt and his certainty of her guilt cut with the acuity of a surgeon's blade.

"If someone took something of yours by mistake?" Esmie asked, not looking at him. "And it was then lost before it could be returned?" The words sprang from her lips before she could stop them. She dared peek at him out of the corner of her eye. He laid his fork aside and sat back in his chair.

"Mercy would not be my first instinct, Miss Fortune. Perhaps then I should follow Mr. Lambton's counsel and seek retribution rather than restitution."

For the first time, Esmie knew real fear, and yet she did not believe he would summon the authorities. No, he would seek retribution in his own way.

"Do you see no difference, my lord, between a crime and a mistake? Does intent count for nothing?"

"Intent is all, Miss Fortune. Indeed, it is all."

Mr. Lambton frowned at this interchange. Miss Lambton's eyes held a glint of suspicion. The earl's brow creased for the briefest of moments, and then he relaxed his shoulders and lifted his knife and fork to attack the fillet of beef. "So, Lambton, have you any suggestions for resolving the drainage difficulty behind the stables?"

He could not have chosen a topic more likely to engross Mr. Lambton. The two men launched into a detailed discussion of sluices as Esmie pushed the peas around her plate. Miss Lambton seemed content to let her eyes wander about the room and admire the paintings. When the drainage problem had been thoroughly discussed, the earl indicated his intention to forego brandy and cigars and the gentlemen accompanied Miss Lambton and Esmie to the gilt salon for coffee. Esmie almost wept with relief when the earl gave her permission to retire so she might check on the children. Mr. Lambton opened his mouth as if to object, but Esmie forestalled him, grateful for the opportunity to escape. To her dismay, the earl accompanied her from the room and into the corridor. He pulled the door to the salon shut behind them.

"A moment, Miss Fortune."

She despised the way he said her name, as if he relished its double meaning and found great pleasure in reminding her of how very *unfortunate* it sounded. "My lord? I thought you wished me to look in on the children?"

"It was merely an excuse to extricate you from an uncomfortable situation."

"Uncomfortable? What makes you think so, my lord?"

He clasped his hands behind his back and frowned at her, but the ferocity of his expression did nothing to dim his attractiveness—an attractiveness that made no sense at all. "Do not play games with me, madam. We are both far too intelligent for anything less than plain speaking. The sooner you are dismissed for the evening, the sooner you may return the manuscript. I trust you will do so in the next few moments, if you have not already."

Esmie bristled. She had made a mistake, true. She had been impulsive and not used her best judgment, but she had not meant to steal anything. Surely he could see that.

"If I knew where the manuscript was, my lord, I should return it."

"If you do not have it, madam, who does?"

"I do not know, my lord. Perhaps one of the servants, though I can't imagine why they would be interested."

"The manuscript is worth a great deal of money, even to those who would not appreciate its scholarly value. You are the only person in this household who would know its true worth. You are the only person with motive and means to steal it."

His words wounded her more deeply than his dismissal of her as a scholar. She might protest her innocence until dawn, and he would not change his opinion of her. The man who epitomized her highest ideals thought her to have no more morals than the mangy cat she'd introduced into his household.

"I will not stand here and be abused."

The earl's expression took on thundercloud intensity. "Even if you did not steal the manuscript, it disappeared while in your care. You alone are responsible." He moved closer until Esmie had to crane her neck to look up at him. To her amazement, he reached out and, unaccountably, laid one hand against her cheek. The shock of the contact almost sent her into a faint. She could feel his palm strong and warm against her face. At such close proximity, she could smell him as well, and the mingled scents of coffee and bay rum were far more intoxicating than the wine she'd drunk at dinner. Esmie's heart thrummed and warmth suffused her cheeks to match that imparted by his hand. Her eyes locked with his, and for a long, taut moment, neither said a word. She wondered whether, in his anger, he even knew he touched her so inappropriately.

"Why are you here?" His soft words wrapped Esmie in an odd sort of warmth, seductive and frightening. His dark eyes centered on her as if no other being existed. Long fingers stroked her cheek, a gesture as unconscious as it was improper.

"I am here to serve as the children's governess, my lord." The lie squeezed past the tightness in her throat. Her limbs were aflame, and she feared to acknowledge the feeling deep in her belly. He looked at her. Her. The unfortunate Miss Fortune. He had laid his hand against her cheek. He had caressed her, perhaps more from bewilderment than from any more passionate motivation, but Esmie knew with a flash of insight that this moment would live in her memory forever. When she grew old, she would feast upon it like a starving man at a banquet.

Behind them, the door to the gilt salon opened, and Miss Lambton stepped into the corridor.

"Oh!" The young woman's exclamation caused the earl to drop his hand. Esmie stepped backward, hardly able to feel the carpet beneath her slippers.

"Miss Fortune had something in her eye," the earl said. "That will do the trick, madam. 'Twas merely a lash."

He lied with such ease Esmie was astonished, but she was also grateful. Miss Lambton looked suspicious, and then her face relaxed into its beautiful, smooth lines. "You are kind, my lord, to take such an interest in a servant's misfortunes."

Esmie lowered her head in embarrassment. The earl bid her a curt good night, and turned with Miss Lambton back to the salon. The door closed behind them, leaving Esmie alone once again to quell the flames of embarrassment—and longing.

Chapter Seven

When he was unsettled, Julian Ashforth often as not paced the darkened corridors of the Abbey. The symmetry of the exercise soothed him as he stepped off each wing floor by floor until he completed the circuit that enclosed the central courtyard. Tonight, the practice did not calm him. What could, after his earlier behavior?

He had touched the governess. Had caressed her face like the veriest schoolboy. The remembrance of her cheek beneath his fingertips increased the speed of his steps.

The most difficult corridor to march was the one outside the schoolroom, and the length of hallway proved doubly difficult tonight. His steps paused outside that particular door. Of their own volition, his fingers curled around the doorknob. He did not turn it to enter and look upon his sleeping children with longing and regret as he sometimes did. Beyond that door lay the truth, and truth had a way of destroying all semblance of perfection. So, apparently, did Esmerelda Fortune.

His fingers released the knob. If he'd still been in possession of the manuscript, he would be in his library, sunk deep into the translation of the ancient text. He valued the *Life of Corinna* for its scholarly importance, but even more he valued the release it afforded from the prison of his life. Lost in the particularities of ancient Greek idiom, he could leave behind the demands of the Abbey and even, if he was very lucky, forget his imprudent action with Miss Fortune.

The earl resumed his determined march. His boots

made no sound against the thick carpets as he moved away from the nursery and its occupants. What he could never leave behind, however, were thoughts of his children. His children. He did not know what else to call them, the five smallish strangers that were so much a part of his life, and yet no part at all. They were his; they bore his name. In time, James would bear the title as well. The girls would marry to advantage—he would see to it. Phillip would be given an estate that would support him in a manner befitting a gentleman. In ten years, fifteen at most, they might all be gone from the Abbey, for even James would want the independence of young manhood. His son would not linger at Ashford once his university days were behind him. The thought of James, a vulnerable young buck on the town in London, caused a slight hitch in Julian's step as he rounded a corner and entered the east wing. He was not close enough to James to offer the paternal advice that his own father had given to him. Julian swallowed past the tightness in his throat. Heeding his own father's advice had landed him in his current straits.

At the end of the corridor, he descended the stairs to the floor below. Here lay the suite of rooms his mother had used in her day. The bedchamber, the morning room, the dressing room—all had been draped in the classical splendor that befitted the Countess of Ashforth. His late wife had redone the rooms, and Julian still missed the elegant simplicity of his mother's décor. Now, it was all chinoiserie, embroidered silk, and japanned cabinets. He stopped outside the door to the bedchamber. He had seldom been in the room since his wife's death five years before. Mrs. Robbins had packed away his wife's things because he could not bear to look upon them.

Slowly, he turned the knob. The lantern light trembled from his shaking hand. A sudden, unexpected surge of anger coursed through him. He had held his fury in check since the day he discovered his wife's infidelities, and it surprised him that those feelings would resurface now. Normally, he could harness any emotion. The only time his control slipped was in the company of his children, and so he spent little time with them.

His lantern barely penetrated the eerie shadows of the bedchamber. The red embroidery of the bed hangings looked strangely muted; in the daylight, it had often reminded him of the colors he'd seen in the one brothel he'd visited when he left university. Once his grandfather had gotten wind of the escapade, he'd set up a respectable, older mistress for Julian in a discreet part of London. Apparently, even fornication could be conducted with an aura of perfection.

He'd given up Julia when he'd married. The truth of the matter was that other than his initiation in the brothel, he'd only been with two women in his life. When Lillian died, he'd returned to Julia's comforts, but it was not the same, and he rarely visited her when he was in town. He wanted more, needed more, but now he was old enough to know he would never have what he wanted or needed in a life's companion.

A vision of Miss Lambton rose in his mind's eye. She was the image of a Greek goddess with her golden curls and shapely form, but he could hardly imagine making love to her. So pristine. So insipid. His mistress had won his respect and admiration. His wife had inspired devotion—until he'd discovered how one-sided his feelings and conduct had been. But Miss Lambton? The thought of her brought only a dampening sense of resignation.

A sudden flash of white to his right startled him. He raised the lantern higher. Reason dictated it was no ghost, but a human trespasser. He strode to the giant wardrobe in the corner. When he peered around the edge, he was somehow unsurprised to find the pale face of Miss Esmerelda Fortune.

She was, of course, clad in nothing but her nightgown and wrapper. The unexpected sight of Miss Fortune in dishabille stunned him. She looked as if she'd just come from her bed, and the image of her lying against rumpled sheets reawakened the unwanted feelings that had stirred in him earlier.

"M-m-my lord." She stumbled over the words, but didn't lose her composure. "I can ex-explain."

The heat began in his midsection and rose to consume his chest. Her unbound hair fell around her face in a riot of corkscrew curls like a wild, untamed creature. Her pale face flushed a bright pink, and the color lent an attractive sparkle to her eyes. Her mouth, slightly open, caused Julian to swallow as a sudden, fierce desire to claim her lips poured through him. Damn her eyes! And damn him for a fool for this insane attraction. He stepped back and shuttered his expression.

"I would say I am surprised, madam, but somehow this seems quite in character. I presume you have come here to retrieve my manuscript. No one else would dare disturb these rooms."

"No, my lord." She looked him boldly in the eye.

"No?"

"I've not come to retrieve the manuscript. I've come to find it."

The sincerity in her tone took Julian aback. He looked down and could see bare toes peeking out from beneath the hem of her nightgown. "So, you are searching for lost treasure?" Skepticism underscored each word.

"Yes, you might say that." She had drawn herself away from the wardrobe, and no longer cowered against it. Indeed, her spine had achieved its customary ramrod straightness. "A thorough search of the Abbey is the only way to locate it."

He believed her. The thought surprised him, but the truth struck him to the core. He had been wrong. She had not taken the manuscript, and now she prowled about his house in the night without a lantern, bent on retrieving it for him. Their dinner repartee came back to him, and suddenly that conversation acquired a new level of meaning.

The Earl of Ashforth was seldom wrong. It discomfited him greatly to be in error, almost as much as it discomfited him to find such intriguing pleasure in Miss Fortune's company.

"You did not take it." He pronounced the words as if he wanted to convince her of the fact.

She gave him a measuring stare. "I told you so in the beginning."

"Yes, you did." He was like a ship's sail that had lost the wind. Esmie sidled around him and made for the door, but he could not let her go.

"Wait."

She turned. Her hair fell over her shoulder, almost to her waist. The moonlight through the open doorway lit her figure, and he could see the dim outlines of her form beneath the nightgown. Desire stirred again, but he tamped it down.

"Have you made a thorough search, then?"

She hesitated, as if considering whether to lie or not. "No. You interrupted my efforts. Perhaps you wish to continue the search alone. Shall I return to my own part of the house?"

Despite her offer, she made no move to leave. He both wanted her presence and despised himself for wanting it. The challenge of Miss Esmerelda Fortune made him feel alive for the first time in a very long while. She had not stolen the manuscript. He had misjudged her in that. But if she had not stolen it, then who had? And where was it now?

"Perhaps we should join forces, madam. Two people will double the pace of the search."

She stared at him as if he had grown horns, and then a shadow crossed her face. Perhaps she remembered with distaste his forwardness in touching her cheek. At length, she nodded in agreement. "That would seem the quickest course, my lord."

Her acquiescence surprised and pleased him. He shouldn't allow himself the pleasure of her prickly, provoking company, but he found himself glad he had been abroad that night to catch Miss Fortune in her midnight wanderings.

Esmie had thought it frightening to canvass the darkened house alone, but having the earl so near alarmed her more. She feared she would betray her agitation at his nearness. Somehow she could not connect him in her mind with the arrogant scholar who had penned that scathing letter of rejection, or the man who stood between her and her dream of Athena Hall. Side by side, they searched the suite of rooms where he'd found her—to no avail. When he questioned her about the possibility of the manuscript being hidden in one of the attics, she acknowledged it. Her room and her trunk were not very far from such a honeycomb of hiding places. It had seemed like a good idea at the time, to follow him up two flights of stairs, through the attic door, and into the silent storage areas.

She had blown out her candle just before the earl discovered her, so he relit it from his lantern. The task required Esmie to stand quite near him, and her hands shook. The candle's flame bobbed and danced, and at the very moment she looked up, she saw understanding dawn in the earl's eyes. Her breath caught in her chest. Afraid that he would make some mention of her trembling, she dropped her gaze. At least he no longer believed her a thief. That was something.

They entered a long, narrow room under the eaves. Esmie could barely stand upright, and the earl stooped as he made his way down the center aisle formed by precise lines of furniture, wooden crates, trunks and chests, and other, less recognizable bundles. The same perfection that ruled the floors below was no less evident in the attics.

Esmie sighed with despair. "It could be anywhere. Lady Caroline might make her debut before we find it."

The earl ignored the reference to his youngest child. "Alexander conquered the known world one province at a time. Our task is considerably smaller. I shall start here. Why don't you try those trunks?"

Esmie was grateful for some distance between them. He was wearing his dressing gown again. His informal attire enticed her, for the dark green silk softened him somehow. Determined to discipline her thoughts, she lifted the lid of the nearest trunk.

The contents belonged to a lady, and Esmie was surprised at the fashionable style of the garments. She would have expected to find gowns and bonnets belonging to the earl's grandmother, or perhaps his mother, but these items were entirely modern. Her fingers caressed a beautiful rose silk, painstakingly stored in layers of tissue. Who would have left such a beautiful gown behind?

Esmie's chin lifted from her contemplation of the contents, and her eyes darted down the row of similar trunks. She counted twelve before they passed beyond the light of her candle. Her breath caught in her throat as realization struck. The clothes belonged, of course, to the earl's late wife. Esmie swallowed. Guiltily, she withdrew her hand from the trunk and softly closed the lid. He must have loved her very much if he had not parted with a single item of her belongings.

Reluctantly, she opened the next trunk. It contained a hodgepodge of objects from the countess's dressing table. A silver hairbrush. A pot of rouge. Some combs and hairpins. And a small bundle of letters, tied with a faded red ribbon. They had begun to yellow around the edges, but she could make out the direction on the topmost one, to a Sir Richard Clark in Northumberland. It bore no sign of having been franked. With a glance over her shoulder at the earl, who had waded into a sea of furniture, and was noisily opening and closing wardrobes, Esmie withdrew the packet. The movement dislodged the loosely bound ribbon, and the letters spilled across the contents of the trunk.

There were a number of letters, addressed to a variety of gentlemen, and none appearing to have been posted. Esmie supposed they must be relatives of the late countess, for it would be improper to have corresponded with a gentleman who was not a member of the family.

The earl slammed a drawer, and Esmie jumped. She looked toward him and found his eyes on her. The raised lid of the trunk concealed the letters. Esmie forced herself to smile. "No luck." The words came out little more than a whisper.

"None here, either."

She bent her head as though continuing her search, but instead she gathered the letters and retied the ribbon, before tucking them back inside the trunk. Depression settled on her chest like a weight. She despised the man. He was arrogant, pompous, conceited. . . . But to know that his affections still belonged to his long-dead wife—somehow that made her loneliness harder to bear.

They worked in near silence for the better part of an hour, Esmie keenly aware of the earl's movements. Finally the entire attic room had been searched. "It is not here," he said. "We should adjourn for the night."

"It is late." A secret part of her was relieved they'd not uncovered the manuscript. Perhaps he would invite her to search with him again. And then she cursed herself for her foolishness. This was a man who despised her and all she stood for. Together, they left the room. The darkness of the corridors and stairways compounded the delicious sense of intimacy. The earl steered her in the direction of the schoolroom, but when they passed the door to his private library, he hesitated. To Esmie's surprise, he reached toward her. With a gulp, she placed her hand in his.

"As I thought. You are cold." He squeezed her fingers. "Even in summer, the Abbey can be chilly, and you have no fire to warm your room. Perhaps some brandy would substitute."

A poor apology, but it was the only sort of peace offering a man as proud as the earl would make. Esmie was wise enough, and foolish enough, to accept it.

"Yes. Brandy might help." Esmie could hardly believe he was not bundling her into the schoolroom and rushing away. For an instant, she let herself pretend that his need for her companionship—more than concern for her well-being or regret for his accusations—motivated him.

He led her into the library. She swallowed around the sudden lump in her throat. "Can you forgive me, my lord, for my imprudent actions that led to this situation?"

He paused in the act of pouring the brandy. "Miss Fortune, I find you are secretly given to acts of imprudence. A most disconcerting trait in a governess." The words might have been tart, except that he said them with a softness that belied any upbraiding. "What's more, when I am in your presence, I find myself given to acts of imprudence as well. That is even more disconcerting."

"You, my lord? Imprudent?" They were both thinking of his actions earlier in the evening. Esmie had never dreamed a man's hand against her cheek would evoke such longing.

He gave her the brandy, and she could feel the warmth on the glass where his fingers had been. She wrapped her hand around the snifter and gently swirled the contents, as she had seen her Italian stepfather do. The rich scent of the liquor floated upward.

"Most imprudent acts, madam. I should not have al-

lowed you to accompany me this evening. I should have
sent you straight back to the schoolroom." His dark eyes
fixed on her.

Esmie turned away, so he would not see her blush.
"The Abbey is very large, and two people can make a
search more efficiently. Our actions tonight were only
logical. Besides, the manuscript is my responsibility."

"Hmm." He neither agreed nor disagreed, which
caused Esmie to blush even more. When she turned back
toward him, he smiled at her, and her heart skipped a
beat. "And how shall you repay me if it is not found?"
he asked, one eyebrow arched.

Esmie gulped down a swallow of brandy. How, indeed? "I will find the means, my lord."

He lifted his own glass to his lips. After an apprecia-
tive taste, he said, "It would take a very long time on a
governess's wages to repay such a sum. You would be
here until Caroline made her debut, if not longer."

Esmie would not let her longing show on her face.
She carefully schooled her features. "You will not have
need of me that long, my lord."

"You do not think that present circumstances might
supersede our agreement?"

His gaze held hers, and Esmie wished she were the
kind of woman who could simper and flirt. She wished
she had some hope of enchanting Julian Armstrong, Earl
of Ashforth, even temporarily. But she was plain Esmerelda Fortune. Men did not look at her more than once,
if they looked at all, and a man like the earl would never
entertain any thoughts of her beyond how efficacious she
might be in educating his children. He was merely being
kind. She would be wrong to mistake it for anything
other than the offhand apology it was.

She took a sip of the brandy. It burned its way down
her throat, and she did indeed feel warmer, which she
hardly needed. The earl's company produced a bonfire
within.

"Would you like to see some of my other treasures?"
He looked at her strangely, and Esmie wondered if he
might have changed his mind again about considering
her a thief.

"Yes. Of course." She would have agreed to peruse Mrs. Robbins's household accounts for more time in his company.

He crossed to a bookcase and withdrew a large folio. "You will know this, of course. Not as grand as the *Corinna,* but a respectable find by any account."

He laid the leather-bound volume on the table and motioned her to stand beside him. "You may examine it, if you wish."

Esmie moved next to him, though it sent shivers of pleasure at his nearness tripping across her skin. She forced her attention to the book. It was a copy of *The Odyssey* dating from the thirteenth century. "I wonder if Homer thought his work would find its way into such form," she mused. Detailed illuminations depicted Penelope at her loom and Odysseus bound to the mast of his ship by his men to escape the Siren's call.

"I should think Homer, like any author, had such hopes."

"Yes, all authors secretly desire to live on beyond their days." Esmie knew that hope well enough from her own dreams.

His hand pressed flat against the tabletop. "You speak as if you have some knowledge of that desire."

Esmie lowered her head, disconcerted at how the very word *desire,* spoken by him, turned her into a mass of emotion.

"A desire to live beyond my time? Of course not, my lord." Clearly he had not connected her with the woman whose scholarship he had so rudely spurned. What's more, here in his library, she could see he was the true scholar, educated by the most learned men in England, his lectures at All Souls College always well received. She was merely a self-educated dabbler. She might be a dreamer, but she was wise enough in the ways of the world to know what was what. His letter had been rude, but perhaps it had been the truth. Perhaps she had no business dreaming of a school or of a scholarly reputation.

He did not respond to her denial. Instead, he leafed through several pages of the book to show her another illumination. His sleeve brushed hers. "Here is the siege of Troy. A rather odd-looking horse, I must admit. Not at all as I've pictured it."

Indeed, the horse looked more like an oversized hunting dog. Esmie smiled. "He looks as if he would point if a rabbit darted across his path."

The earl laughed, and Esmie joined in. Their eyes locked, and the humor evaporated, leaving a raw emptiness in its place. His nearness made his gaze more disconcerting than usual. Her pulse beat so strongly in her throat, he must surely see it.

"I did not think seminaries for young ladies placed great emphasis on the classics. Where did you study?"

The soft question caught her off guard. She groped for a vague answer. "Here and there. Nowhere in particular."

"Had you a tutor?"

"No. Never." She should turn away, break free, but how could she, when the attention of a man of knowledge was all she'd ever longed for? Such a night might never come again.

"You really are a remarkable creature."

He said the words as calmly as if he were commenting on the weather. Esmie hardly dared breathe. Surely she was dreaming?

Tiny lines marked the corners of his eyes. Golden flecks dusted his dark hair. Her face angled upward, to accommodate his greater height, and her body trembled with awareness of his strong form so close to her. She had never felt this way in her entire life. She had never dreamed there was any possibility she might.

"Miss Fortune." He breathed her name, and for the first time his voice held no ironic undertone. "Esmerelda."

She wanted to urge him to call her Esmie, but she feared breaking the spell. Her fear, though, did not compare to the inescapable joy of his complete attention.

But she was not prepared for his head to dip toward hers. And nothing could have readied her for the feel of his lips against her own. Sweet warmth spread over her, through her, inside her. His lips felt like satin and tasted like brandy. His warm breath mingled with hers.

His mouth moved against hers, strong and soft, mobile and firm.

Esmie wanted to die in that very moment, to expire in the arms of her perfect earl, for what could life offer after this? She had assumed his kiss would be brief, that he would come to his senses and end it, but instead his arms wrapped around her. He drew her against him, and for the first time in her life she was pressed against a male form. Sensation clogged her brain. No rational thought, only feelings—feelings she had only dared to hope for in the most secret parts of her soul. The Earl of Ashforth, the paragon earl, held plain Esmerelda Fortune in his arms as if she were the most desirable commodity in the world.

He lifted his head, then, and Esmie knew herself foolish to hope for tender words, but she did. She wanted them desperately. She lifted her gaze to his.

It was like looking at a stranger. The depths of his brown eyes had gone flat. His arms loosened and fell to his sides. He pulled back and turned away, but not before Esmie saw the horror in his expression.

Her perfect earl had come to his senses.

Chapter Eight

*J*ulian's first instinct was to flee. He feared the stones of Ashworth Abbey might crumble at any moment. He spun away from Esmerelda and took two steps toward the door before years of training stopped him cold. He must bear the blame, he and he alone. Slowly, he turned to face Esmerelda Fortune.

Her lips were red and slightly swollen. The sight sent an arrow of need and desire straight to his groin. A rosy flush covered her face, and her eyes were wide with hurt. Her hair curled in every possible direction, and he could only wonder that he had thought her plain. He could certainly never again think her undesirable. No woman had made him so forget himself or what he owed his position. She was a respectable woman under his protection, and he had compromised her. The truly honorable thing would be to offer for her, but of course he could not. He had sacrificed his own life for the preservation of the Abbey and all it stood for; he had not expected those around him to sacrifice theirs as well. Like him, Miss Esmerelda Fortune was fodder for the perpetuation of the Ashforth perfection.

"Miss Fortune . . ." How did one apologize for taking advantage in such a manner—especially to a woman in one's employ? "Miss Fortune, I cannot express my regret enough." The words came out as formally as if he addressed a queen. "Please forgive me. There is no excuse."

Her cheeks flushed an even deeper hue. He wanted to offer her some reason for his behavior, wanted to blame her for what had happened. But the burden was his, as was the task of making this right. Only how could he contemplate making such a thing right when what he really wanted was to take her in his arms again and discover if a second kiss could equal the sheer pleasure of the first?

Despite her high color, she maintained her composure. "There is no need for you to make excuses, sir. I have got what I deserved. It is late, and this whole evening has been quite improper. I should never have agreed to search with you. What you must think of me . . ."

Her mortification pierced him to the depths of his heart, or what remained of it. "The fault is entirely mine, madam. Without doubt. I can only beg your forgiveness and promise never to repeat such extraordinary behavior." Even though he wanted to repeat it very much, and would have been all too glad to do so at that very moment. Why couldn't Miss Lambton inspire this sort of feeling? Why was she not the one who could share in the pleasure of his library and make him feel as if his very being was on fire? Instead, he must wed a blond beauty who simpered and shopped and never appeared to have a thought that didn't concern her bonnet or her frock.

He sighed and shoved his hands into the pockets of his dressing gown. At least with them imprisoned there, they would not be able to reach for Esmerelda and pull her into his arms.

"Repeat such behavior?" she echoed rather weakly. "I can't imagine what would tempt you to do so."

The light had gone from her eyes. He had taken it. The knowledge filled him with despair. She had thought his kiss inspired by her availability. She had no conception of the feelings she stirred within him—which was to the good, he told himself. He should not be tempted. He would not be tempted. Too much was at stake.

"Miss Fortune . . ."

"Please, do not abuse yourself so. This is best forgotten." She stepped away from him and moved toward the door. "I will find the manuscript and return it to you. Have no fear on that score. Good night."

She slipped from the room like a wraith. Julian stood

immobile next to the long table and watched her go. All the air left the room with her, and he had the strangest feeling she had taken his last bit of hope as well. His hands trembled in the pockets of his dressing gown. He did not care for the feelings Esmerelda Fortune stirred within him.

"Liar," he whispered into the void. For he did care. He cared very much indeed, and such longings could never be satisfied. Not when they belonged to the Earl of Ashforth.

Esmie had suffered every sort of indignity imaginable during her two seasons in London. She had been scorned by society and by her own mother. She had seen her stepsister capture a prince, while Esmie received no offers of marriage whatsoever. She had sat among the elderly widows at balls when no partners appeared to claim her hand. She had hidden in grottos at garden parties, and when she could not hide, she had endured her mother's painful attempts to play the coquette. She had stood mortified as her mother flung her at one eligible gentleman after another. Esmie had pirouetted in front of the modiste's mirror and listened to every possible flaw of her person cataloged in a painfully thorough manner. She had bowed her head meekly when gentlemen scolded her for offering an opinion, and she had once been given the cut direct by the reigning beauty of society.

But none of these humiliations compared to what Esmie felt now, as she stumbled toward the schoolroom. Her lungs pressed against her ribs as if they had no room to expand. She held her tears in check until she gained the sanctuary of her barren little chamber. With her door closed safely behind her, she allowed the dam to burst. Rough, ragged sobs shook her shoulders. She moved to fling herself on the bed, but even that dramatic gesture could not express the horror and disgust and utter shame that filled her.

He had kissed her merely because she was there. She had placed herself with him in a darkened library late at night. She had been wearing nothing but a night rail and wrapper. No wonder he had kissed her. A wonder he hadn't thought she was asking for him to make love to her.

Esmie sobbed harder. He would never look at her as he did Miss Lambton. He would never lead her decorously into dinner. She would never grace his table and charm his guests. In his eyes, not only was she a failure as a scholar, she was not fit to be the Countess of Ashforth. No, she was merely worthy to be a tawdry interlude in his library.

Agitated, she paced from the door to her trunk and back again, wringing her hands like a character in a Cheltenham tragedy. She must leave. But, no, she couldn't leave—not until she returned the manuscript. Honor demanded that, even if all hope for her scholarship and her school was gone. She would have to see him again, perhaps several more times, before she could make her escape. She no longer cared about using the manuscript for her own dreams. She only cared about distancing herself from the Earl of Ashforth.

Esmie sank down on the top of the trunk and lifted her fingers to her lips. She could still feel the warmth of him there, and when she ran the tip of her tongue across her lower lip she could taste the brandy they'd shared. Clearly, she did not need her mother to humiliate her. She was perfectly capable of humiliating herself.

Esmie jumped in alarm at the soft knock on her door. Surely he would not follow her to her room? Unless, of course, he had reconsidered his attempt at chivalry and thought to avail himself of what she had so blatantly offered.

The knock came again. Esmie pushed her hair behind her ears and cleared her throat. She wiped away her tears. "Come in."

The door opened. To her surprise, Sophie appeared.

Esmie's tears dried immediately.

"Miss Fortune?" The child's dark ringlets were concealed under a white nightcap. "Why are you still awake?"

Esmie knew her only defense was to assert her position as governess. "More to the point, Lady Sophie, why are you? It is the middle of the night."

Sophie eyed her shrewdly. "Yes, it is, isn't it? I heard you come through the schoolroom just now."

Though Sophie was only ten, she had the brittle,

weary air of a person five times her age, as if life had already beaten her down and she had accepted the pummeling with little resistance. Esmie knew better than to lie, for she had no idea what the girl had seen. A chill swept over her. What if Sophie had witnessed her emerging from the library in tears at this late hour? That would be all the situation needed—public exposure of her excessively private humiliation.

"I was looking for something," Esmie offered vaguely. She hoped the child would let it go, but she could tell from the way Sophie's eyes hardened that the girl sensed her advantage.

"What could you possibly be looking for in the middle of the night?" Sophie folded her arms across her chest and assumed a stance that reminded Esmie of Mrs. Robbins.

Esmie stared helplessly at her. "Looking for? Why . . ." And then a vision of her first day at the Abbey rose in her mind. "I was looking for Plutarch, of course."

"Your cat?" Sophie looked doubtful.

"Yes."

"The earl banished him to the stables."

Esmie tried her best to look innocent. "Did he?"

Sophie still frowned with suspicion, but she didn't press the point.

"You should return to bed," Esmie told the girl. "As I am planning to do."

Sophie shot a glance at Esmie's narrow iron bedstead. The coverlet and pillow lay quite undisturbed. "Return to bed?" the girl asked, one eyebrow raised.

Brusquely, Esmie rose from the trunk and shooed the girl from her room. "Yes. Immediately. Now off you go." She followed Sophie halfway across the schoolroom until the girl reached the door to her own bedchamber. "Good night, Sophie," Esmie whispered, but the girl pretended not to hear. Instead, she tossed her head— the nightcap dampened the effect of swinging ringlets— and disappeared into her room, closing the door firmly behind her.

Esmie did the same. She slipped off her wrapper and hung it on a peg before she climbed between the cool sheets. She did not feel cold, though. Instead she felt

quite warm, for she could not turn her thoughts from
the feel of the earl's lips against hers. It should never
have happened. She would pay the price on the morrow.
He might dismiss her. Worse, he might ignore her. But
whatever tomorrow might bring, she had the memory of
the earl's eyes as they gazed into hers and the feel of
his kiss to treasure always. It would never be enough,
but it was better than nothing at all.

Julian closed the library door behind him. No point
in pretending to sleep. He might as well continue to look
for the manuscript.

What had possessed him to indulge in such an act of
insanity? Perhaps it had been the location, for his private
library was his and his alone—it had nothing to do with
the Ashforth legacy or the practice of perfection. Or
perhaps it was the lateness of the hour. He could try to
manufacture all manner of excuses for his conduct, but
no justification existed. He had allowed instinct to over-
ride duty and training. He must make amends to Miss
Fortune, and he must not allow such a thing to happen
again.

But as he strode through the darkened corridors of
the Abbey, he could not lie to himself. He would never
make the proper amends to Esmerelda, because he
would never marry her. Besides, it was not mere honor
that first set the notion of offering for Esmerelda Fortune in his brain. He must be honest about that. It was
inclination. Unexpected, unsettling inclination that had
culminated in the most remarkable kiss of his life. He
wanted such a thing to happen again. He wanted to feel
her against him, beneath him, above him.

Julian turned the corner and tromped resolutely down
the length of the east wing corridor. He doubted he
would do much searching, but if he walked for the remainder of the night, he might escape the hounds of
desire that nipped at his heels.

"James." Phillip and Phoebe nudged their older brother
who slept soundly. Caroline tugged his foot at the end of
the bed. "James," they hissed in concert. They hadn't
dared bring a candle, and when they'd heard their father's

footsteps in the hallway, it had almost ended their mission. But the earl had not paused at the schoolroom door, and the children had slipped into their older brother's room.

"Hmm . . . what?" James woke abruptly to find three sets of eyes staring down at him in the moonlight.

"Something's happened," Phoebe whispered. "Father and Miss Esmie were in the library. We heard them talking. And then it was quiet, and she ran out. We think we heard her crying."

This news brought James fully awake. "Are you sure?"

Caroline nodded solemnly. "Quite. Do you think he's sacked her, James? Will she leave, like the others?"

"We don't want *her* to leave," added Phillip. "She's not like the others."

James scratched his head. "No, she's not. Though I should be surprised if father's dismissed her. He needs her too much."

Phoebe looked puzzled. "What ever for?"

"For us, you goose. Somebody's got to keep us from scaring off Miss Lambton."

"Oh."

"He didn't look at Miss Lambton like she was cakes and sweets," Caroline said. "He looked at her like a china doll."

"Yes. Cold and still," added Phillip.

"And she doesn't look at him like he's a new bonnet," Caroline added. "In fact, she doesn't look at him very much at all. She looks at the house, at the carpets and furnishings and things. As if she's doing sums in her head."

James sighed. He had observed the same thing. "She is not the one," he pronounced. The others nodded in agreement.

"So," ventured Phillip, "how do we get rid of the Lambtons?"

"If he won't see to his own interests," Phoebe chimed in, "then we will have to see to them on his behalf."

James studied his brother and sisters. "The consequences will be far worse than when we ran off the other governesses. Father will be quite angry."

Phillip squared his shoulders manfully. "Better to be

angry with us than wed to someone who doesn't love him—or his children."

"Yes," James agreed, "but we might be sent away to school. This is a far more serious business than running off those harpies Mrs. Hazelwood sends."

Phoebe sniffled. "If father marries Miss Lambton, I have a feeling we shall all be sent off to school in any event."

James nodded. "Very well, then. We shall need a plan."

"The lake works well," said Phillip. "Miss Clark and Miss Johnston resigned on the spot."

James pulled back the bedclothes and motioned to the others to climb in. "Settle in, then. We shall need to plan carefully to insure our success."

The moon had almost set before the children had finished plotting.

Dawn came too quickly for Esmerelda's peace of mind. She took her breakfast with the housekeeper. The bounty of food on the table in the servants' dining room never ceased to astonish her. If she continued to eat in this manner, she would grow quite fat.

"So, my dear," Mrs. Robbins said as she buttered her toast. "The gossip among the servants is that the earl will propose within the week. What do you think?"

Esmie was surprised the dour housekeeper would indulge in such speculation, but the hope of the house having a mistress must have loosened her tongue.

"I'm sure I could not say what the earl's intentions are," Esmie demurred, turning her attention to her own breakfast. But Mrs. Robbins would not let the matter drop.

"Miss Lambton seems the proper sort to be mistress of the Abbey. She is fashionable, and will lavish attention on the house in ways only a woman can do. It is regrettable her father made his fortune in trade, but I suppose that is the only way money is to be got these days."

"Yes, I suppose it is." The toast, which only moments before had slipped with buttery ease down Esmie's throat, tasted like sawdust.

"I hope they will wed before summer's end," the housekeeper said as she reached for the jam pot. "When there's a marriage to be made, it is best not to wait."

Esmie pasted a false smile on her face. "I agree, Mrs. Robbins. Once there is an engagement, it is best to marry as quickly as possible."

"I knew you would see it that way." The housekeeper's smile was only slightly less ferocious than her frown. "You are a sensible girl, Miss Fortune."

A sensible girl. A dull girl. A bookish girl. An unattractive girl. It was all of a piece.

"The children will be ready for their lessons." Esmie laid her napkin beside her plate and rose from the table.

"Miss Fortune?" The housekeeper's sharp tone stopped Esmie at the door.

"Yes?"

"I should think it unsafe to wander the house at night. Perhaps you should not venture from the schoolroom in the dark. One never knows what ghosts might be about."

The shrewd light in the other woman's eyes caused a knot to form in Esmie's stomach. "Wander the house at night? Why ever would I do such a thing, Mrs. Robbins?"

"Hmm. Perhaps I am mistaken, then. One of the maids thought she saw you near the countess's rooms."

"Then it is the maid you need to lecture, ma'am, if she was abroad in the darkness."

The older woman pursed her lips. "Do not get ideas above your station, Miss Fortune. I warn you as a friend."

Esmie refused to flinch. "What you imply is distasteful, ma'am. Good day."

The lie lodged in Esmie's throat. She should have known that no one's actions in such a house would go unnoticed. Servants and children were everywhere. Still, she would have to continue to search at night. She could not leave the Abbey with her head high until she returned the manuscript to the earl. Of course, the height of her head would merely conceal the depths of her spirits.

Chapter Nine

*M*iss Maria Lambton was not a young woman to be trifled with, though the ladies and gentlemen of the *ton* were by and large unaware of the shrewd, self-serving heart that beat in her fashionable breast. Guinea-gold curls and china blue eyes could prove deceptive, indeed.

"Papa, you must divert his attentions from that governess. Heaven knows how he can stand to look at her, but she holds his interest with her conversation." Father and daughter had ensconced themselves in the morning sun of the grand salon.

Mr. Lambton shook his head. "She is not so difficult to look upon, my dear. In fact, she appeared almost passable last night." Mr. Lambton paused to take snuff from the back of his hand. The resulting sneeze echoed through the long room.

Miss Lambton lifted her head and arched her swanlike neck. "Papa, you are not infatuated yourself? Men are impossible." She brushed imaginary crumbs from her lap and set her dish of tea on the marble-topped table next to the settee.

"Infatuated? No, no, my dear." He tucked his snuff-box into his pocket. "Still, if I must make love to a woman to obtain this Abbey, Miss Fortune is not the worst of fates."

"You will not be obtaining Ashforth Abbey, Papa." Miss Lambton raised her chin. "All this shall be mine." She waved her hand to indicate the mantelpiece of Italian marble, crystal chandeliers from Austria, and Axminster carpets. "You will, however, be welcome to visit as often as you like."

Mr. Lambton could hardly fault his daughter for the selfishness and greed he had worked so diligently to instill. "Visit? If you become mistress of all this, Maria, then I shall take up residence. I could occupy an entire wing without you or the earl perceiving the difference." He chuckled. "You seem quite certain of yourself for a woman who is worried about the governess."

Her eyes flashed. "I never said I was worried, merely that I do not want his lordship's attention diverted from me." Miss Lambton bristled in the manner of a cat whose territory has been disturbed. "You will keep the aptly named Miss Fortune occupied, if you want the Lambtons to become the rightful residents of Ashforth Abbey."

"Pity I can't just call in the mortgage," Mr. Lambton observed as he rubbed his chin. " 'Twould be much simpler."

"Money cannot buy a title, only marriage to one," Miss Lambton reminded him. "In one generation, we may wipe out the stench of trade. My children will be welcome in every drawing room in London."

Mr. Lambton's smirk matched his daughter's. "As will my daughter, when she is Countess of Ashforth." He bent to brush a kiss across her cheek. "And that was the dearest wish of your mother. Very well, my dear. I'll run the governess to earth. I hope she doesn't fall too desperately in love with me. These affairs can become quite messy. Remember Tunbridge Wells?"

"La, Papa, that Miss Smith would have expected a proposal from any man who so much as bid her good day. You take it too much to heart."

Mr. Lambton paused, serious for a moment. "And you, Maria, perhaps do not take it enough to heart."

She looked at him blankly. "I have no idea what you mean."

"Of course you don't, my dear." He patted her cheek, and then glanced around the drawing room. "It is that very quality which will gain you all this." He retrieved his gloves and hat from a side table. "Perhaps the governess might fancy a ramble through the gardens. Where might one find Miss Fortune on a sunny day, do you think?"

"Involved in some dreary task, I suppose." Miss Lambton yawned very prettily. "Perhaps washing ink stains from her fingers."

Mr. Lambton chuckled and left the room. Miss Lambton remained where she was, and continued to contemplate the pride of possession one might take in a room such as the grand salon.

Esmie was enjoying a rare moment's peace in the garden. The children had dispersed after luncheon to their various pursuits. The old nurse had appeared in the schoolroom and offered to put Caroline down for her nap. The girl had protested, but since her objections had been punctuated by vigorous yawns, Esmie had insisted.

Sophie had disappeared somewhere to indulge in a good sulk. A groom had promised the twins a trip to the stables to visit Plutarch, and James was bent over one of the schoolroom desks as he worked on his mysterious translation. Esmie wondered what the boy found so interesting. All she could determine was that it was Greek and he seemed to have no trouble with the task.

The summer sun warmed her shoulders, and she removed her bonnet so she might feel the welcome touch on her hair. She had never enjoyed the out of doors, but somehow the Oxfordshire summer worked its magic. The caress of the sun led to thoughts of the earl's kiss, and in moments she was overheated, indeed.

Esmie started with guilt when she heard someone approach. Her heart raced, for she both feared and hoped it was the earl who advanced down the path through the azaleas. When the figure rounded the curve, however, it was not the earl, but Mr. Lambton instead.

"Miss Fortune." He smiled with pleasure. "I'm delighted to find you here." And he was happy to see her, she could tell. His manners were easy and unaffected. If she must have company, she was glad it was Mr. Lambton. Truly she was.

"Good day, Mr. Lambton." She was unsure whether to invite him to sit with her. Suddenly the bench seemed very small.

"May I join you?" He gestured toward the seat beside her. The decision made for her, Esmie moved to one end. Mr. Lambton sat next to her, not too near and not too far. Really, she was allowing her agitation with the earl to spread to perfectly innocent encounters.

"I'm glad for a bit of company." She wished she hadn't taken off her bonnet, but at least her sidelong view would not be restricted, and she might read Mr. Lambton's expression clearly.

"You are right to be outside enjoying such a day. I attempted to persuade my daughter to accompany me in a turn about the grounds, but she would not be moved from the grand salon."

"Have you visited the Abbey before?" she inquired politely.

"No, no. Though I anticipate being a frequent guest in the future."

"Oh." So both sides intended the marriage. She had known that, but somehow Mr. Lambton's words transformed the notion from possibility to certainty.

"Since my daughter would not accompany me, perhaps you will take my arm for a short stroll? I do want to see the folly bridge, on the other side of the formal garden."

The beautiful Palladian bridge was renowned throughout England for its perfect proportions. "Yes, indeed, Mr. Lambton. I should be glad to accompany you."

"Shall we, then?" He rose and offered his arm. She took it without hesitation.

Mr. Lambton proved himself a charming conversationalist, and Esmie relaxed in his company. They moved through the symmetry of the Italianate garden and beyond, to the path that wound through the meadow towards the bridge in the distance.

"You find your position here tolerable?" he asked, when they had almost reached the bridge. "I should think five children would be a difficult charge."

"I have always enjoyed a challenge," Esmie demurred.

"Ah, I see you mean to be circumspect. I understand, my dear. A woman in your position cannot be too careful. But . . ."

"Yes?"

"Perhaps you will not always be in such a position."

Esmie glanced up at him, startled. He smiled in a pleasant manner, and she wondered if she was wrong to read some deeper meaning into his words. Heavens, had Mr. Lambton formed a *tendre* for her?

"I suspect I shall always earn my bread, sir."

He patted her hand where it rested against his sleeve. "Come, Miss Fortune, you are far too young to resign yourself to a life of servitude. Surely some dashing suitor will happen along. Is that not the way of the world?"

"Perhaps it is the way of your world, sir."

He stopped, and she stopped next to him of necessity, for her hand still rested on his sleeve. "Do not be too sure, madam. One never knows when the heart may take a tumble."

He was looking at her oddly. It reminded her of how the earl had looked at her in the library, just before he had kissed her. Esmie stepped back in alarm.

She slipped her hand from his arm and turned as if to take in the view. "I suppose one doesn't know what will happen in the future. The heart is the most volatile of creatures." Esmie smiled. "We are very close to the bridge. Shall we cross it and enjoy the prospect toward the house? I have heard it is most picturesque."

"As you wish, my dear. You will find I am a most amiable fellow, despite my advanced age."

Esmie smiled woodenly. Mr. Lambton was flirting with her. Should she ignore him or humor him? Suddenly, she saw the middle-aged merchant in a new light. What if he did nurture an attraction for her? She could never have the earl, but she might have a man such as Mr. Lambton. She need never be hungry or cold—or starved for books. He was wealthy. She might even have her school. Though she could not love him, she would be faithful and loyal.

Faithful and loyal. Like a hunting dog. A wave of distaste rolled over her. But once the seed had been planted, she could not quite cull it from the fertile ground of her thoughts. Last night had shown that though the earl might be so imperfect as to kiss her, he could never form any serious attachment. She had seen the look of horror in his eyes before she'd fled the library.

"You? Advanced age? Do not deal in Spanish coin, sir." The reply was more coquettish than she intended, but Mr. Lambton did not look displeased. She set off for the bridge before he could offer her his arm again, feeling like Odysseus as he navigated between Scylla and Charybdis.

Julian had closeted himself in his study with the account books. Twice, the butler had brought tea, and the hours of the morning passed swiftly, but still, no escape appeared in the neat rows of figures that marched across each page. He had mortgaged the Abbey almost past redemption. Much of the debt had been accrued by his late wife. The interest alone alarmed him, but such had been the price he'd paid for her silence about the children and their varied paternities. Since her death, Julian had spent what was necessary to maintain his legacy, but even by retrenching in every possible area, he had not been able to keep pace with the debts.

With an oath, he slapped the last ledger closed. How ironic that a new wife should prove the only way to save the Abbey from the havoc wreaked by the first one. Miss Lambton was the means for passing the Ashforth perfection on to James intact, who in his turn would be held prisoner by the family façade. The thought depressed Julian, though not as much as the reminder it brought—that though James would inherit the title and estate, he was not Julian's true heir. Indeed, Julian had no heir, merely a collection of children his unfaithful wife had whelped.

Her betrayals and blackmail hurt more than the debts or the necessity of marrying Maria Lambton. From their wedding day, he had looked forward to the birth of his first child. He had loved each one in succession—loved them as only a lonely man could love his children—until his wife had perceived the depth of his attachment to them. Then she had spilt her poison, forever ruining the one thing that had made his life worth living. He had known for years that Lillian bore him no love, and he

had resigned himself to the void of affection that was
his marriage. But when she had taken the children from
him. . . . She had not taken them physically, but her
defiant confession and the price she had demanded to
keep her infidelities secret had changed his feelings forever. Though the children would always bear his name
and enjoy his protection, he had built a wall around
his heart.

Yet the wall was vulnerable. Julian sank back in the
leather chair and pushed away from the massive desk.
That was why he stayed away as much as possible. If he
was too often near them, he might betray the truth, and
they deserved to be protected. It was the least he could
do for them, these children who bore his name but not
his blood.

With an oath, Julian swung back to the desk and
opened the ledger once more. There must be another
way besides a loveless marriage. He flipped a few pages
and bent his head in study.

They had lingered too long on the bridge. Esmie knew
she must tread a fine line between appearing amiable
and seeming overeager for Mr. Lambton's company. It
was wrong to think of attaching him when her own feelings were otherwise engaged, but perhaps her mother
was right. She should be more practical. She must look
to her own interests, for who else would?

When a quarter of an hour had passed in idle conversation and contemplation of the view, she turned to her
escort with the intention of bringing their stroll to an
end. "The children will need me, sir. I had better return
to the house."

Mr. Lambton smiled congenially. "You are very con-
scientious in your duties, my dear, and that trait is much
to be admired. But first . . ." He took her hand and
drew her behind one of the pillars that supported the
portico. From their position, they could not be seen from
the house. "Perhaps I overstep myself, ma'am, but when
one feels as I do, propriety is an unwelcome restraint."

Before Esmie could react, Mr. Lambton had pressed
his mouth upon hers. Kissed twice in the space of
twenty-four hours! Esmie stood shocked as he made

sounds of pleasure and then lifted his head. He smiled broadly at her and winked, and her face went scarlet.

"Sir . . ." She had no idea what to say, but she did have the presence of mind to slip away from him.

He hurried after her. "Miss Fortune, I am sorry. I believe I have rushed my fences."

For the first time, Esmie comprehended the precarious nature of her position. She couldn't afford to offend Mr. Lambton, for Miss Lambton might persuade the earl to send her away before she found the manuscript. And the children—she didn't like to think of them left to Miss Lambton's mercy.

"Yes. . . . I mean, no. . . . I'm not sure what I mean, sir." He stood far too close to her again.

"You blush most charmingly, madam, and that alone tells me I have imposed upon you." He stepped even closer. "But since you do not run away, that tells me my imposition is perhaps not unwelcome."

He meant to kiss her again! Heavens, how had an innocent stroll through the gardens turned into a tryst?

"Sir—"

A scream shattered the summer air, followed by a loud splash. Esmie whirled around to see James and the twins standing on the bank of the lake just below the bridge. Maria Lambton stood next to them, one hand clutching her parasol and the other covering her mouth, from which the scream had issued.

"Caroline!" Phoebe yelled, and Esmie saw the ripples in the water as they moved outward.

Esmie raced to the edge of the lake. The children waved frantically at the water, and Miss Lambton looked as if she might swoon.

"She fell, Miss Esmie. She's in there." Phillip's face was white, but not as white as Miss Lambton's.

The lake was murky, and thick reeds grew next to the bank. Esmie didn't hesitate. She waded into the water as she called instructions to the children over her shoulder. "Phillip, run to the stables and fetch some rope. James, find your father. And Phoebe . . ." She broke off as she floundered into the water. "Mind Miss Lambton. She looks like she may faint."

Though it was summer, the lake held a chill worthy

of the harshest winter. For the first time in her life, Esmie thanked her stepfather for the swimming lessons he'd forced her to endure. She drew a deep breath and dove beneath the water, eyes burning and hands outstretched, as she searched desperately for her youngest charge.

"My lord! My lord! Come quickly!"

Julian's head shot up, and he was on his feet in an instant. The butler appeared in the doorway. "Lady Caroline, sir." The older man gasped for breath.

"Good God, not the roof!" Julian swept around the corner of the desk and across the room. "She's not fallen from the roof!" The chit liked to amuse herself by tormenting the servants from the parapets, but Julian had lectured her so sternly last time he could not believe she would have done so again.

"Not the roof, sir. The lake."

"The lake? What was she doing by the lake? And where was Miss Fortune?"

"Miss Fortune is in the lake as well, my lord."

Understanding dawned. The near-drowning charade had run off two previous governesses in the blink of an eye. Suddenly, the fear returned full force. Caroline was a perfectly able swimmer, but Julian had no idea whether Miss Fortune could keep her head above water. "Can she swim?"

"Lady Caroline, sir? Of course. But you did ask me to tell you when she got herself into another of her scrapes."

"Not Lady Caroline, Miss Fortune! Can she swim?"

The butler mopped his brow with a handkerchief. "I don't know, my lord. I didn't think to ask."

Julian brushed by him. "Didn't think to ask?" He raced across the foyer and threw open the terrace doors above the formal garden. The small meadow had never seemed so long, as he raced along the gravel path. Ahead, several grooms stood huddled by the water. One of them held a rope.

Julian stripped himself of cravat and waistcoat as he ran.

"Where are they?" he demanded of the groom.

"Who, sir?"

"Lady Caroline and the governess, imbecile." It was all he could do not to grab the man by the throat and shake him. His eyes darted to the smooth surface of the lake.

"Miss Fortune, my lord? She's there." He jerked his head farther up the the bank. "Fit as a fiddle. Swims like a fish, does that one. Almost as well as Lady Caroline."

Julian swung around. There on the grass, wrapped in a blanket, Esmie sat with his youngest daughter clutched in her arms. Esmie's hair tangled about her face in damp ringlets, as she used a corner of the blanket to dry Caroline's face. His heart, which he had thought might burst in his chest, settled into an unsteady rhythm at the sight of the pair. Then he noticed that not ten feet away, Miss Lambton lay sprawled upon the grass, her maid administering a reviving dose of hartshorn.

"You have gone too far this time, miss," he whispered to himself, unsure of whether he addressed his daughter or the woman in his employ.

"Madam, what is this?" He hadn't meant to raise his voice, but the words rang out, and the grooms turned toward him with keen interest. Esmie blushed a bright red.

"I am sorry, my lord. I had no idea—"

"You are paid to have *every* idea!" He stepped closer and lowered his voice. "Can you not see through a childhood prank? Did you not know you were lured into the lake?"

He knew he was being unreasonable. The whole episode was a childish trick, but the depth of the fear that had gripped him went beyond reason.

Esmie pushed back a damp strand of hair from her forehead, her gray eyes cloudy. "All I saw, my lord, were ripples on the surface. Somehow it seemed imprudent to stop and conduct an inquiry."

Julian paused, for once completely at a loss. Thankfully, Caroline interrupted by flinging herself at Esmie.

"I'm sorry, Miss Esmie. I am sorry." The little girl's remorse was as apparent as it was unusual. Generally she was defiant after her pranks, but now she clung to Esmerelda like a limpet and sobbed with guilt. A pang of envy pierced Julian. He could not remember Caroline ever turning to him for comfort. She was far more likely to thrust her tongue out at him and run the opposite direction.

"Sh. . . ." Esmie held the girl close and stroked her hair. The warm summer sun had already begun to dry their clothing. " 'Tis of no account, Lady Caroline. As long as you are safe."

Bewildered, Julian towered above the blasted governess and her charge. If he punished Caroline, Esmie would think him heartless. But if he did not? Someday, one of her tricks might get her into far more trouble than she bargained for.

"Well, sir?" Esmie looked at him over Caroline's head. "We all make mistakes, do we not? Shall we simply be thankful this one did not have severe consequences?"

Julian cast a glance at the limp figure of Miss Lambton. Esmerelda Fortune meant to shame him, he could see, by reminding him of his own behavior in the library, and the tactic was remarkably effective. At that moment, he realized he stood before her with his shirt open, his suspenders hanging down his hips. The remainder of his clothing lay somewhere on the gravel path between the lake and the house. The sun heated his skin, but not as much as the attraction he felt for the confounded governess. Her eyes strayed from his as her gaze locked on his chest. For one brief second, her tongue darted out to touch her lips.

God, she would kill him. Fear and desire proved an unaccountably erotic combination. He would give up the Abbey if he could turn and dive unceremoniously into the cold waters of the lake, but Miss Lambton's presence precluded that course. Instead, without another word, he turned on his heel and marched toward the prostrate woman, his pride intact but his heart in shambles.

Chapter Ten

*T*hat night, Esmie again slipped from her chamber with only a candle to light her way. She had never been more thankful to see night fall in her life. Bad enough to have been an unwilling participant in Mr. Lambton's embrace, but she had been beyond mortification when the earl caught her staring at his chest. He had evidently been so repulsed by the longing in her expression he'd pivoted without a word and moved past her to see the prostrate from of Maria Lambton.

The memory of the earl's response lent new urgency to her steps as she descended the back staircase. She must find the manuscript, and quickly. Her scholarship would have to stand on its own merits, and her school would have to wait—for even the *Life of Corinna* and the making of Athena Hall were not worth her last bit of pride.

The darkened corridors of the Abbey lay blessedly empty. A prodigious amount of house remained to be searched. If she had taken the manuscript, where would she conceal it? After a long moment, she set out down the corridor toward the rear of the house. This portion of the Abbey was the least used. It contained a ballroom on the ground floor, guest chambers above, and rooms for visitors' servants at the top. Very well. She would begin with the ballroom. It would be the simplest to search, though as a rule she despised them. She had never had a pleasant experience in one.

The Earl of Ashforth's ballroom was not difficult to find. Immense double doors opened noiselessly as Esmie stepped inside. Moonlight flooded through the long windows, providing far more illumination than her lone candle could. The smooth wood floor stretched before her like a sea of dark glass, and opposite the door, high in the wall, sat the musicians' gallery. What Esmie noticed most, though, were the walls. She had spent a great deal of time examining ballroom walls, for they had been her most frequent social companions. The earl's walls were a pale blue and covered with plaster ornaments. There would be little chance to blend into such a wall unless one's gown was of a matching color. Esmie preferred the gilding and frescoes of bygone days, where one could blend more easily with the decoration.

She trailed around the ballroom as she searched in the dim light for any hiding places that might conceal the *Corinna*. Her eyes traveled upward. Perhaps the musicians' gallery, but that would be accessed from some other room. Society frowned on any mixing of the servants and the wellborn.

At the end of the room hung a portrait of a grand lady of the last century, her wide skirts and high-piled hair as different from modern fashions as Esmie could imagine. What must it have been like, to be imprisoned in panniers and wigs and tightly laced bodices? Perhaps that was why she was drawn to the classical period. The mobility allowed by dressing *à la grècque* gave women far more freedom. Resentment at society's strictures welled within her, but there was little point to such feeling, for it could produce only bitterness. Yet sometimes acceptance failed her, and she rued what she did not have.

Her gaze swept the magnificent ballroom. She wished she were the earl. He had everything, and yet it had not given him any more happiness than Esmie's nothingness had given her. She glanced around the circle of light cast by her candle. How could one have all this and not be content?

Footsteps sounded in the hallway, and her heart leapt to her throat. Drat! She prayed it was a footman or the butler who had heard her scratching about, but in her heart of hearts she knew to whom the footsteps belonged. She saw no point in hiding. He would find her eventually. Besides, her anger and resentment gave her newfound armor. Though his contempt still stung, she felt stronger in his presence than she'd been when she first arrived at the Abbey.

A shadow stepped through the doorway, and a pool of lantern light met the circle of her candle's glow.

"Good evening, Miss Fortune." His greeting echoed in the empty ballroom.

Was there sarcasm in his voice? Surprisingly, no. The earl was clad in his dressing gown again, an infinite improvement over his undone shirt. Well, not an improvement, exactly, but far better for her peace of mind.

"Good evening, my lord."

"I trust you are searching for the manuscript."

"No, my lord. I mean to rob you, and thought I'd best strip the ballroom of valuables before starting on the main part of the house."

To her surprise, he laughed and crossed the room toward her. She had expected him to poker up, not to advance on her in that slow, measured way. "Touché, Miss Fortune. I deserve that. And I owe you an apology for my behavior this afternoon. I had no right to scold you for Caroline's antics, when I'd failed to warn you of her favorite trick."

Esmie smiled, despite her gloom. "I had thought dangling from the rooftop was her torment of choice."

The earl's face sobered. "I trust you suffered no ill effects from your impromptu swim." He glanced around the room. "You have had no luck finding the *Corinna* I take it?"

Esmie sighed. "None. It is hard to know where the manuscript would be hidden, when we have no idea who filched it."

"Puzzling, indeed." He moved about the ballroom with an uncharacteristic absentmindedness. "One floor above, and you will be in the Lambtons' quarters," he said in a soft tone.

Esmie's heart raced in alarm. Suppose she had stumbled into one of their rooms by mistake? The earl looked at her as if to measure her response. Did he somehow know about Mr. Lambton's kiss?

"Then I am glad you arrived to prevent me any further embarrassment. I should not have liked to barge into their bedchambers unawares."

"Miss Lambton would have balked although I suspect Mr. Lambton would not have minded."

Their gazes met and locked, and even in the darkness Esmie could feel his scrutiny. "Pardon?" Feigning ignorance seemed the best course.

"I believe the gentleman finds you attractive, Miss Fortune." The hollow ring of his words made Esmie's knees weak. Only her vanity—and her desperation—could make her think she heard a note of jealousy in his tone.

"Mr. Lambton is very kind."

"Is he?"

"What do you mean?"

"Only that I believe Miss Lambton perceives the tension between us, and feels threatened. Her father means to remove you from my notice."

So he thought her a pawn in the matrimonial chess he played with the Lambtons. His assumption that Mr. Lambton could have no real interest in her stung her pride.

"I find Mr. Lambton quite an agreeable gentleman." Her tone implied she found the earl entirely otherwise.

He arched one eyebrow. "Hmm. Lambton is also a shrewd businessman, madam. That is how he made his fortune, and it would not pay to underestimate his dedication to his course. He wants the Abbey, and what's more he wants the title of countess for his daughter."

Well, that was plain speaking. Still, she resented his assumption that her person and conversation could hold no attraction for Mr. Lambton.

"You seem very sure of your own attractions, my lord. Have you not considered that Miss Lambton may reject your suit?"

His comical look of disbelief might have made Esmie laugh, had she found anything remotely amusing in the situation. As it was, she fought back tears.

"Reject my suit?" He sounded wistful at the thought, and Esmie's heartbeat quickened. Did she dare hope the earl had changed his mind? "I should think not. Mr. Lambton and I understand one another. Our purposes dovetail exactly."

Foolish hope withered at his words. The earl would not sacrifice all for love any more than he would give his heart to a scrawny, sharp-tongued governess.

"I should finish my search," she said, wanting only to be out of his presence. He was not perfect at all. He only appeared as such. Underneath, he was as self-serving as any other member of the aristocracy.

"Wait." His soft command stopped her as she stepped toward the door. "I apologize, Miss Fortune. You do not deserve such treatment. Would you allow me to search with you again?"

His question roused an image of the night before in his library. Her eyes must have revealed her thoughts, for he ran a hand through his hair and said, "If you feel you can trust me not to repeat my actions of last evening, of course. For that, I do owe you the most profound of apologies."

Esmie hardly knew what to think of the man now. He was by turns imperious and placating, and she could never be certain which facet of the earl's nature might hold sway in a given moment.

"No apology is necessary, my lord. I have not thought of it twice," she lied.

It occurred to Esmie that if she were of higher birth, much more than a simple apology would be in order. If she were Miss Lambton, honor would dictate the earl offer for her after having compromised her to such a degree. But she was not Miss Lambton, and a governess held no claim on a gentleman's honor. Clearly, the notion had not even crossed his mind.

"Good. Good." He tightened the belt of his dressing gown. "I should like it if we could find the manuscript tonight."

"Are you certain it is still in the house, my lord?" She was glad to turn his attention to the manuscript. No doubt he planned to enter his translation of the work in the competition. If he did, her chances for the prize would be nil. Once again, her association with the earl found her working against her own interests.

"Yes. The footmen have searched every cart, carriage and rider leaving the estate. It is either about the house or somewhere on the grounds, and the house seems the most likely hiding place."

"Very well. I do not see it here, but I'd thought to search the musicians' gallery." She looked upward. "Dawn approaches soon enough."

She had not dared to hope for a second night alone with him. Even to consider the possibility was foolish in the extreme. She had thought she would never feel comfortable with him again, but as she followed him into the hall and through the narrow door that led to a winding staircase, they fell into a disconcerting companionship.

"Now that you have seen the manuscript, do you think a case may be made for the *Corinna*'s authenticity?" he asked over his shoulder as they climbed to the gallery.

She looked up, startled that he would seek her opinion. "I am no expert, sir."

"But no doubt you have a view on the matter?"

"What details I observed were consistent with what I know of the poetess. But so little of her work survives, and much of what we know of her is most likely legend. If it proves authentic, it would be a great boon to classical scholarship."

"Yes, it would." He held open the small door to the gallery and nodded at her to pass through. Such proximity sent Esmie's stomach into motion once more. The earl set his lantern on a ledge. "But I wonder why the *Corinna* has not been discovered before. Why is it not referred to in other works? Would not Ovid have drawn from it when he likened his beloved to her? There is no evidence he did so."

Esmie looked around the ghostly ballroom below. "But is there evidence he did not? A close comparison of the two works would reveal if details or phrases are found that seem to be more than coincidence." Her eyes went back to his face in the lantern light. The earl's eyebrows arched.

"An excellent suggestion, madam." He paused and studied her face. Esmie's discomfort reappeared under his scrutiny. There was no prurient interest in his gaze now; no, his look was measuring rather than amorous. "I am impressed with the knowledge you have obtained without a formal education. It must have required a great deal of discipline."

"And solitude," Esmie said with a self-deprecating smile. "It filled the hours that we remained at home for lack of invitations." The moment the words were uttered, she wished with all her heart she might call them back. They seemed to echo over the ballroom.

He looked at her even more closely now. "Were you out in society?"

Her heart raced. "Yes." She swallowed. "My first stepfather was the Duke of Nottingham."

"Nottingham? Then it was your sister who married the Crown Prince of Santadorra."

"My stepsister. Yes."

"I am surprised. Surely your stepsister might have kept you from service. Her husband is among the richest men in Europe."

"I would not permit Mama to ask." Esmie wished she could turn the subject.

"No?" He examined her as if she were some undiscovered species he should catalog for posterity.

"It was not an honor I felt worthy of."

"So instead you became a governess."

The time for confession had come. Without something as unique as the *Corinna* to lend it a bit of glamour, her recounting of Greek and Roman women stood little chance in the competition. She had chosen her pride over her dreams already. Now she must choose her honor over his good opinion. "I came to your house under false pretenses, my lord. I had heard you were in possession of the *Corinna*, and wanted her to supplement my own work."

"Indeed?"

She had not thought his eyebrow could arch quite so high. "Yes. The paper I submitted to the Classics Society was soundly dismissed. I needed something to stand my work apart."

His eyes widened with understanding. At last he had connected her with the aspiring scholar he had so brusquely rejected. "And you were roundly rebuffed by a certain member of the Society."

"Yes, my lord."

"And in the most arrogant and condescending fashion, I should warrant." He smiled with self-deprecation.

"Yes."

He stepped closer, until they both stood within the circle of the lantern's light. Would her heart never beat at a normal pace when he was near?

"I am sorry, Miss Fortune. What I wrote was inexcusable. I fear I vented my anger at someone else in my letter to you. I did not know you then."

His apology only increased her agitation. "There is no reason you would have known me, my lord. In the eyes of true scholars, I am a dilettante."

"So you came to the Abbey in hopes of finding the *Corinna*? That was your design in coming here?"

"Yes." What an odd conversation to have in the darkness of the musician's gallery. But somehow all their most important exchanges took place in the dark of night.

"The cat was hardly a brilliant stratagem, if you meant to ingratiate yourself here. What possessed you to bring it along?"

Esmie ducked her head. "An uncharacteristic bout of empathy, my lord."

He smiled—a lovely smile that transformed his stern features into a far more youthful mien. "I don't find your compassion for that wretched creature uncharacteristic at all."

An awkward silence followed.

"You no doubt wish me to Hades, my lord, since the disappearance of the manuscript, but I must remain until it is found. As a point of honor."

He looked dubious. "A point of honor?"

"I am responsible for its loss, so I must be responsible for its recovery."

"And when it is found? If I do not sanction your use of it?"

"I will stay to the end of our agreed upon period."

A look of relief relaxed the tight planes of his face.

"I had no idea governesses were so scheming, but I admire your ingenuity, ma'am. And your belated honesty."

"Then you have changed your estimation of my character?"

He frowned for a moment. "You are intelligent, not above schemes and stratagems, and yet you do have a sense of honor. My estimation of your character remains much the same as it was when you arrived, madam." His mouth slid into a more companionable line. Despite the asperity of his words, his tone held such warmth that Esmie could hardly stop the way her pulse pounded in her ears. She turned away in confusion.

"You overestimate me, my lord."

"I don't believe I do."

Esmie, unnerved, made no reply. His approbation was as potent to her as opium, and she dared not fall under its influence.

"So your mother married again after Nottingham cocked up his toes?"

The darkness did indeed invite confidences. "Her jointure as the duke's widow was quickly spent. After my stepsister's departure, we traveled to the Continent. She met the count in Rome. He has a villa there." She kept her tone neutral.

"But little money?"

"What he has is spent on brandy, my lord. And life in London is far more costly than in Italy."

"I would have thought Nottingham's widow would always find a place amongst the *ton*."

Esmie wished she could flee, for she could see what was coming as clearly as she could see him in the lantern light. "You have made my mother's acquaintance, my lord, but you will not recall it. I daresay you meet with a great many officious, fawning people in the course of a season."

She saw the moment when comprehension dawned, for her mother's toadeating ways had made her infamous amongst the *ton*. "That woman is your mother?"

Esmie could at least console herself with the look of disbelief in his eyes. "The lady is my mother, yes."

He frowned. "I am sorry. I meant no disrespect."

"There is no disrespect in the truth, sir. Merely a great

deal of embarrassment." The words leapt from her lips, and she could only half wish to retrieve them.

His brow furrowed. "Our relatives do not always do us credit, madam, but their actions are not our own."

"But they reflect on us, sir, most often to our detriment. At least, that has been the case for me."

"Hmm." His wordless response neither confirmed nor disputed her statement. He retrieved the lantern from the ledge and opened the gallery door. "I fear there is nothing to be discovered up here, ma'am. Perhaps we should continue on."

He had discovered far too much already, but she followed him down from the musicians' gallery without comment. They walked to the end of the hallway and climbed the stairs. On the next floor, the earl opened the first door they came to. "Most of the guest chambers have not been used in some time. You may find them a bit dusty."

"I do not mind a bit of dirt, sir."

"No, you are made of stern stuff. Not one to turn craven at the first difficulty. Not like . . ." His voice trailed away as they entered the bedchamber.

Esmie glanced around the splendid room.

"It is grander than anything I have seen in London," Esmie breathed. "A shame it should not be used."

"My wife was fond of guests." He looked away for a moment, and Esmie felt a twinge of envy at the heaviness in his voice. "Since her death, I have found no occasion for large parties."

"Perhaps when your engagement to Miss Lambton is announced, you will feel the necessity for entertainment." The thought filled Esmie with despair.

The earl stepped to the middle of the guest chamber and surveyed it as if seeing the room for the first time.

"No doubt we will announce our engagement in London. We may even marry there. Miss Lambton will wish it."

"You have proposed, then?" Esmie's audacity amazed her, but she must know. She needed every proof of the earl's intention to attach himself to Miss Lambton, to counter her own foolish feelings.

"No." He said the word with a sad quietness. "Not yet."

"Why do you hesitate?" Why could he not commit himself and leave Esmie to her misery?

She thought he would give her a setdown for her impertinence, but instead he turned and eyed her thoughtfully. Ten feet must have separated them, but she was as aware of him as if he stood next to her.

"Why do I hesitate? That is what I have asked myself, Miss Fortune."

"You do not love her, then." The words slipped from her lips, both a release and a challenge.

To Esmie's consternation, he laughed. "Love Miss Lambton?" He reached up to rub his temples with a thumb and forefinger. "This is an aristocratic marriage, my dear. What romantic notions you have."

The part of her that could detach itself from the intimacy of the moment knew his words should frighten her as much as they enticed her. "Then why? What possible motive could compel you to offer for a woman whom you do not esteem?"

Saying the words aloud brought home the ruthlessness of his course to Esmie. He did not love Miss Lambton, and Miss Lambton only loved the earl's title and property. Esmie knew a recipe for disaster when she saw one, and his marriage to Miss Lambton would be as disastrous as if he married Esmie Fortune. There, she had thought it. Had acknowledged it. She only hoped he couldn't see her thoughts in her expression.

"I esteem what she will bring to the marriage, my dear. Perfection does not come cheap, particularly when one has debts." He broke off and turned away. "I have no business telling you such things."

"You do not feel the need to marry for love again?" She tormented herself with the question, but it was impossible not to press him on the issue.

"Again?" He looked genuinely puzzled.

"As you did with your first wife."

"Marrying for love, Miss Fortune, is an extremely dangerous business. I would not recommend it to my bitterest enemy."

Confusion brought a blush to her cheeks. "But . . . Your wife's rooms are untouched. Her clothes are so neatly stored away. And you have not used the ballroom." The perfect earl must have had the perfect marriage. He must have.

The earl snorted and paced in a circle like a caged lion. "Her room is untouched and her clothes stored in the attic because I have no desire to revive the memory of such a woman. And I have not used the ballroom because I have been raising the money to redeem the mortgages on this place. I see you have attributed my actions to a motive of love." He crossed his arms and raised his chin. "I am sorry to disillusion you, my dear, but I am as grasping as your mama. I simply perform my officiousness with greater polish."

Esmie didn't want to understand the very plain meaning of his speech. "But, the children . . ."

"What of them?" His cold expression warned her off, but she persisted.

"Your children. You have so many."

"Yes?"

"You must have loved your wife at one time." Her mouth had grown almost too dry for speech.

"Indeed, I did. Unfortunately, she loved a great many men other than myself."

"My lord?"

"The children are not mine, madam. Not one of them."

Like a conundrum understood at last, it all fell into place. A cool rush flooded her body. She had misunderstood. The countess did not claim his love but his contempt, and his children inherited that bitter legacy. Esmie knew in that moment how deeply wrong she had been in her estimation of him—as wrong as he had been in his estimation of her. His perfect veneer concealed a gentleman as flawed as any other in the kingdom. And while a perfect earl might have been beyond her touch, the very real, very troubled Julian Armstrong was not.

The thought sent a flush to her cheeks, and her knees went weak. Foolish, foolish girl. She looked up at him, into his dark eyes, and saw the wounded man so carefully concealed beneath the perfect exterior. And the woman within—the woman who had desired him in all his perfection—could only desire him all the more for his deficiencies.

Chapter Eleven

*T*he confusion on Esmerelda's face doubled the press of anxiety in Julian's chest. He had never foisted the skeleton in his cupboard on anyone, much less a servant, but Esmerelda elicited the most unexpected behavior. He waited for her condemnation, aware that her reaction mattered more than that of any peer of the realm. When she remained still, his discomfort increased. He tried to swallow his disappointment.

"I apologize, madam. You did not invite such a confidence. It was wrong to impose it on you." The formal words did not cover the break in his voice. He wanted only to escape from her presence; he did not care for the novelty of shame, and he hated how he shifted from one foot to another like a penitent child. "I will leave you. You cannot wish for my companionship now." He strode toward the door.

"If I wished to avoid confidences, my lord, I would do better not to wander the house in the dark hours." Her voice, though not loud, rang out in the quiet of the night, and her declaration stopped him in his tracks. Hardly daring to draw breath, he turned toward her. In the soft glow of his lantern, she looked as ethereal as Aphrodite descended. No, not Aphrodite. Rather, Athena, goddess of wisdom. Despite her slight frame, it was no stretch to envision her with a shield and spear in hand. In her own way, she was a warrior.

Her words planted the tormenting seeds of hope in his chest. "You are not required to tolerate my every behavior, Miss Fortune, merely because you are in my employ."

"You would exempt me from the requirements you impose upon the rest of the staff, my lord?" The sly gleam in her gray eyes further tightened the invisible bands around his chest.

"Where is your shock, madam? Your distaste? Now is indeed the time to be missish." He wanted her to be appalled. If she offered understanding and then withdrew it, he could bear it.

"My lord, if I intended to cut up stiff at the irregularities of this household, I should have done so long before now." Her eyes still held a glint of worry, but no distaste showed in the determined set of her mouth.

"Your opinion of me will have changed." His limbs might as well have been made of wood.

"It would not be the first time." She studied him, and the sensation was not unpleasant, though he feared to ask what she meant by her last words.

"You will see my children quite differently now." That was the worst of it. However much she discomfited him, she had engaged the children as none of the previous governesses had. He dreaded for them to lose her regard.

Esmie's shoulders squared, a gesture he recognized and had grown rather fond of. "I will continue to see five children who are in desperate need of discipline and order. And five children who have great need of their father."

Her words might as well have been delivered with an axe. "Not father." His words were low and bitter. "*Fathers*. If the children need such a parent, then you must look about England, madam, and attempt to round up the gentlemen in question."

"I speak of no other man but you, sir." Her eyes bore straight into his; he'd been much more comfortable when her gaze flitted about the room. He had thought to engage her sympathy, not to be challenged in this manner.

"I have done for them what many other gentlemen would not. They have the protection of my name. I take responsibility for their futures."

"That means nothing if they do not have your love." Esmie's censure clouded her face. " 'Tis the most expensive gift, my lord, for it comes very dear."

The anger he concealed bubbled beneath the surface. The dim emptiness of the deserted bedchamber blurred the demands of position and duty, for it cocooned him in the anonymity of darkness, where he might express what he most deeply felt.

"I have sacrificed nearly everything to fulfill my duties," he bit out.

"Sacrificed everything?" She actually laughed aloud, and Julian's fists clenched.

"This is a jest to you."

"No, my lord, I am perfectly serious. What have you sacrificed for the place you hold? You have everything a man could want—position, power, title, breeding. The grandest house in the kingdom. A library that rivals any in the land. You may come and go as you please, with no accounting to anyone. A hundred people await your every command, and your five children would adore you, given the slightest opportunity. Now that you intend to marry, you might have any woman you choose. No, my lord, I perceive no sacrifice on your part."

"Then you have not the intellect with which I credited you." Hope died within him, and anger poured from his soul like lava raining down upon Pompeii. "You look no deeper than your preconceptions and prejudices, madam. When the realities of life conflict with your romantic views, you have no patience, no acceptance." His lantern flickered, and then went out, leaving only the faint light from Esmie's candle. Darkness closed in around him. He had been a fool to think Esmie might do anything to alleviate the growing shadow. He wanted to lash out at her. He knew that such actions were unforgivable, and yet the temptation was so strong he could taste it on his tongue.

Just as he had tasted her. The thought hit with the force of a blow. In two strides, he was in front of her. With a quick puff, he blew out her candle and plunged them into darkness. He reached for her. The candle and its tin holder fell to the floor and she was in his arms again.

He kissed her because he was angry, because she had

not offered the sympathy he craved, because he wanted
her more than he had ever wanted any woman, and because she was not Miss Lambton. She was Esmie, intelligent and sharp-tongued and delicious. Her curves pressed
against him in the best places. If he could, he would pull
her around him, inside him, through him. He wanted to
be lost, so he separated her lips with his tongue and delved
into the sweetness of her mouth. To his satisfaction, she
responded. Anger and passion fed their duel, one gaining
the upper hand and then the other. Julian pressed his advantage as he brought one hand from her back to cup her
head, to control the angle of her mouth. She replied by
sliding both hands into his hair and tugging lightly. Pleasure slid across his scalp, down his spine, and lower. He
wanted her now, even if it meant taking her in a deserted
chamber. Was he not due one moment of pure self-
indulgence? She pressed closer, and he made no attempt
to hide his body's response. He thought she might push
away in shock, but instead she clung to him with a strength
that might have frightened a lesser man. She was Athena,
daughter of Zeus, the thunder god.

His other hand smoothed its way around her ribcage
and up the bodice of her dress. With more care than he
would have thought himself capable, he cupped her
breast and molded it with his fingers. Her figure was
neither too small nor overlarge, and satisfaction flooded
him when her nipple hardened beneath his touch.

God, he wanted her. She moaned softly, and the low,
throaty sound pushed him to the brink. She was not
perfection. No, she was better. Real and warm, she challenged him at every turn. He would never rest easy while
Esmerelda Fortune remained in his house. He would
never be bored, either.

He tightened his arms about her, and she clung to his
shoulders in return. No one need know. Ashforth Abbey
had concealed a great many secrets for years. Was it not
his turn to avail himself of its cloaking? He had done his
duty every day of his life. He had lived up to the appearance of perfection, and kept the Ashforth name wrapped
in its façade. One night with Esmerelda was all he asked.

His skin burned everywhere her hands touched him,
and he hoped his caresses made her feel the same. They

must, for she continued to return his kisses with fervor. She was not as expert as his mistress or his wife, but her taste proved a great deal sweeter and far more erotic.

He had her bodice undone before she knew it. He quelled the flashes of conscience that tried to make themselves known through the haze of desire. He would deal with the consequences tomorrow. Tonight, he would immerse himself in the knowledge that the woman he desired burned for him as well.

His mistress had taught him the quickest way to divest a woman of her clothing. Moonlight poured through the windows just as it had in the ballroom below. Esmie's eyes were as dark as the night, but they sparkled with need and desire. Her lips were swollen with his kisses, and her mouth had never looked more desirable. Julian wanted to stop and fling away his own garments, but he feared to let her out of his arms, afraid she might come to her senses at any moment.

He would make amends tomorrow. He would set her up as his mistress. She would have gowns, jewels, a carriage, and books. Many, many books. She might have his library for the asking. The *Corinna*. Anything, as long as she stayed in his arms.

She gasped when he scooped her up and laid her on the bed. He followed her down onto the mattress, pinning and protecting her with his weight. She responded by capturing his mouth with hers, and he let her tongue explore it. Her kiss was not practiced, but it was fueled by desire for him and him only. The thought was sweet balm after his wife's betrayals.

"Esmerelda." He breathed her name into her ear, and then let his tongue follow the word with light, circular strokes. With one hand, he reached down to unbutton his breeches and free himself. Her fingers followed his, and Julian thought he might explode. He captured her hands, pulling them away and pushing them above her head. He covered her fully, and pressed into the crevice between her thighs.

Would he take her without even removing his clothing? She deserved more than that, though she had made no move to divest him of his dressing gown, much less his trousers and boots.

"Do not move." He bit out each word, and rolled away to free himself of his garments. He sat on the edge of the bed and tugged at his boots. Suddenly, something hit the mattress next to him with a thump, and a pair of slitted yellow eyes stared into his.

The itching began in his throat and then spread to his nose. Tears stung his eyes, and his chest tightened until he found it difficult to draw breath. The first sneeze erupted like cannon fire, and Esmie shot up next to him.

"Julian?" It was the first time he had heard her say his given name, but he could not savor it.

"Cat," he wheezed.

"Plutarch!" Esmie cried. "Phillip and Phoebe must have smuggled him in from the stables."

Julian neither knew nor cared how the beast had gained entry. He only wanted to force oxygen into his lungs, so he would not fall to the floor in an ignominious faint. Esmie scrambled from the bed and searched blindly about the room for her clothing. The cat purred with delight at the disruption it had caused, and sauntered across the mattress past Julian.

"Devil's spawn," he wanted to hiss, but the words required breath he did not have.

Esmie fastened her bodice with shaking hands. "I will remove him at once, my lord." She snatched up the cat and then backed away, her eyes locked on Julian's.

He should offer tender words of reassurance. He should beg her pardon, but he was too intent upon drawing his next breath to be overmuch concerned with honor. Amends would have to wait until he could be certain he would live to see the morrow.

With a soulful glance backward, Esmie escaped the room. Julian rolled from the bed to his feet and staggered to the basin and pitcher that rested on top of the dressing table. No water was to be had in an unused guest chamber. Instead, he took the towel that lay next to the basin and began to scrub at his face. The cat had no doubt slept cozily in the bedding. It would take a hot bath and a washing of his hair, along with some of the apothecary's prescribed herbs in a strong tea, to find relief.

Julian took two steps into the hallway before he

looked down and saw that his trousers were still undone. Grimacing, he fastened them and made for the staircase.

What the earl did not see was the door that stood ajar halfway down the corridor behind him. Nor did he notice Miss Lambton's golden curls as she observed his actions, and then withdrew to her room.

Plutarch struggled in the blanket as Esmie hurried across the stable yard, choking back tears. She would deposit the cat in the stables and then . . . And then? She had no idea. Her thoughts tumbled about like jackstraws, and she feared to examine her feelings, which were in an even more chaotic state than her thoughts.

The night air cooled her blushes as she remembered her acquiescence to—nay, her participation in—their encounter. No wonder men had died for love and women betrayed themselves for it. She had never dreamed feelings could be expressed in such a way. What would he think of her now? He had been so violently racked with sneezes when she fled. She had been afraid of what he might say when he came to his senses. She could not have endured a repetition of the look of horror that had settled on his features last night in the library. She did not want to see him despise himself for desiring her; she did not want to despise herself for desiring him.

Esmie was keenly aware that she knew little of passion. No, to own the truth, she had known nothing. But surely such feelings were not in the common way. He wanted her, at least physically, but had been scarred by betrayal. His veneer of perfection was as false as her mother's claims to gentility. He hurt, just as she herself hurt, and the knowledge filled her with a mix of elation and sorrow. Had he turned to her for comfort or from desire? Was she unique to him, or merely a novelty, neither servant nor equal, and thus a likely candidate for his confidences?

The stables lay quiet as she slipped inside. She could hear the snores of the grooms from the sleeping quarters in the loft. Plutarch gave a plaintive meow when she released him, and darted off in search of mice. Esmie sank down upon the nearest pile of straw. She had almost lain with him. She had never thought of herself as a carnal creature, but there it was. She, Esmerelda Fortune, was no different from the rest of the men and women in the world. She could fall prey to indiscretion as easily as the next person.

The humbling thought caused her to wiggle upon her mound of straw. She had studied Herodotus and Ovid and Seneca, and thought that such fine thoughts put her on a plane above that of mere mortals. Though she could not compete in beauty with other women, she knew her intellect to be superior. With limited resources, she had cultivated her mind and embarked on scholarship. She had fancied herself better than the people who disdained her, had looked down upon them for their vanities and worldliness, but, in the end, neither she nor the earl were any different. No one was truly perfect.

Deeply troubled, she clambered to her feet and left the stables, latching the door behind her, then crossed the darkened yard again. If she'd had a shawl, she might have sat in the garden to gather her thoughts, but despite the day's heat, the night air proved too cool for comfort. She let herself into the house through a servants' door and climbed the back stairs to the third floor. For a moment, she started toward her room, and then her feet turned her back toward the stairs. *The bundle of letters she had found in the attic.* Letters addressed to several different gentlemen, but apparently never sent. Curiosity planted its seed, which quickly took root.

Before she knew it, she had climbed the last set of stairs and let herself into the attic storage room. It took several minutes of opening and closing trunk lids before her trembling fingers located the items from the countess's dressing table. The letters were still there, and Esmie shook as she lifted them from the trunk and slid the ribbon away. She took the topmost one from the stack, opened it, and began to read.

> *My dearest Edward,*
>   *Such a thing has happened, and I know you will count it a great joke, but I must say I have lost the humor in it now that Ashforth has cut up stiff. I am with child, you see, and he knows it cannot be his. I am weary of such indisposition, but as I seem*

*to have the knack for breeding, I am resigned to
my fate. You, of course, will have a very good idea
of who the father is. . . .*

Bile rose in her throat. The paper dropped from her
fingers. With trepidation, Esmie opened the next letter.
Its direction addressed a gentleman in Kent. The hand-
writing was the same, as were the sentiments expressed.
More letters followed, all of a piece. Esmie thought she
might be physically ill. The earl had lived in his own
private hell, and none of the world had known it.

The bottommost letter was addressed to a woman.

*. . . I have told Julian that the child is not his,
merely to have the satisfaction of distressing him.
Men are so easily fooled; can they not count? But
he deserves this trickery. He denies me every pleasure and will not allow me to go to London. I do
not see why he does not take a lover as well, for it
would settle matters to my satisfaction. If he complies with my wishes, I will tell him the truth, that
he has already his precious heir—that James is his
child.*

Esmie glanced at the top of the page. The letter bore
no name or direction for its delivery. Evidently, the late
countess had traded on the lie for years. The earl did in
fact have an heir of his blood. Esmie's head swam. She
might have cost Julian the *Corinna* manuscript, but here
was something far more valuable that she might restore
to him. She wondered why he had never looked at these
letters, then remembered he'd said Mrs. Robbins packed
away the countess's belongings after her death. For five
years, the truth that might have provided some peace
had been tucked away in the attic. Though she had no
desire to see the earl again so soon, she could not withhold such information for a moment.

Her candle sputtered and threatened to go out. Esmie
slipped the one letter into her pocket and closed the
trunk. Heart in her throat at the prospect of knocking
on the door of the earl's bedchamber, she crept from
the attic.

Chapter Twelve

*J*ulian lingered in the hip bath as he drew in great lungfuls of air. He had downed two cups of the prescribed tea and scrubbed himself within an inch of his life. His valet had borne off his clothes to be burnt. An hour after he'd entered his bedchamber, every trace of cat had been banished. The footman had poured the last pail of hot water into the bath and disappeared. Now there was only the firelight, the warmth of the water, and the sweet, blessed air in his lungs.

His honor—nay, Esmie's honor—had been saved by a cat. With a groan, Julian leaned forward and splashed his face, then took the pitcher the footman had left, scooped some water, and poured it over his head. The impromptu shower could not compare with the shame that spilled over him. The abandonment of his principles appalled him. He had never lost control in such a manner. He was not a man to justify his own desires with self-serving excuses.

With a towel, he wiped the water from his eyes. If it were only his own honor, he would offer for her without delay. Damnation, if it were only his own future and his own name, he would seize Esmerelda Fortune with both hands and drag her to the nearest parson. But he could not consider himself. Since the day his father had marched him into the study and driven home with his cane what it meant to be the future Earl of Ashforth, Julian had not regarded himself or his own wishes. Perfection, his father had said through clenched teeth as he lashed Julian's backside, was worth any pain, any price.

He had believed his father's words. He had striven to
be what was expected of him. He knew he was intelligent and capable and a leader of men. An Ashforth
could be nothing less. An Ashforth could marry no one
less perfect than himself. No, he could only burn for a
thin, gray-eyed termagant who thwarted him at every
turn and drove him to distraction.

Julian shivered. The water had grown cool.

He would have to send her away. Her loss pained him
far more than the disappearance of the *Corinna,* for one
was a prize for the intellect, but the other had been salve
for his soul. He shoved himself upward and reached for
a dry piece of toweling. A knock sounded at the door,
and he cursed under his breath. Far too many people
prowled his house in the middle of the night.

He climbed from the bath and wrapped the toweling
around his waist as he crossed the room. His valet was
a stickler for modesty, a rather odd quality in a manser-
vant. Perhaps he should remind the man that servants
were meant to make life simpler, not more complex.

"Come in, and be quick about it." He flung open the
door and stood to the side so he would not be in full
view of the corridor.

"My lord!"

Julian's head whipped around. Esmie stood in the
doorway, swollen eyes and all, but her expression was
not one of sorrow. Instead, she looked as he felt—
horrified. But also fascinated.

For the first time in many years, the Earl of Ashforth
blushed. Instinctively, he tried to push the door closed
to shut her out, but she was already inside the room.
Since he had the use of only one hand, he could scarcely
throw her out. What had possessed her to come to his
room? He doubted she had come to renew their earlier lovemaking.

"I thought you were my valet." He glanced about for
his dressing gown. He had no screen behind which to
dress and he could hardly drop the toweling to don the
gown. "You should not be here, madam." The words
dripped with disapproval.

"It is a matter of some urgency, my lord." Despite
her high color, she kept her composure well. He forced

himself to keep his eyes focused on her face. To let them roam about her person was a recipe for disaster.

"What could possibly be so urgent?" He must discipline himself to not desire Esmie Fortune.

"I found something, my lord, which should be of interest to you. . . ." She trailed off, looking anywhere but at him, and her previous certainty drained away. He wished he wouldn't notice how her hair hung about her breasts or how her wrapper molded her slender hips. If he did not distract himself, the toweling would be of little use in disguising his interest in her.

"Which can surely wait 'til morning, madam." He couldn't abide her presence any longer, not without dropping the toweling and scooping her into his arms to carry her to his bed.

"I know 'tis not proper, my lord—"

"Not proper!" Julian laughed, the sound like a pistol shot in the quiet of his darkened bedchamber. "My dear, we passed proper somewhat earlier this evening. I must insist you leave."

"But, sir . . ."

Julian couldn't allow her to linger. Already, he could feel his iron will weakening. If she moved any further into the room, she'd be in the path of the firelight, and who knew what he might see through her thin night rail. . . .

"Miss Fortune, my earlier behavior seems to have left you with a misconception. You are here to educate and supervise my children. If you would like to share my bed, I should not object, but there will be no familiarity between us. And you will not act in a way as to cause scandal."

The odious, unfair words fell as easily from his lips as polite ballroom conversation. He used them like a knife, determined to carve away his own feelings and hers. There could be nothing between them, and if he must hurt and humiliate them both to protect the Ashforth name, he would do so. But, oh, the pain of the knife he wielded. He'd never dreamt how sorely words might wound him or the woman he—

No, he did not love her. He merely desired her, for who would not? Her gray eyes burned with embarrassment and anger, her body beneath her wrapper was everything a man might wish for, and she was his intellectual equal.

Dear God, was there no other way? The pain of his casual offer to bed her showed in every detail of her person—in the lines of hurt that framed her eyes and mouth, in the rigidity of her spine, in the slight trembling in her frame.

"No, my lord." She held herself like a queen, like a duchess, like a . . . countess. If he could but marry her, he had no doubt she would do him proud. But the world would never know her true worth. Only he would know, and remember, and pine even as he pledged his troth to Miss Lambton.

"No?" He turned his back on her, and moved as if he intended to return to the bath. "Then you will please see yourself out. I am not yet clean of your wretched cat's dander." Another lie. He turned away so she would not see the ambivalence in his expression. His father had taught him never to show his feelings on his face. By the time he turned twelve, he could endure a caning without so much as a flicker of an eyelash. Esmie Fortune, though, threatened his hard-earned control as no one had ever done.

She wavered, damn her eyes. He could feel it. The attraction between them was strong enough to tempt a young woman of even stronger mind. She had never stolen the *Corinna*. He only wished he could say the same for his heart.

When his hands reached for the knot in the toweling, he heard her indrawn breath. When he released it, she gasped, and he heard her whirl and fling open the door. Naked, he stepped into the cold water. Every ounce of warmth had evaporated, in his bath and in his soul.

The door slammed behind Esmie Fortune. Julian reached for the pitcher again. The cold water sluiced over his head and shoulders, camouflaging any other moisture he might have been foolish enough to allow to collect in his eyes.

Esmie fled to the schoolroom. Her feet found their way of their own accord, for she could only concentrate on drawing each breath as she put as much space as possible between herself and the Earl of Ashforth. Humiliation, anger, grief—yes, that was it. Grief surrounded her like a cloud and she could barely see through the mist.

With the schoolroom door safely closed behind her and the earl half a world away in his wing of the house, Esmie sank onto the window seat. The night's damp already clung to the windowpane. Caroline should have a clean slate in the morning, but Esmie would not. She knew what he had been about. He had feelings for her as well. He must have, or he would not have worked so hard to drive her away. He had feelings for her, but he would never act upon them. Whatever lay between them was not to be. It could not be. Passion could not give way to position, and she would not be the means for bringing down the man she loved.

The man she loved. The pain of the thought far outweighed the pleasure. Her finger reached for the windowpane and she drew absently, marring the surface. If her heart were any heavier, it would sink out of her body and tumble to the floor.

Love without hope was the most devastating of truths. Esmie had read her share of history's wisest men, its greatest philosophers. What would they say to her now? "If you would marry suitably, marry your equal." Ovid's words rang in her ears.

She would never have Julian. She would learn to accept that. She might never have the *Corinna* or the prize or Athena Hall. Her dreamed-of students must remain figments of her imagination, clutching their phantom volumes of *The Odyssey*. She could not have what she wanted, but she knew five children who could.

She had not expected her life to change in the dark of night on the schoolroom window seat, but her priorities shifted of their own volition. She was glad she'd not stayed to tell Julian her news. For it would have been too easy an answer to his dilemma. He must build a bridge over the torrent of deception and shame that cut him off from his sons and daughters. If he could come to love the children for themselves, then and only then would she tell him the truth of James's paternity. When it would be too late, when it would not matter, because he had already accepted the children and given them his love. Then there would be no distinction between James and the others. Julian would not be torn between them, forever questioning his love for James and whether his partiality was fair to the others.

His children. The one gift she could give him before she left. Children who would be the one oasis of love when Julian married the cold Miss Lambton and deprived himself of ever giving and receiving love again.

The thought of Miss Lambton in his arms made Esmie twist in the window seat. Would Miss Lambton merely acquiesce in her marriage bed, or would she find Julian's touch as thrilling as Esmie had found it? Her fingers moved furiously across the moist windowpane, and she looked up to see the design. She'd written one word across the glass.

No. No to her feelings for Julian. To her dreams of the future. But when all else was lost, she would retain her sense of pride. That must be enough. She would make it be enough.

The next day brought the opportunity to act on her decision. The schoolroom made a rather fetching theater, Esmie decided, as she stood on the edge of a chair, arms stretched upward as she tacked a makeshift curtain into place. In the night, she'd hit upon an idea for involving the earl with his children. Now the children were busy at their various tasks. The twins bustled about gathering props and costumes while James sat at a desk, painstakingly copying out the parts for the tableau. Caroline drew scenery on an old linen sheet, her pastels providing more color than shape to the backdrop. Sophie sulked in the window seat.

"Here, Soph." Phillip dumped an armload of worn linen sheets into his sister's lap. "You are costume mistress. None of us can do it as well as you."

Esmie smothered a grin as first Sophie flashed a small smile at her brother's acknowledgment of her, then quickly hid the offending expression. She had been longing to participate all morning. Phillip had been wise to take the decision out of his sister's hands.

"Why do we have to do a Greek tableau?" Sophie asked with slightly less petulance than usual. "Why could we not do *Lovers' Vows*?"

Esmie turned back to tacking her curtain so the girl would not see her amusement. "*Lovers' Vows* is hardly appropriate for a schoolroom, Sophie. Besides, we are performing this for your father and Miss Lambton. And you know how he loves the Greeks."

Sophie tossed her curls, but she did begin sorting through the linens her brother had dumped upon her. "Yes, well, it is the only thing in this house he loves."

The other children fell silent, and even James's pen ceased its scratching. Caroline looked up, lower lip trembling, and Phillip and Phoebe bit their lips in identical places. Sophie looked around at her brothers and sisters with a mixture of defiance and pleading. "It's true, is it not? He loves this house, he loves his Greeks, and he loves his money. But he does not love Miss Lambton or us." She looked toward Esmie. "Or Miss Fortune."

"I should hardly think your father would love the governess," Esmie teased, though it cost her to maintain her sangfroid. With the last tack firmly in place, she climbed down from the chair and planted her feet on the floor. Her handling of the next few moments would prove critical in carrying out her plan to make Julian and his children a true family. "He does love you. I'm sure of it." For if Julian did not love the children, he would never have cut himself off from them so thoroughly. A man who loved either shouted it from the rooftops or alienated himself from the source of his pain. Julian wanted desperately to love his children. She need only maneuver him into admitting the truth.

"Will he come to our performance?" Caroline asked.

Esmie pasted on her face the brightest smile she could manage. "I will make sure of it."

"When?" This from James, who studied her with the dark, brooding eyes so like his father's.

Esmie swallowed. Facing the earl did not appear on her list of pleasant activities for the day, but she would swallow her pride and do what she must for the sake of the children.

"Today. I shall make an appointment with him, so we may fix a time and date. Then we shall practice our lines in earnest so our performance rivals that of any theater company in England." Esmie finished her words with a twirl and a flourish of her arms, and the children giggled.

"Come along, then. We've lots to do. James, are the parts ready?

The boy held up a sheaf of papers. "Finished, Miss Esmie."

"Excellent. We shall read through our lines this morning and then spend the afternoon fitting costumes. Oh, and we'll need the atlas as well. If we're to be famous Greeks, we need to know where they lived. Your father's sure to ask if you've learned anything in all this fuss."

James eyed her thoughtfully. "I suspect we've learned more than you think, Miss Esmie."

She looked at him, puzzled, but whatever his thoughts, he did not reveal them. So much like his father. How could Julian not see it? But he would. Eventually. First, though, she would ensure that he saw much more than any physical resemblance. Once he loved the children for themselves, Esmie could leave in good conscience. With a heavy heart, 'twas true. A broken one, even. But her life had changed in the last week. Her goals differed. Her future might be uncertain, but for now she had a task, and she would see it fulfilled.

Julian strolled toward the folly bridge with Miss Lambton on his arm and the sun on his face. The woman beside him chattered enough for three magpies, so he saw no need to do more than offer the occasional grunt of acknowledgement. To their right, the surface of the lake mirrored the blue summer sky and wisps of trailing clouds. A perfect English summer day, and he could be nothing but miserable—at his own actions with Esmie, at the prospect of wedding the woman on his arm, and at the longing to fling away his responsibilities before it was too late.

"Do you not think so, my lord?"

Miss Lambton's question startled him, but he did not show it. He had been such an apt pupil of his father that he could be a world away, lost in thoughts of Thrace and Sparta, and his companion might never know.

"Of course, madam." He had fallen into the dangerous habit of agreeing with Maria Lambton.

She tapped him playfully on the arm with her fan. "Imagine, the Earl of Ashforth admitting to growing bored with society." She smiled, and the hint of victory in her eyes alarmed him. He drew in a deep breath to stave off the lightheadedness that threatened.

"Everyone grows bored of balls and routs at some time or other. It is why the *ton* retires to the country at regular intervals," he said.

"Yes, even the *ton* cannot deny the virtues of some time spent at home and hearth." She smiled in an attempt to be beguiling. Julian could see all too clearly where this conversation was leading. Miss Lambton was nothing if not masterful in manipulating a situation. Talk of home fires and repairing to the country could only lead to talk of marriage and family. And children.

Could hearts really turn leaden? His chest ached as if he'd caught a bad cold, but no mustard plaster could alleviate this heaviness. Now was no time to consider what sort of mother Miss Lambton might make. The money she would bring to the marriage would see to their futures. And now was certainly no time to think of Esmie Fortune, her body beneath his, her gray eyes dark with passion.

"My thoughts, too, have turned to home and hearth of late, Miss Lambton. Particularly of my own wishes and my own comfort." He paused on the pathway, and she stopped beside him. He had meant to wait until they were on the magnificent Palladian bridge, the perfect spot for a romantic proposal. But he found nothing romantic about this one.

"How could you be anything but comfortable, my lord, when you have all this?" Maria Lambton looked about, her eyes sparkling with avarice and triumph.

"I could only be comfortable here, madam, with the proper companion by my side." He swallowed, the words lodging in his throat. He took her hands in his, for he refused to kneel. This was no time to play the supplicant. She would not expect it. "I could only be comfortable here if you were my wife." The lie slipped with such ease from his lips. "Would you consider my suit, Miss Lambton? Will you make me the happiest of men?"

Her mouth curved in a cold, feline smile. No, not feline. That was an insult to the wretched creatures. Her beautiful smile was as cold as if it had been sculpted from ice.

"But of course, my lord, I will marry you."

She tilted her face up, rightly expecting to be kissed. Not allowing himself to think, he brushed his lips against hers before he released her hands and stepped back. He drew a breath against the darkness that fluttered at the edge of his vision. *I will regret this.* He knew it with every part of his being, but the words had been uttered, and he could not turn back.

Chapter Thirteen

The engagement announcement of Miss Maria Lambton and the Earl of Ashforth appeared in the London papers within the week. Esmie sat at the breakfast table in the housekeeper's room one morning as Mrs. Robbins scrutinized them with the intensity she applied to overseeing the work of the maids.

"Now this one—this one is elegance itself."

Esmie had no choice but to stiffen her spine and join in the housekeeper's admiration for the wording of the notice. But for all her effusions of pleasure, she could barely keep down the tea and toast the housekeeper had set before her.

"Imagine." The housekeeper broke off to slurp her tea. "St. George's, Hanover Square. With the fashionable world in attendance."

Esmie's only balm was that she would not be expected to attend or to join in the preparations if the wedding was held in London. Her own preparations, though, must be finished before then. For afterward, Miss Lambton would do anything within her power to prevent Esmie's plans from happening.

"There's more." Mrs. Robbins rustled the pages as she folded the broadsheet. "Here, amongst the *on-dits*. Miss Lambton's trousseau will cost . . ." The housekeeper drew a sharp breath. "Well, we shall just say her father will be considerably lighter in the purse."

Esmie turned a deaf ear to the housekeeper and thought instead upon her own difficulties. She had made no further progress in finding the *Corinna*. The earl had sent her a curt note informing her he had engaged men to watch the booksellers in London and Edinburgh. His disappointment had been palpable in the terse lines, and Esmie's guilt increased. Still, she held fast to the belief that his children were of more worth than any manuscript.

She lifted her cup of tea and sipped the last of it. She'd already begun correspondence with the employment agency to procure her next position. Mrs. Hazelwood had suggested an arrangement as a companion to an elderly widow in Oxford, and Esmie consoled herself with the thought that when she was not preparing tisanes and pushing the widow about in a Bath chair, she might wander among the majestic spires of the colleges and think of what might have been.

"I must bid you good morning, ma'am. The children will be ready for their lessons." She rose from her chair, and the housekeeper waved her on her way with one hand.

Esmie slipped from the housekeeper's room and made for the stairs. She longed to see Cortland Manor again. The time had come to sell the property. The money it would bring was in no way substantial, given the condition of the house, but it would be enough to reimburse the earl for the *Corinna* and then, with any luck, purchase a small cottage in an obscure village. She might even contrive to buy the occasional book. With prudence, it would maintain her for her lifetime. No growth, no stimulation, no engagement of her mind, but enough to see to her basic needs. Except for the need to love and be loved, the need to engage in the world of ideas and to share her thoughts with those who might appreciate their value.

She passed the long gallery, and climbed the last set of stairs leading to the schoolroom. She knew she had no hope now of winning the prize from the Classics Society. She wondered if she ought even to enter, but some last bit of hope, some fading wisp of pride in her work had forced her to copy out a clean version of her manuscript, bundle it in oilskin and twine, and ride with James into the village to post it, for he had a parcel of his own for his godparents. She had not given her entry directly to the earl, for she did not want him to know that it came from her. Even the registration she completed under a false name. *Athena Hall.* The impulsive choice had brought a rare smile to her lips.

The next weeks would pass quickly, indeed. The Society would announce its prizewinner, the children would perform their tableau for the earl, and he and Miss Lambton would depart the Abbey for their wedding in London. And after that, she would never see him again. Esmie paused at the schoolroom door, unsteady upon her feet. No more glimpses of him striding across the lawn while she perched in the schoolroom window seat. No sound of him moving about in his private library. And no reminders of him in James's dark eyes, or in the boy's head bent studiously over his assignments.

Esmie leaned her forehead against the cool wood of the schoolroom door. For now, she would soak in all she could of Julian Armstrong, Earl of Ashforth, so she might steel herself against the lonely days ahead. She would allow Caroline to climb into her lap so she might sniff the violet water the nurse used to rinse the girl's hair. She would revel in the sights, sounds, and feel of his family. When the time came, she would slip away. No tears, at least none the earl or the children might see. She would go to Oxford and push a Bath chair until she could sell Cortland Manor and secure her little cottage. And then she would find something to do with the rest of her days besides ponder, again and again, what might have been.

The expedition into Oxford was not to Julian's liking, but the petulance of his betrothed and the persistence of his children drove him to accept the inevitable. He called for the enormous traveling carriage—really, he should take two carriages, but that would mean taking the horses from the farms, which he could not afford, even for a day. Maria was prepared to shop in celebration of their engagement, the children were eager for a change of scene, and he would have no peace until he agreed.

"I shall have the window!" Caroline shouted as they bounded toward the carriage. He held the children off

so Maria could take her seat first, but then the dam
burst, and in a tangle of arms and legs the five children
clambered into the carriage. He climbed in after them,
prepared to sort out the mess, but found Maria had
cowed them already with her sharp tongue. Julian bristled at her tone but said nothing. He took the only unoc-
cupied space, opposite Maria, and the footman shut
the door.

"Wait!" wailed Phoebe as she glanced around. "What
of Miss Esmie?"

"Yes, yes, what about Miss Esmie?" Caroline echoed.
Phillip, James, and even the sullen Sophie joined the
chorus.

Julian sat motionless. He was embarrassed that he had
not found the strength of purpose to send her away. The
mere mention of her name heightened his color, and so
he called on every ounce of sangfroid.

"Miss Fortune? I have given her the day off. She was
pleased to have a bit of time to herself."

"But we want her!" Phillip protested. "We can't go
into Oxford without her. Who will show us the sights?"

"I will show you what I can until it is time for my
lecture." He patted the leather case next to him that
contained his notes. Not the translation of the *Life of
Corinna,* but a respectable lecture on Ovid's allusions to
the ancient poetess in his *Amores*. "Afterwards, we will
have luncheon at an inn."

"But we want to see the Radcliffe Camera," James
protested. "And the Bodleian Library, and all the colleges. You shan't have time for that, sir."

The earl swallowed. Thank goodness he would not
have the time. That expedition would entail far too
many hours in the company of his children. He did not
want to see their pleasure or their excitement at the
impressive sights of the ancient town. If he had, he
would have escorted them himself long before now.

"Perhaps Miss Lambton will show you the things you
would like to see. You might picnic by the river, if
you'd rather."

"I want Miss Esmie!" Caroline flounced against the
squabs.

"Yes, yes, Miss Esmie!" the twins chorused.

At that moment, the lady in question appeared at the top of the Abbey stairs. She descended the steps toward the carriage, dressed in a drab pelisse and wilted bonnet.

"Look—there she is." James's voice cracked on the last word.

"Miss Esmie! Miss Esmie!" Caroline half hung out the window, and Julian grabbed the back of her skirt to prevent her from falling from the carriage.

Esmie approached, and her fine eyes took in the throng of people in the vehicle. The amusement that lit her expression made Julian more disgruntled than ever. How had it come to this?

"Miss Esmie, come with us," Caroline pleaded.

"No!" Maria Lambton barked out the word and then quickly softened her voice and her expression. "I mean, Miss Fortune deserves a little time away from the burden of her duties. I have no objection to showing you about Oxford." She clapped her hands in a forced attempt to express delight at the thought. "What fun we shall have."

Julian smothered a groan, and Esmie's smile grew wider. "Indeed, Miss Lambton. What a lovely idea," she said through the carriage window. "Be sure, though, not to let Caroline indulge in more cake than is good for her. She has a tendency to be sick when she's excited."

Miss Lambton blanched, Julian bit back a smile of his own, and Esmie remained as serene and poised as a goddess.

Goaded by her air of satisfaction at his predicament, he did something very rare for the paragon Earl of Ashforth. He acted on impulse. If he was to be miserable, why should the cause of his discomfort not have a share of it as well?

"You are going out, Miss Fortune? Perhaps you should like to clamber aboard and travel to Oxford with us. You would not be responsible for the children, and I know your interest in education. Surely you would not turn down an opportunity to stroll among the spires?"

He regretted his words as soon as they left his lips. The mixture of longing and hunger that flooded her expression made him feel like a brutish schoolboy tormenting a motherless lamb.

"Oxford?" She considered the offer. If the longing of
the children for her company had been any more palpable, it would have swept her off the drive and deposited
her in the carriage. She wavered for a moment, biting
her lip, before she reached her decision. "Very well. I
accept."

Miss Lambton groaned, but covered her frustration
with her handkerchief. The children cheered, and Julian
felt the familiar rush of pleasure and fear that Esmie
Fortune's presence evoked. The sensation only heightened when the footman opened the door and handed
Esmie into the carriage. James, who had been sitting
next to him, quickly scooted away and created a sliver
of space for her between them. Miss Lambton's eyes
shot daggers, but he could hardly decline to sit next to
his children's governess. The refusal would only confirm
his uneasiness in her presence.

No, not uneasiness. That wasn't the truth, and Julian
had always tried to be truthful with himself. It was often
the only thing that kept him sane behind the façade of
perfection he promulgated. Her presence did not make
him uneasy; rather, it made his stomach churn with the
desire to wrap himself around her, take her mouth with
his, and forget the Abbey, Miss Lambton, his debts and
dependents, and anyone or anything else that might have
a claim upon him. Yet years of self-control ensured that
no such travesty occurred. No, his torment was entirely
self-contained, as Esmerelda wriggled onto the seat beside him. James seemed determined to give her as little
room as possible, and Julian was already pressed against
the side of the carriage. The curve of her hip pushed
against his own, the length of her thigh lay alongside his,
her shoulder met his sleeve. If he forced himself to think
of the icy waters of the lake beside the bridge, he might
possibly survive the journey to Oxford without embarrassing himself. But if he did not . . . Stifling a groan,
he ignored the children's animated chatter, and imagined
gallons of icy water rushing over his body. The carriage
rolled forward, Miss Lambton shot him a frustrated
glance that she converted to a simpering smile, and
Esmie chattered as happily as Caroline or Phoebe.

When they left the drive, though, and entered the

rougher road, the first bump brought Esmie's body flush against his.

Why in the name of all the gods did it have to be Esmerelda Fortune who proved to be his personal Lyssa, his own goddess of madness? Fixing his eyes on the hedgerows that ran alongside the lane, he recited the opening of *The Odyssey* under his breath. Anything to distract him from the enticing figure pressed against him.

Esmie had passed through the city of Oxford on several occasions. Still, the sight of the towering spires was something she could never take for granted. She should have liked to have been a bird for an hour and soared above the colleges, viewing the quadrangles and chapel towers from on high, and tracing the joining of the Isis and the Cherwell to form the Thames. She should have liked to peer down upon the black-gowned students who hurried along the narrow streets, and watched the aimless meanderings of the cows that dotted Christ Church Meadow.

Instead, she contented herself with approaching in the relative comfort of the earl's traveling carriage—the comfort being relative, due to the disturbing fit of the aforementioned earl against her side. By sheer dint of will, Esmie ignored the effect his presence had on her senses. Soon enough the ancient stone walls of the colleges towered around them, and they were circling the Sheldonian Theatre. The coachman pulled the carriage to the side, and the footman came around to open the door. The children tumbled out with their usual chaos.

"We shall meet here at three o'clock." The earl tapped his pocket watch.

Miss Lambton drew breath as if to protest, but must have thought the better of it. Before she could smooth her light pelisse and open her parasol, James and Phillip had taken their future stepmother by the arm and propelled her away. Phoebe and Caroline skipped behind, and Sophie followed feet.

"Boys—mind Miss Lambton's frock!" the earl shouted after them but they gave no sign of having heard. Esmie covered her mouth to hide her smile. Beside her, the earl looked down with annoyance, but she did not allow

him to discomfit her. She had been almost as intimate
with this man as a woman might possibly be. In a few
more weeks, he would be out of her life forever. He had
made it clear that whatever might lay between them
should be given no consequence. He could do nothing
to shame her now that he'd not already done.

"You will come to the lecture, Miss Fortune?" His
stern question had all the authority of a general's
command.

"I shall, my lord."

If her acquiescence surprised him, he did not show it.
Indeed, it seemed they had both determined to hide any
and all emotion. Esmie knew it was for the best, that
she must forget whatever had passed between them. She
must not think of the warmth of his touch, or of the
similar warmth his understanding of her intellect produced in her breast. No, she must be merely an employee and he, her employer. No matter that she loved
him, or that he might love her. He had decided the matter for both of them. No use in longing for what would
never be.

Still, to walk into the Sheldonian Theatre on his arm
was a pleasure not to be discounted. She recognized
many of the people gathered there as some of the leading classics scholars in the kingdom. The stalls above
were open to the public, so those who wished might
attend the proceedings, but the esteemed members of
the Society held the positions of distinction about the
gilded Chancellor's Throne. The earl spoke to several of
his peers, but made no move to introduce her. Instead,
he led her to a seat in an obscure part of the theater,
and then excused himself. The press of his hand when
he moved her toward her chair felt icy, and she wondered whether he might be nervous.

Esmie had seen drawings of the Sheldonian's unusual
circular design, the flat ceiling constructed of the same
ropes and canopy that might have shielded an audience
in ancient Rome. The Sheldonian had been the first public building of the great Christopher Wren, whose re-
building of London after the Great Fire of 1666 had
transformed the capital from a city of medieval and
Tudor buildings into a panoply of classical columns,

friezes, and porticos. No building could have been more
calculated to make Esmie feel her own inadequacies.
Still, she settled into the hard chair as the president of
the Society moved to the podium. He introduced the
earl, who received a flattering round of applause, and
Esmie put aside the ache within her heart. Instead, she
gave herself over to the pleasure of seeing the man she
loved shine before the assembly.

"Ouch! Drat these cobblestones!" Miss Lambton
halted despite James's and Phillip's relentless escort, and
reached down to rub her foot. "I can't stand this another
moment. If I see another quadrangle or spire, I shall
scream."

Phoebe smothered a giggle, but not enough to prevent
her future stepmother from hearing.

"You!" She glowered at the children, her china blue
eyes full of malice. "All of you! You don't deceive me
for a moment. Best remember, *mes enfants,* once I am
your mama, I shall do with you as I see fit. Your father
has no interest in you, so you would do well to humor
me."

The venomous words produced the sobering effect
Miss Lambton intended.

James cleared his throat. "Perhaps we could see to
the picnic things, madam. The river is not far, and you
may rest along the bank while the younger ones amuse
themselves."

"Very well." Miss Lambton raised her nose in the
air and marched determinedly forward. One by one, the
children fell in line behind her, for none of them dared
to let her know she was headed in the entirely wrong
direction.

Those assembled in the Sheldonian Theatre received
the Earl of Ashforth's lecture with an approving round of
applause at its end. Afterward, a number of people
surrounded the earl, quite cutting him off from Esmie's
view. She sat still for several moments, afraid to stand
on legs that seemed unusually wobbly. The weakness in
her limbs could be traced to the strangest combination
of admiration and jealousy. She had never been so proud

of a man in her life as she had when Julian addressed the Society. But her pride had been undermined by stirrings of envy. His lecture had been intelligent, clever, and informative. His view of Ovid's work was unique and interesting. She could easily grant he had studied more than she had; one or two of the references she would have to look up in his library at the Abbey. And yet . . .

If Julian's lecture was the standard the Society set, she knew she could meet that standard herself. It was not beyond her reach in terms of ability or scholarship. A sharp pain, like the grip of a vise, clamped her midsection. Had she been born to breeches, she very well might have stood where Julian stood now, and received the approbation of her peers. But she had been destined for skirts and chaperones, had been born for no purpose other than marriage and children.

To own the truth, she would not mind marriage. She had found she rather liked children, even half-grown ones who were petulant, needy, or aloof. But still . . . Must a woman never fulfill the longings of her heart? Was she limited by her gender from following all the paths that could be hers?

This very lecture proved why her school would be so important. A first step on a long journey her sex must undertake before they, too, could stand before the Classics Society in the Sheldonian Theatre. The import of her recent decision could not be clearer. She had chosen her heart over her calling. She had elected to sacrifice her future students, whoever they might be, for five motherless children. She had decided that instead of following her dream, she would leave her immediate circle better than she'd found it. And she had, in the process, relinquished her hopes for that which might mean more to the wider world. Was this what had kept women from improving their place in the world? Little wonder, then, so little of Corinna's life and the lives of those like her had survived.

Esmie rose from the chair, wobbly legs and all, and slipped around the edge of the crowd until she found the door. She glanced toward Julian, but could only see the top of his dark head among the throng of admirers.

In a few weeks, these same people would meet in a closed session to determine the winner of the prize. Esmie knew who they would choose. And it would not be her.

Tears should have threatened as she made her way past the Divinity School and down a side lane toward Cornmarket Street. Once, long ago, she'd purchased a penny guidebook, and she pulled it now from her reticule, determined not to let her day's freedom go to waste. She would guide herself through the ancient streets, wander through any quadrangles where the porter would let her past the gates, and finally find her way to the river to see the students glide by in their punts. Along the way, she'd buy a bit of bread and cheese and dream of what might have been. Then she would make her way to the widow's house for a brief interview to see if they should suit. Rather, they would meet so the widow might see if Esmie would suit. The prospect of the Bath chair filled her with despair. Well, the only remedy for that was to make use of the precious day ahead. She set off, the hard cobblestones merciless beneath her feet.

The crowd had thinned before Julian had a moment to look about for Esmie. He glanced around the room. It would not do for the Earl of Ashforth to be seen casting about for his children's governess.

Three times in his lecture, he had indulged himself by looking at her to gauge her response to his work. He had not been disappointed. Even though she perched in the shadows, he could see the intensity of her gaze and the slight furrow of her brow. For a long moment, he'd thought perhaps his work hadn't pleased her, that she'd thought it inferior. But at the conclusion of the lecture, she'd smiled and applauded with genuine approbation. Strangely, her applause mattered more to him than that of all the members of the Society.

Perhaps she'd slipped outside for a breath of air. After bidding his good-byes, he went in search of her.

She was nowhere to be found outside the theater, either, much to Julian's growing consternation. He'd thought to invite her to join him for luncheon, since Miss

Lambton had taken the children on their picnic. Could the dratted woman not stay put? And why hadn't she come forth to congratulate him? Her neglect pricked his pride. Very well. If Miss Fortune would not linger, then he would seek out Miss Lambton and the children along the river. His peace of mind would be much better served by attending to his betrothed than by mooning about for a woman he could never have. The very thought set his footsteps in the direction of the Thames, even if his heart would not follow.

Chapter Fourteen

*J*ulian had no difficulty locating his children along the stretch of river adjacent to Christ Church Meadow. He could hear their shrieks as he strode down the New Walk, the long gravel avenue lined with towering trees like some outdoor cathedral. The awe it inspired reminded him, a mere human, of the grandeur and power of institutions—whether that institution was the monarchy, the university, or the aristocracy. With each step, his spine grew more rigid, his cravat cinched tighter, and his heart shrank. This was the end he'd been raised to serve. Nothing else was possible, no matter what emotions Esmie Fortune might bring forth in his breast.

The New Walk ended abruptly at the river. He'd stopped to buy some provisions at a greengrocer to supplement the picnic things, and the heavy basket hung like an anchor at the end of his hand. The children frolicked on the bank of the river, and Miss Lambton sat beneath the low, sheltering branches of a plane tree, her parasol raised unnecessarily, for she sat entirely in the shade.

"I see you've found a comfortable place for repose."

Her head snapped up from her contemplation of her slippers. "My lord! I did not hear you approach."

"You were quite lost in thought."

She patted the grass beside her. "Won't you join me?"

Though Miss Lambton had invited him to sit beside her, she made no move to share the small blanket that shielded her jonquil muslin. With a rueful shrug, he settled in beside her and hoped his doeskin breeches would not collect a mark that might make him cower before his valet. He hated being so fastidious. Phillip found a frog, and chased his sisters with it, much to their protesting delight. Even James had joined in the teasing, and Sophie shrieked as loudly as any of them.

It all seemed so ordinary. The antics of any family on a day's outing, yet having Maria Lambton seated next to him felt wrong, as if his valet had brought him the wrong coat. The children caught sight of him and waved, their faces shiny with exertion and the warmth of the summer day. He waved back with uncharacteristic enthusiasm. Miss Lambton shot him a glance.

"They have rather a lot of energy, do they not?" She smiled, but the happy expression fell far short of her eyes.

"They *are* children."

"James is well beyond the age of being sent to school," Miss Lambton said. The remark was not casual.

"I have procrastinated sending him to Eton, but he shall go this autumn, for the Michaelmas term." He had done far more than procrastinate.

"And Phillip will not join him? He is of an age to go as well."

"I have not decided. They seem so young."

Miss Lambton made a dismissive gesture with her hand. "Most boys are sent at the age of eight. It is good for them. . . ." She trailed off at the earl's expression. "Or so I am told."

"If you had ever been to Eton, Miss Lambton, you might have the same reluctance as I."

Her bark of laughter was most uncharacteristic. "I? Sent to Eton?" She came close to snorting with amusement. "You are a wit, my lord. What would I, a mere female, find to do at Eton?"

A vision of Esmie Fortune rose in his mind, a younger Esmie, her head bent over a desk with manuscripts piled around her, and ink staining her fingers and her gown. She would have known exactly what to do, had she been sent to Eton.

Miss Lambton did not wait for him to answer her question. "Sophie is old enough for a seminary for young ladies. Where shall she go in the autumn?"

An ache started in Julian's chest that he could not discount. Send Sophie away? Next, Miss Lambton would suggest Phoebe go as well. Which would leave only Caroline, and Julian could not imagine the energetic child on her own in the schoolroom with no brothers and sisters for company or guidance. Left to her own devices, she would find far more trouble than climbing upon the roof or falling into the lake.

"The girls will remain at home for now."

Miss Lambton's face tightened. "I see."

As did Julian. He had known what course of events was inevitable once he offered for Maria Lambton. Caroline would be shut up in the schoolroom with a governess—a governess who was not Esmie Fortune. The rest of the children would be sent away to school, despite his assurances to the contrary.

Children. There might be more of them. In fact, there likely would be more. He did not plan to procure a mistress after his marriage, for he had rather traditional views on the fidelity required of the marriage bed. He assumed Miss Lambton would want offspring of her own, but now, sitting beside her and listening to her mentally pack his children off to school, he wondered if she would welcome a child of her own.

And his. Perhaps this time, in this marriage, he could be certain of the paternity of his children. All it would cost him were the other children he had owned in name, if not in blood.

His thoughts were interrupted by a loud splash from the direction of the river. Miss Lambton gasped, and Julian ducked his head to hide the cringe of embarrassment, for Caroline was up to her old tricks. He could see her from where he sat, not fifty feet away, as she flailed about in the water.

"My lord!" Maria Lambton snapped her parasol shut and prodded him with the tip. "This is the outside of enough. Do something!"

Some demon prodded him into a devious choice. "I am not a strong swimmer, my dear. Are you?"

"Of course," she snapped. "But if you think I would ruin my gown for that . . ."

Julian thought of another young woman who had not

hesitated to plunge into a lake after his youngest daughter. He remembered her hair and her dress plastered to her form, and the way she had looked at him with his shirt open. Why could not Esmie Fortune be the one with the Cit of a father and the piles of guineas?

"My lord, you must do the saving." Miss Lambton appeared more annoyed than frightened. Apparently she had learned her lesson after the last incident.

Julian sighed. "James! Grab that pole and fish your sister out of the river."

The boy did as instructed, and grabbed an abandoned pole a punter had left on the bank. He held the length of it out to Caroline, and the girl, seeing that her father and Miss Lambton were not inclined to dive into the water after her, grabbed hold of its length and allowed her brother to tow her to shore. Dripping, she climbed up the bank. Julian rose to his feet without looking at Miss Lambton again.

"Caroline!" He wanted to laugh at her ploy but he knew he must put the fear of the Almighty into her. She stumbled toward him, head bowed, water dripping from her curls, and cattails caught on her clothing.

"Sir?" She thrust her lower lip out in hopes that petulance might be mistaken for penance.

"I will not abide these tricks, Caroline. Come with me." He must discipline her, or one day her foolery would bring her real harm.

For the first time, she showed real fear for what she'd done. The other children stepped up behind her, but he stopped them with a stern glance. "I'm sure your sister was not alone in choosing to employ this stratagem, but she will be the one to bear the consequences for it."

James opened his mouth to protest but stopped when he saw his father's stormy expression. Julian held out his hand to his youngest daughter and she placed her wet fingers in his. "Come, then, Caroline."

Sophie, of all people, started to weep, and Phoebe quickly followed. The boys hung their heads and scuffed their toes in the dirt of the path that ran along the river.

"Miss Lambton? Will you allow the boys to escort you back to the carriage?"

She smiled with a strange sort of triumph that made Julian nauseated. "Of course, my lord."

He left the picnic basket forgotten on the riverbank. With long strides, he moved away from the others, little Caroline in tow. He had no idea where he was taking her or what he would say, and could only pray that the gods would send some messenger to inspire him.

Esmie had not even begun to drink her fill of Oxford, but the chimes from Tom Tower warned her of the approaching hour of three o'clock. She turned her steps toward the river in search of the children, Miss Lambton, and the earl. Knowing the children as she did, she doubted they would prove too difficult to find, and the chance to stroll along the river held almost as strong an appeal as the city's spires.

She reached a portion of the bank where the path took her beneath a canopy of overhanging willows. Two swans dawdled in the shade. Despite their regal air, swans were among the most loyal of creatures and mated for life. The thought brought a blush to Esmie's cheeks, for since that night with the earl, she understood more fully what that meant, to mate for life. Lost in thought, she didn't see the angry paragon and dripping little girl until they were already upon her.

"My lord! Caroline!"

She fell to her knees in front of the child, who flung her arms around Esmie's neck and pressed her damp body close against Esmie's breast. The girl reeked of the river, but Esmie cradled her as if she were the most precious of all creatures.

"Oh, Caroline. Not again." Esmie leaned back so she could see the child's face. For now, she preferred to ignore the earl's thunderous expression. "You promised me."

Caroline bit her lip and kept her eyes glued to Esmie's.

"I b-b-broke my promise." With that trembling confession, Caroline burst into sobs and fell against her. They would have tumbled to the path if the earl's hands had not reached for them. His arm came around Esmie's shoulders, supporting her, sustaining her, and she shot

him a look of gratitude. His eyes held that strange light
again, half hope and half despair. She must not read
anything into the man's expression. No, she must repeat
his words of denial of anything between them until she
hardened her heart as he had hardened his own.

"Caroline, were you playing a trick upon Miss Lambton?"

The girl only shook harder in Esmie's arms, and she
took that for assent.

"Indeed, Miss Fortune, she was up to her usual tricks,
and I am prepared to discipline her. Someday her
schemes will lead to real trouble, for herself or for her
victim."

His harsh tone grated, but Esmie knew the words
must be spoken. Still, Caroline shook from the damp
and she would catch cold if not dried off properly.

There were a few linens left at Cortland Manor. They
could take Caroline there—it lay within walking distance, but Esmie had kept herself from going there
today, anxious to avoid further pain now that she knew
the hope for her dream was gone. Visiting the beloved
place could only lead to regrets and recriminations. But
Caroline's needs must come first, above Esmie's own
bruised feelings.

"She needs to get out of these wet things, my lord. I
know a place nearby where we may dry her out."

"Indeed?" The earl raised a skeptical eyebrow. "I
should let her endure the carriage ride home as a
soggy lesson."

"With the press of people in your carriage today, my
lord, we will all suffer for her sins. Are you prepared for
her to snuggle next to you all the way to the Abbey?"

He scowled. "Where shall we take her, then?"

"Follow me."

She rose, Caroline in her arms, prepared to carry the
girl to the bridge she'd just passed, and then across the
open field to Cortland Hall, but the earl reached out and
took the girl from her. "She is far too heavy for you."

Surprised, Esmie released her to her father's care.
Caroline cast one longing glance at Esmie, and then a
cautious one at her father. When he showed no signs of

further scolding, she settled her damp curls against the superlatively tailored Bath superfine of his coat.

Esmie turned and led the way. They crossed the bridge, the earl muffling his grunts of exertion, his step determined. Caroline was no longer a babe, and warmth grew around Esmie's heart at this demonstration of fatherly affection. They crossed the field behind Cortland Manor and approached the tumbledown house from the rear. Sadly, this view was even less impressive than the front prospect. Rather than use the gate, Esmie stepped through a large hole in the garden wall, thereby saving the earl a number of steps. Esmie could see the tight lines of distaste around the earl's mouth as they made their way through the tangle of the gardens to the kitchen door.

"What is this place?"

Esmie needed no skill reading minds to know he was comparing her derelict property with the elegance of Ashforth Abbey. "It is my house, my lord." She relished the words, said them with pride, and lifted her nose while she straightened her spine. Let him think of it what he might. Cortland Manor was not a very worthy place, just as she was not a very worthy person. Still, this was her house, he and Caroline were her guests, and she was indeed a person, whatever her shortcomings might be.

"No need to cut up stiff. It's yours? Why don't you live here?"

The infuriating innocence of the question dug into her skin like a nettle. Only someone of great wealth would ask such a thing.

"I do not live here, my lord, because to live here would require a significant infusion of cash. I'm hardly likely to earn enough as a governess to restore this place to its proper state."

He grimaced and shifted the sleeping Caroline in his arms. "You will have quite a bit of cash, indeed, if you fulfill the terms of our bargain."

"Indeed, I shall not. The money you promised you may keep as payment against the value of the *Corinna*."

"The value of the *Corinna*?"

"I am responsible for its loss, my lord, as you have pointed out. I will repay you the value of the work."

He raised one eyebrow. "That would be thousands of pounds. You said yourself you had no money."

Esmie unlocked the kitchen door and it swung open on rusty hinges. She stepped across the threshold and motioned for the earl to follow. "I have already contacted my solicitor in regard to conducting an auction of this house."

He followed her through the kitchen and up the stairs. "Why have you not disposed of it already? The proceeds would secure you a modest establishment of your own and your independence."

Esmie bit her lip against the tears that threatened. Such a casual question, but to answer would require baring her soul to a man who had already rejected her on two humiliating occasions.

They had reached an empty bedroom. Esmie passed through it to the small dressing room beyond. The tiny space contained a daybed and a trunk. Esmie opened the trunk and pulled out several worn linen sheets. With practiced hands, she made up the daybed while the earl continued to cradle Caroline. When she finished, she motioned for him to lay the drowsing girl on the bed.

"We need to get her out of these wet things." Esmie worked at the buttons of her dress and the earl reached down to untie the laces of Caroline's little half-boots. Her hair had begun to dry.

"You've not answered my question. Why have you not sold this house before and secured your independence?"

"Perhaps I find too much pleasure in being a governess." The bite of sarcasm stung her mouth as well as her words.

"You might teach at any village school in the country. And I'm sure any parish would be delighted to have you."

Esmie refused to meet his eyes. "Very well. Perhaps I have placed myself in service merely to ferret out rare manuscripts like the *Life of Corinna*."

"Hmm." He succeeded in loosening Caroline's first boot, worked it from her foot, and began on the second.

"That sounds more like the Miss Fortune with whom I have become acquainted. So, mine is not the only house in England where you've skulked about in the dead of night?"

He smiled at her as she worked next to him, untying Caroline's sash and slipping the dress from her shoulders. Esmie ignored the trembling that his smile initiated in her limbs. Caroline frowned in her sleep and mumbled the word *cat* twice before settling back to her slumber.

Finally, though, Esmie looked at Julian and his smile brought an answering one to her own lips. "No, my lord, I have not made it a practice of playing the wraith."

Caroline curled onto the mattress in her chemise. Esmie reached for the other linens and draped them over the girl. Again her eyes met the earl's, and his scrutiny sent tiny darts of awareness down her spine.

"We should hang her clothes in the garden and put her boots in the sun."

"Yes." The laconic reply did little to stop the quickening of Esmie's pulse. How could she have any other response when the earl's full attention fell upon her?

With one last gesture of care, she smoothed the sheet over Caroline, and then picked up the girl's things. Without looking back at the earl, she left the room. He followed hard on her heels as she descended the stairs and retraced her steps through the kitchen, out the door, and into the garden.

The overgrown hedges provided ample space for laying out Caroline's wet dress and stockings. Esmie set the little boots on top of a pile of stones that formed a sort of pyre where the garden wall had fallen in.

"I'm afraid I have no refreshment to offer you, my lord. Not even a dish of tea." What would she do with him now, while Caroline slept?

Julian's mouth twisted in frustration. "I had a full picnic basket, but I left it by the river. I hope the children picked it up."

"The children!" For the first time, Esmie spared a thought from Caroline to wonder where the rest of her charges might be. "Are they waiting for you by the river? I had no idea. We should not have come here.

We'd best return." She reached for the clothes she'd just laid out on the gooseberry bush, but the earl's hand stopped her.

The contact of his fingers against the bare skin of her arm sent warmth shooting through her entire body. She jumped away from his touch, and he snatched his hand back as if he'd been bitten.

"James will see to Sophie and the twins. They were to escort Miss Lambton back to my carriage."

"But they will be waiting. We must get back." Now that she was alone with him, she panicked. What only days ago would have seemed the most precious thing in the world was now entirely too painful.

"Miss Lambton and the children can wait another half an hour. Let Caroline have her rest. Her clothes will dry quickly in this heat, and then we can return to the carriage. Besides," he smiled with wry forlornness, "I have no doubt Miss Lambton will make herself comfortable in a private dining room at the nearest inn. No doubt they are all at this moment feasting upon cold ham, bread, and cheese."

The mention of food set Esmie's stomach to rumbling. She had not eaten luncheon, and the afternoon grew late. "There is a small well just beyond the garden. If nothing else, we can have a drink of water."

"Very well. We shall content ourselves with a cooling drink, and then you may tell me the true reason you have never parted with this house."

Esmie started at the command in his tone. Her feelings of intimidation irritated her. Who was this man to demand any explanations? He had made it plain she was of no consequence to him. She should practice despising him. But just when she thought she might manage it, he did something out of character like carry Caroline through the field, and help with caring for the tired, wet child.

"You have no right to pry into my affairs, my lord."

"No, I do not. But that has never stopped me before." The challenge in his eyes warmed Esmie even as it set her to trembling. He was a worthy opponent, an intelligent and perceptive man, and so determined to avoid his feelings for his children and for her. She could do nothing to alter his refusal to acknowledge his own emotions. It was pointless to think she might. Somehow, though, her common sense did not seem to hold sway over the undisciplined vagaries of her heart.

"Very well, then, my lord. If you will draw the water, I will tell you what you want to know."

Chapter Fifteen

*J*ulian offered Esmie the first turn with the dipper from the well. She sipped thirstily, and Julian's eyes could focus nowhere but on her lips, cool and wet with the water he had drawn. She finished before he could drink his fill of her face, and when she looked up and lifted the dipper to him, she caught him staring. Her cheeks went red, and she turned away.

Julian placed his lips where hers had been and savored the coolness of the water on his tongue. He fancied he could still taste her there. He tilted his head back and let the water run down his throat. How unfortunate that he couldn't dip a third time and pour the water directly over his head. By Jove, every time Esmie Fortune came near, he found himself wanting to douse himself with cold water. Hardly the response of a man schooled to a lifetime of indifference—or at least to the showing of it.

He dropped the bucket into the well and strode after Esmie, who made her way through the opening in the garden wall. The house, if one might call it that, was in remarkably horrid condition. Her first stepfather had been a duke. Julian suspected that was how she had come to be in possession of this ramshackle pile of stones. But why had she kept it? Its disposition would produce sufficient funds to secure her independence, leaving no need for paid employment.

"Miss Fortune, you have had your water. Now I should like my story."

Esmie paused and looked back at him. He stood within ten feet of her and could read her expression.

Wariness lined her face. She bit her lip in consideration. If they had been at Ashforth Abbey, he might have ordered her to tell him the truth. But here, it was as if they inhabited a different world, one far from the usual strictures of time, custom, and society. Despite its sad state, the house had a timelessness that made him think of the holy places he had visited—ancient temples, cathedrals, and even the chapels within the colleges of Oxford.

"Are you ordering the information, my lord?" She arched an eyebrow at him.

He drew a deep breath. "I am asking, madam. Not commanding." And to his surprise, he found it was true.

"The house was left me by my stepfather." She looked around for a place to sit, and settled on the pile of stones near Caroline's drying clothes.

"A bequest from the Duke of Nottingham, then?"

"Yes. He wanted me to have some security. Unfortunately, with my mother's spendthrift ways, there was no money left to accompany the house. As there is no farm attached to generate the income needed to sustain such a place, it has been left empty since my stepfather's death." Her careful words did not conceal the wealth of her disappointment.

"I'm surprised your mother has not sold it."

"It is not hers to sell, though the contents were, which is why there are few furnishings. I did manage to rescue one or two odd pieces and a small trunk of worn linen. But as for the rest . . ."

The regret in her eyes and the longing in her tone unnerved him. In his life, he made a habit of not looking at other people too closely. He could not afford the wear upon his emotions. He made his decisions with a cold, calculating precision that would have done his father proud. He had never weighed his own emotions into his decisions, either. At least, not until Esmie Fortune had arrived upon his doorstep.

"You must have had some plans for this house, else you would have relinquished it long ago." He turned his attention to Esmie, eager to escape too much self-reflection.

"I did have plans. Once. But not now."

"What changed?"

"A great many things." She kicked the heels of her half-boots against the pile of stones much as Caroline might have.

Julian looked up, taking in the uneven line of the roof and the missing slates there. No doubt the place leaked like a sieve. "I do not see what possible use you might have envisioned for it. A small cottage somewhere would suit your needs far better."

She bristled. "This house is mine, to do with as I wish."

"And what is it that you wish to do with it?" His persistence would pay off, and he would hear the truth.

She bit her lip again, and the sight of her teeth against the tender flesh made him want to reach out and take her mouth with his own to soothe it. He clenched his hands to keep them immobile at his side, and willed his boots to remain planted in the weed-strewn garden path.

Esmie straightened her spine, and he knew from her posture that she meant to tell the truth.

"I wish to establish a school, my lord."

"A school?"

"Yes. A school for young women."

Julian frowned. Esmie hardly seemed the type to preside over thirty silly girls who were content to paint screens and squabble over the latest issue of *La Belle Assemblée.*

"Why ever would you want to do that?"

Her hands tightened at her side, and Julian almost laughed out loud at the pair of them, fists clenched as if preparing to engage in fisticuffs.

"Because young women have a right, my lord, to their Greek and Latin and logic. They can learn astronomy and botany and literature. Their scholarship should not be suppressed or diverted merely because of their sex."

Julian's bark of laughter startled even him. "You want to educate them like men? You sound like Mrs. Wollstonecraft." He had been discomfited when he'd first read the reformer's work, though he could concede the merits of furthering women's education—to some degree. But Latin? Logic? Absurd.

"I thank you for the comparison to that great lady.

That is a compliment, indeed." Esmie's eyes flashed a warning Julian had no intention of heeding.

"How do you propose to bring this school about? Where will you find masters who will so humble themselves as to try to drum ancient languages into the empty heads of young women? And for that matter, where would you find young women who cared a fig for Homer or Aeschylus or Aristophanes?" He laughed again at the absurdity, and then waved his hand at the tumbledown house. "Not to mention the cost of repairing this place so it might be habitable."

He said the words without thinking, a visceral response to a ridiculous suggestion. The hurt in her eyes, though, signaled that she didn't find her plans for the school absurd in the least.

"We should look in on Caroline." Esmie's voice had gone flat. She jumped up from the pile of stones and spun on her heel, marching off through the garden.

"Miss Fortune! Wait."

He should apologize. He must apologize. No one deserved to have a dream trampled upon so cruelly. He should know, for his father had trod upon his in a manner that made his treatment of Esmie look doting.

He caught her arm halfway across the garden.

"I do apologize." He came to a stop just behind her and she continued to ignore him, her head turned away. "But it is a strange idea, you must admit. Even the most radical reformers do not push so far."

Esmie spun around, her eyes blazing and her color high. "One day, women will sit beside men in the examination schools at every university in the land."

Julian choked back a laugh and kept his face impassive. Although, now that she'd said it, he had a strange vision of Sophie, head bent over her desk, pen flying across the page. He could see it of her. Not of Caroline—heavens, he would do well to keep her from drowning before she reached the age to be thrown on the marriage mart.

"I know you well enough to know that you must have some sort of plan. How will you begin your school?"

Esmie went bright red. "I'd thought to use the money from our agreement."

"A large amount, but not sufficient for the purpose. Surely you had some other scheme before you came to the Abbey?"

Her color remained high. She looked everywhere but at his face.

"Miss Fortune?"

"Please stop calling me that!"

"How did you plan to secure the funds for this?" He waved his free hand at the sooty walls of the house.

She shook off his grip on her arm. "With the prize money." The mumbled words took a moment to make out.

"Prize money? What prize money?"

"From the Society's competition."

"The Society? The Classics Society?" She might as well have told him she intended to fly to the moon.

"The prize money would have been sufficient to start repairs upon the house. And perhaps secure my first masters."

"The prize money?" he repeated, an incredulous echo. "You have entered the competition, then?" For some reason, he grew alarmed. He himself had counted on winning. Invested in some of the outlying areas of his property, such a sum would greatly increase his yields and someday decrease his indebtedness. But why should he worry about competing with the frizzy-headed Miss Fortune?

She looked him in the eye. "I told you I came for the *Corinna*."

"For what purpose?"

"For my compendium of ancient Greek and Roman women."

"Your compendium?"

"Yes. Plutarch catalogued the men in his *Lives of the Noble Greeks and Romans*. I wanted to record the women. Perhaps someday they will be of more interest to scholars than they are at present."

Julian hardly heard her reply, for he was too busy puzzling out this new side of her to fully comprehend her statement.

"How did you know I had the *Corinna*?" He had not thought to ask before.

"By the process of logical deduction, sir."

"You must have known for some time, then, that the manuscript was in my possession. What took you so long?"

"I did not want to come to the Abbey, my lord."

"Not want to? Why not?"

"Because of your reputation for perfection. I was far too aware of how short I should fall of your expectations."

Her eyes dropped to the ground, but her statement swept across Julian's skin like tiny knives. He snorted. "Now, though, you see the legendary perfection of the Earl of Ashforth for the sham it is."

She did not raise her eyes. "Yes, my lord."

God, he hated the way she said, "my lord," with every other breath. Could he not simply be *Julian*? If only for her?

"Enough!"

She lifted her chin. "Are you dismissing me, sir?"

"No. By Jove, woman, you work rather diligently to get turned off for a woman who claims to need money."

"I do need the money, my lord. . . . I need the money, but not for what you think."

"Not for what I think?" He rubbed his eyes with the palms of his hands. And this woman wanted to teach other women the fine points of logic?

Finally, she lifted her eyes to his. "I will fulfill my duty, but not to secure money from you."

"You are refusing the money?" Had there ever been a more confusing chit of a girl?

"No. I am giving it back to you, in lieu of the *Corinna*. I will pay the rest back as well. In time."

Julian could hardly follow the twisted pathway of her reason. "How do you intend to repay such a sum?"

She waved her hand toward the house. " 'Tis in abominable condition, but still it has value."

"No!" His own vehemence surprised him.

"It is not sufficient?"

"You think I would accept such a sacrifice?"

"I thought you demanded such sacrifices, my lord. Did you not inform me of that fact yourself?"

Julian's shoulders sank. "I would not accept such a thing," he said in a low voice.

"Then you impugn my honor."

"Your honor?" His eyes met hers.

"Do you not believe I possess such a quality?" Her chin lifted.

"I think, my dear, you possess too much of it."

She was prepared to give it all away, everything that might be hers. She would dump it into his lap for the sake of a mistake she'd made in pursuit of a dream. Julian thought of the mistakes he'd made. The wife he'd failed to keep from straying from his side. The children he both loved and could not endure to be in company with. He'd sacrificed his own desires and the desires of those around him for what? For an illusion? For an ideal? For a lie?

The first raindrop fell, thick and fat, and it landed on his nose. A second followed it, cold and wet against the back of his neck. Esmie looked up at the sky and held her hands out, as if testing the wetness. The summer shower broke over them, and though the sun still shone around the thick, dark cloud above, Julian did not see the light. He saw only the ominous thunderhead, and felt only the chill sting of the rain.

"Come on." Esmie grabbed his hand and towed him toward the house. He followed, and in his raw emotional state would have followed anywhere the warmth of her hand might have led him.

Esmie paused in the garden long enough to snatch Caroline's dress and boots. She dropped Julian's hand to retrieve the items, but still he followed her as if under her spell. She'd seen the shift in his eyes, just now, as they'd talked. Something had happened that both frightened her and intrigued her. She glanced at him over her shoulder, at the sudden slope to his shoulders and the air of . . . what? Dejection? Resignation? Relief? Whatever it was, it had enveloped him, and it seemed to buffer him, for the moment, from the outside world.

She was so busy assessing him that she almost walked into the door frame. His hand shot out to stop her, and his grip brought her up short. She looked down at his fingers wrapped around her arm and then up at him. He met her gaze, and there was such sadness in his eyes that tears welled in her own.

He had said she possessed too much honor. What did he mean? Still, the acknowledgement from a man of his stature warmed her, though not nearly as much as the warmth of his fingers as they slid down her arm, and then took her hand in his. She led him over the threshold and into the kitchen. The sudden rain had brought a chill with it, and Esmie shivered. Without a word, he reached for her.

She fit so neatly against him and slid into his embrace so easily, his throat knotted with emotion. Soft in his arms and still shivering, she was far more pliant than he would have ever imagined. Memories of their nighttime embraces followed, but he tamped them down as quickly as they came.

"Oh, Esmie, what have I done?" He expected no answer, and she gave none, other than to slip her arms around his waist and clasp him loosely. Her cheek pressed against his chest.

"We are being very foolish, my lord."

"Indeed, we are. Indeed, we are."

But foolishness had never prevented a man from acting as his heart dictated. With one hand he lifted her chin, and with the other he reached to cup the nape of her neck. "You will be the ruin of me. And I shall certainly be the ruin of you."

He shouldn't kiss her, shouldn't run his hands down the length of her back or twine his fingers in her hair. He should push her away from him and admonish her for her hoydenish ways. But he did no such thing. Instead, he held her as if she were the most precious commodity in the entire world.

Esmie looped her arms around his neck and gave in to the pulse that drummed through her body. She was no longer chilled. Clearly, she had not an ounce of pride left, to cling to him after he'd spurned her. It was a hopeless embrace, but perhaps the inevitability of its end made it all the sweeter. She had no honor, to stand and kiss another woman's betrothed. This would be the last time, though.

"Come upstairs," she whispered and stepped back, once more threading his fingers through hers. "Caroline is still asleep. Come upstairs." It would only be the once, and she would have the memory to feast upon in the lonely years to come in her damp little cottage. Could it be so wrong? Could she not have just this one memory to treasure?

Julian's eyes widened at her suggestion. The rain drummed softly against the kitchen windowpanes. There was no question of returning to Oxford and finding the others until the storm abated, and the exhausted little girl might sleep for hours.

He stepped forward and, to Esmie's surprise, scooped her up in his arms. She started to protest—for she was no child to be carried about, even in a moment of passion—but the intensity of his expression stopped her. He looked at her, the most imperfect woman in the world, as if she were without equal.

His muscles tightened and rolled beneath her fingers as he strode into the hall and mounted the stairs. She directed him down the corridor with a nod of her head. They passed the sleeping Caroline's room. At the end of the hall, he set her down and her treacherous knees nearly gave way beneath her. Esmie opened the door and they stepped inside.

It was the one room she'd managed to persuade her mother to leave untouched. The large tester bed with its medieval proportions loomed in the shadows. A step stool stood at the ready, the mattress bare and dusty.

He looked down at her, and for the first time she saw his heart in his eyes. "Esmie, are you sure?"

"Yes." She reached for his hand. "If this is all there is, then it will be enough."

"No, it won't. It will never be enough." His voice broke on the last words, and he leaned down to take her mouth with his. Pleasure shot through her with the same intensity as the onset of the storm outside. She was a mere mortal being seduced by a god, and for the first time she understood why those foolish women had fallen prey to their immortal lovers.

Then he lifted her to the bed and followed her onto

the mattress. This time there would be no Plutarch to shed his dander and interrupt their tryst.

His hands moved over her, thorough and gentle. Esmie drank in every movement, every sound, far thirstier for him than she'd been for the water at the well. Julian obliged as she slaked her thirst for the taste of his lips. He smelled of sandalwood and rain. The combination made her head swim. His weight pressed her into the mattress and she let go of any final reservations, any question of good sense or honor. Just this one afternoon. Just this stolen hour. Just one taste of Julian. And then a lifetime of regrets and loneliness.

Chapter Sixteen

"I'll not wait any longer." Miss Lambton glowered down at James with perfect loathing. "Your father and that . . . that . . . *child* may hire a hack. I am returning to the Abbey."

Phillip and Phoebe watched the argument with similar expressions of anxiety. Sophie stood to the side, unsure whether to throw in her lot with her brother or her future stepmother.

"We will wait here, as my father directed." James glanced toward the mullioned windows. Even through their thickness, he could see the great drops of rain wetting everything in sight. "No doubt they have taken shelter as well." His heart lodged in his throat, for Miss Lambton in high dudgeon was an intimidating prospect. But he was the future earl, and if he gave in to Miss Lambton now, he would regret it. He could see her plans for each one of them in her cold blue eyes. Boarding schools for the lot, and they'd be lucky to be allowed home on holidays.

"Then I will call the carriage around myself." She moved to the door. James stepped in front of her.

"No, ma'am. You will not." He made the slightest bow he could and still be called a gentleman. "I am under orders from my father."

He thought her head might pop off her neck, she turned so red and rigid. Sophie moved to stand behind him, evidently deciding that solidarity with her brother would prove more beneficial in the long run. The twins fell in behind her, the four of them a united front against a common enemy.

Miss Lambton's sharp, cold eyes bored through them. "So! This is how we begin. Very well. Know it shall be how we go on as well." She bent forward, and the harsh lines around her mouth erased any beauty society might have celebrated. "In a few weeks' time, when I am the countess, you will not find my desires so easily thwarted."

James stood still so the trembling in his hands would not betray his fear. She spun on her heel with a muttered imprecation and stalked toward the dining table where the remains of their cold collation were still spread about. She looked around, and her eyes caught Sophie's. "Ring for tea, girl. Now!"

Sophie, accustomed to such imperious commands from her father, leapt to attention and yanked the bell pull beside the mantelpiece. An uneasy silence fell over the room, and James wondered if he'd made the right decision. In his heart, he knew he had. He could never abandon his father or Caroline. Yet at the thought of the loyalty due his father, a sudden stab of guilt pressed against his chest. He had something his father wanted very much, but he could not part with it. Not quite yet.

Why had no one told her that pleasure could be so consuming? Esmie bit her lip to keep from moaning when Julian eased her gown down around her shoulders. Her thin chemise did little to hide her form from him, and he growled with satisfaction. She giggled, for who could have imagined the imperious Earl of Ashforth growling at anything?

"You find that amusing?" His eyes lit with laughter, and Esmie drank in the sight. She was the sole object of his considerable powers of concentration, and she found she enjoyed the sensation very much. Her hands tugged at his shirt and pulled it from his trousers. He growled again when her fingers worked their way lower. His physical strength was not something she'd spent much time considering, but with him pressed so tightly against her, she felt every movement of muscle and sinew.

"Esmie." He whispered her name into her ear, and deep shivers ran down her spine. Her skin was ablaze. His hand traced its way up her leg, beneath her skirt, until she felt his palm, warm and strong against the lower part of her belly.

"Julian." She whispered his name into his neck, embarrassed at how she savored the word upon her tongue. And then he savored her tongue with his own.

"Papa?"

The sleepy, bewildered voice from the doorway dowsed them as effectively as cold water. Julian sprang back as if struck by a lightning bolt. He scrambled from the bed, missing the steps entirely, and stood in the midst of the nearly empty room with his shirttail hanging about his hips.

"Caroline. You're awake."

Esmie yanked her bodice back into place, thankful for the height of the bed that hid her from the child's view. Mortification brought a hot blush to her cheeks.

"I was afraid," Caroline whined.

Esmie peeked over the edge of the bed to see the little girl standing uncertainly in the doorway. The child bit her lip, unsure of her welcome, but her body leaning of its own accord toward her father. With a last twist and a tuck, Esmie secured her clothing again. She almost rolled to the edge of the mattress to announce her presence when Julian stepped forward and spoke.

"Come here, poppet." He sank down on one knee and opened his arms. Caroline's eyes widened, and then with a little hiccup of delight she launched herself into her father's arms.

"There was an ogre, my lord." Her sleepy use of the familiar *Papa* giving way to her usual deference to her father. Esmie wondered if Julian had even noticed. But at least he cradled the child in his arms and muttered soft, comforting words.

"It was a dream. You're awake now." He stood and lifted Caroline into his arms. "Let us go see if your things are dry. Miss Esmie has hung them in the kitchen."

"Miss Esmie? Where is she?"

He did not glance back at the bed where Esmie lay.

"She is somewhere about, poppet. Let us see to your clothing and boots, and then we shall find her."

"It is raining," Caroline observed solemnly.

"Yes, it is."

"I'm hungry."

"I know, poppet. So am I. As soon as this cloudburst passes, we shall find a very good inn and eat as much ham and bread as we can hold."

The little girl looked around. "Where are we?"

Esmie watched as Julian reached up to brush a curl from his daughter's eyes. "We are in Miss Fortune's house."

"Miss Esmie has a house?"

"Yes. Come now, and I will tell you all about it."

Caroline looked around the room. "It's not a very good house, is it?"

He tapped her nose with his finger. "You know, I liked it just now, when you called me *Papa*. I think I should like that better than *my lord*. What do you think?"

Caroline murmured her assent, and the pair left the room, taking Esmie's heart with them. She had just witnessed a sea change. Julian had taken Caroline into his arms, called her *poppet* and asked to be called *Papa* in return. It was what she had wanted. Why, then, did it make her feel so hollow?

She would never be on the inside of anything. The realization hit her with suffocating force, almost pinning her against the mattress. She would always stand outside—outside the beau monde, outside the Classics Society and the university, outside the family of the man she loved so desperately. Loneliness robbed her of breath. In a few short weeks, all the things she had desired, all the stuff of dreams she'd never known she had, would be out of her reach forever.

Esmie laid her cheek against the cool damp of the mattress and wished she could disappear into its depths. Tears or despair would gain her nothing. The Earl of Ashforth was not to be hers. He knew it, the cat knew it, even Caroline knew it. Why could she not accept it?

With a heavy heart, she climbed down from the bed and smoothed her rumpled clothing. She would not succumb to the earl again, much as her heart might urge her. She had made a fool of herself more than enough for one lifetime.

Esmie found the pair of them a few moments later. They were in the kitchen, the earl buttoning up Caroline's dress. He bent to lace her boots for her, and the little girl reached out a tentative hand to touch his hair. Neither of them had noticed Esmie's presence yet. The intimacy of the gesture made her breath catch in her throat.

The earl looked up at his daughter and smiled. Caroline grinned, clearly delighted at this newfound aspect of her father. He stood and ruffled her damp curls.

"Miss Esmie!" Caroline noticed her standing in the doorway and rushed forward. "There you are."

"Here I am." She smoothed the girl's ringlets with her own fingers. "And I believe the rain has stopped." All three glanced out the window, where the skies had cleared. "Time to return to the others."

Esmie glanced around for her reticule and found where it had fallen to the floor beside the door. "No doubt your brothers and sisters are impatient to return home. I shudder to think what poor innkeeper they may have been tormenting this last hour."

The earl averted his eyes and reached out a hand for Caroline to grasp. "Miss Fortune is right, poppet. Time to go."

"But I haven't seen Miss Esmie's house!"

"Another time, dear," Esmie soothed. "We shall come back one day."

But they would not. The house would be sold as soon as possible, preferably by the time she left the earl's employ in a few short weeks. Then she could settle her accounts with him and move forward into her future, where the widow with the Bath chair awaited.

She locked the door behind them and, for the last time, placed the key into her reticule. Her fingers shook as she did so, but she kept her face impassive. In a short time, they had passed through the rain-kissed fields and crossed the river. Caroline chattered happily enough, unaware of the tension between her two silent companions.

They spied the earl's carriage outside an inn not far from the examination schools. Inside, they found the rest of their party waiting in a private dining parlor.

"Ham!" Caroline cried and fell upon the remains of her siblings' repast. One glance at Miss Lambton's thundercloud expression and Esmie's hunger receded abruptly.

"My lord." James sketched his father a bow. The boy hesitated, as if to say something. He glanced at Miss Lambton and then fell silent.

"Well done, James. You have seen to Miss Lambton's comfort and managed to keep track of your brother and sisters." The earl placed his hand on the boy's shoulder, and James's head snapped up in surprise. A glow of pleasure spread across his face.

"Thank you, my lord."

The earl turned to his betrothed. "Miss Lambton? You are well?"

Miss Lambton looked anything but well. The rigid set to her shoulders and the hard expression in her eyes radiated displeasure.

"I would have preferred to return to the Abbey, but your son would not allow it." She was clearly prepared for the earl to back her on the matter. "You will instruct him, of course, that in future, my directions carry the same weight as your own."

She could not have said anything more designed to infuriate the earl. His shoulders tightened, and Esmie watched as he transformed himself from doting papa to overbearing aristocrat.

"My son did right, madam. Miss Fortune and I would have been stranded otherwise, and you were perfectly comfortable."

Maria Lambton went a rather unbecoming shade of puce. "We shall discuss this when the children are not present, my lord."

"Shall we?" He drawled the question in a silky tone that made Esmie's skin prickle. One did not give imperious orders to a man who had learned to issue them from his cradle.

Miss Lambton glanced at Esmie. "She is the cause of this, I am sure. Trouble follows wherever she goes."

The children murmured their protest and the earl

quirked one eyebrow. "I believe the rain, madam, is the root of your present discomfort. If you wish to complain, we may stop by a church and you can make your unhappiness known to the divine."

Miss Lambton's mouth formed an "O" of astonishment. Her eyes narrowed, and Esmie shivered in her shoes.

The earl turned toward her. "Miss Fortune? Shall we join Caroline? Neither of us has eaten luncheon."

Esmie's stomach was too knotted by the hostility radiating from Miss Lambton to make eating a good idea. Nonetheless, she nodded her agreement.

He moved to the table and pulled a chair out for her. With Miss Lambton's glare digging into her back like a dagger, Esmie seated herself. Caroline looked at her and grinned, crumbs tumbling from her lips, and her eyes alight with the pleasure of a satisfying meal for her empty stomach.

Esmie wanted only to be back in the carriage and on her way to the Abbey. She cast the earl surreptitious glances. He ate his bread and cheese with grim determination, as Miss Lambton pouted in the corner. James had found some spillikins, and led the other children in a quiet game before the hearth. The tension in the air was thick as treacle. Esmie forced a few bites down her closed throat and then sat back.

The earl finally lifted his eyes to hers, as he'd not done since he'd carried Caroline from the dusty bedchamber. Esmie saw sorrow there, and regret. What she did not see was any light of hope for the feelings that still coursed so vibrantly between them.

The outing to Oxford proved an end as well as a beginning. Several days passed in which the earl studiously continued to avoid her. Esmie kept to the schoolroom as much as possible. The children practiced diligently for the presentation of their tableau. Sophie fashioned Greek and Roman costumes according to their parts. James drilled them until their lines were perfectly memorized. Esmie applauded, consoled, and cajoled by turns, coaxing the best performance from each of them.

The earl spent small amounts of time with each child,

Esmie noted, and the change was one of the few pleasures that lightened her days. He and James continued to ride together over the grounds of the Abbey. With Sophie, he had taken a carriage into the village and bought her a very grown-up-looking bonnet. The twins had been treated to a fishing expedition, and one evening Esmie had retired to the schoolroom after dining with the housekeeper to find the earl ensconced in the window seat with Caroline as he read her a favorite storybook.

They exchanged only the briefest of greetings before she fled to her bedchamber. She did not meet his eyes.

The most alarming development, though, was the increasing attentions of Mr. Lambton. He seemed to be everywhere—house and garden, stables and lane. Whenever Esmie had a moment's peace, she would steal away, but somehow Mr. Lambton always managed to sniff her out.

Late one evening, though, she hit upon the perfect plan to find a few moments of respite. The earl had been invited to a neighboring house for dinner, and so, confident in his absence, Esmie slipped down the hallway and into his library.

She carried a small lantern, much as she had the first time she'd invaded his sanctuary. Tonight, she vowed not to bother so much as a loose sheet of paper. She'd brought her own beloved copy of Plutarch's *Lives* to peruse, but her true purpose was to find solace in the presence of the great works that lined the walls. Solace, and perhaps a firmer resolve, for every day she became more attached to the children. Her feelings for the earl had not abated, either. And she still carried the guilt of not telling him about James's parentage, even if she held the secret for Julian's ultimate good.

She seated herself in the earl's wing chair and set the lantern on the small table beside it. The brandy decanter stood at hand, but Esmie left it undisturbed. She had lost her head enough in the earl's house without further undermining her resolve.

Immersed in the exploits of Heracles, she hardly noticed when her lantern burned low. A rustle sounded outside the door and, panicked that it might be the earl, she doused the light. The sudden loss of illumination paralyzed her, for she could see nothing, and the cloudy night kept any starshine from coming through the windows. The library door opened, and Esmie held her breath. Her pulse thrummed in her ears, and she softly closed the book in her lap. The door opened further, and someone stepped into the room carrying a candle.

"Miss Fortune?"

Mr. Lambton! Drat.

"Yes."

Mr. Lambton laughed and stepped farther into the room. He lifted his candle so the light touched her face. "Have no fear. I am not the earl." He set the candle on the table. "Come out of the shadows, my dear. I shall not deal with you as Ashforth would if he found you here."

Sheepishly, Esmie rose from the chair and stepped forward. "You have caught me out, sir. I pray you, please don't mention this to the earl. He holds me in low enough regard already."

"Does he?" Mr. Lambton half smiled, but no mirth lit his eyes. "I wager he would not be unduly distressed to find you here, madam."

Esmie pretended not to take his meaning. "He has forbidden me this room."

"Has he?" Mr. Lambton's expression turned a bit darker. "I wonder you would cross him, then."

"I needed a bit of peace. And the earl dines out this evening."

"Yes. With my daughter."

"You chose not to accompany them?" A sudden shiver of foreboding raced down Esmie's spine. Mr. Lambton enjoyed parties and dinners of any kind. He must have stayed at the Abbey for a reason, and she feared his choice might have had something to do with her.

"I see you have discerned my motives, Miss Fortune. I hoped to spend a few moments in company with you, and so pleaded a headache."

"A headache?" Esmie had to laugh. "I thought only the female of the species was allowed to employ such a stratagem."

"To spend time with you, my dear, I would employ whatever scheme was necessary."

The frankness of his declaration startled Esmie. "Sir?"

He moved closer, until his nearness discomfited her. Esmie would have liked to step back, but to do so would bring them into the shadows if he followed her. Somehow the light seemed a better choice.

"Miss Fortune, I cannot believe you have not understood my intentions."

His hand reached out and came to rest on her shoulder. His warm touch felt wrong. Awkward. And a bit menacing.

"I am the governess, sir. I would never presume anyone had intentions toward me."

"Is that so?" He studied her with uncomfortable thoroughness. "Let us be frank, my dear. It will save a great deal of time and trouble. The earl is attracted to you—"

"He is not!" But her protest lacked credibility. Mr. Lambton moved in front of her, and his other hand came to rest on her upper arm, so she stood firmly in his grasp.

"Do not be a fool, my dear, and moon about after a man who will never acknowledge you. He will never offer you a future. But I . . ." His fingertips trailed down her arm and when he found her hand, he laced her fingers through his. "I can offer you a great deal more. You have captivated me, Miss Fortune. I am not accustomed to being captivated. I had sworn never to marry again, but then I came here. And met you. And now . . ."

"Sir! I beg you to think before you speak any words that cannot be recalled." The attentions of this attractive, wealthy man flattered her vanity. But he had other motives for pursuing her, and none of them bore any relation to her dubious charms.

"I would not recall them, my dear. Not for the world."

He meant to kiss her again. Esmie stood as still as a marble statue. Fate was offering her an escape from servitude. For whatever his motivations, Mr. Lambton did not offer a slip on the shoulder. He dropped to one knee and looked up at her. Esmie gasped.

"Will you marry me, Esmerelda? I shall make you happy. I am determined to make you happy."

"What of your happiness?" She was still unsure whether he poured out his heart to her or used her in a clever game to ensure his daughter would wed Julian.

"To me, there is no difference between your joy and my own."

The words were right. The. setting was ideal. If she had never met Julian Armstrong, if she did not have doubts about Mr. Lambton's motives, it would be perfect.

Perfect. By Athena's shield, she was sick of that word.

"What do you say, then, my love? We can be married by special license, before my daughter makes her walk down the aisle. You shall be by my side at St. George's when Maria weds the earl, and I will be proud to tell the world you are mine."

Would he? Did he have no qualms about marrying a penniless governess whose mother was an embarrassing shrew?

She wanted to believe him. Her bones ached with yearning for someone who would love her in spite of her flaws and weaknesses. She could take the chance and say yes to his proposal. Julian would never offer her what Mr. Lambton offered now, at this moment. Why did she not grab this opportunity with both hands?

"I do not wish to demean you or flatter myself when I say you are not likely to receive a more attractive offer. What say you, madam?"

Flustered, Esmie looked about the room as if to seek direction from the wise Greeks and Romans who lined the shelves. No answer came from the silent piles of books and papers. A new light, however, appeared in the doorway, and Esmie drew in a sharp breath. The earl stood in the opening, candle in hand.

"Yes, Miss Fortune? What say you? I am sure Mr. Lambton would like an answer to his most generous offer."

Chapter Seventeen

*J*ulian halted in the doorway of the library. Esmie stood in the circle of lamplight with Mr. Lambton's hands upon her shoulders. Julian's insides twisted into hard knots. He regretted his goading words, for all three of them knew they were born of jealousy. His childish desire to prevent another man from having the woman he had spurned sickened him, and yet the knowledge of his envy did nothing to temper his actions.

Esmie's face had gone as white as a death mask. Mr. Lambton's hands tightened on her shoulders, and he drew her to his side.

"This is a private moment, Ashforth. Would you be so kind?" He inclined his head toward the hallway.

But the desperation churning in Julian's stomach made him reckless. He could give her up. Somehow he would manage to remove Esmie Fortune from his mind and heart by sheer dint of will, but not to lose her to Lambton. The man did not deserve her, would not respect her intellect or treasure her insights. For Lambton, she was merely an obstacle to an end he desired.

"As you are trespassing on the goodwill of my employee in my private library, sir, I am reluctant to leave just yet."

Esmie shot him a look that should have felled him on the spot. Panic shot through him. Surely she wouldn't entertain Lambton's offer? Surely she could see through his façade. Besides, even if Lambton wanted more than to remove her from the Abbey, a woman of her classical bent would never be happy trapped in a world of cut-throat commerce and grasping social ambitions. No, she should be in the country somewhere, surrounded by a great library and children and . . .

And all the things he could never give her. For if he did not wed Miss Lambton, he would have nothing but himself to bestow on Esmie Fortune if he asked her to be his wife. It was not enough. He was not enough.

Esmie did not step away from Lambton. "You are kindness itself, my lord, to worry about my well-being, but you need not concern yourself. This is a private matter, and I am well able to manage my affairs."

Her choice of words evoked precious images. Esmie, her eyes alight with joy when he showed her the treasures of his library, and then dark with desire when he kissed her. Esmie, hair loose and standing in the doorway of his bedchamber. Esmie, her body beneath his on the great moldy bed at her tumbledown house.

"You welcome his offer, then?" Julian had to know.

Esmie turned to Mr. Lambton and placed her hand on his arm. "You are kind, sir, but perhaps your daughter's wedding plans have turned your thoughts in an untoward direction."

"No, Miss Fortune. I am not so weak-willed as that." He oozed sincerity as he took her hand from his sleeve and interlaced her fingers with his own. Anger, possessiveness, envy—all welled in Julian's breast and robbed him of breath. Lambton reached out and brushed Esmie's cheek with his fingertips, and Julian almost came out of his boots. His fingers itched to throttle the other man.

"You are sure, then, your offer is sincere?" Esmie leaned toward Lambton with an earnestness that made Julian's teeth hurt. She did not look like a woman about to spurn the most advantageous proposal of marriage she was likely to ever receive.

"I have never meant anything more. I swear it," Lambton said.

Esmie smiled up at the man—a smile Julian felt as much ownership of as he did his own. "Then I would accept, sir, and agree a special license be procured immediately."

Stunned, Julian watched as Mr. Lambton pulled Esmie

into his arms and planted a kiss on her lips. Julian stepped toward them, ready to tear his future father-in-law limb from limb until he saw Esmie return the kiss. His stomach roiled in protest.

"It appears you have settled matters to your satisfaction," Julian bit out between clenched teeth. Esmie did not look at him, but buried her face in Lambton's shoulder. The other man looked at Julian over her head. The message was clear. There was never to be any question of Esmie Fortune becoming the Countess of Ashforth. Lambton would see to it. He was not an evil man, merely a determined one. Julian did not know if Lambton would go through with the marriage, but, either way, he had carried the day. Julian's hands were now tied by two betrothals, neither of which could be broken. Miss Lambton would never release him, and as long as she held him, Esmie would remain engaged to Lambton.

The noose tightened around his neck, and he could almost feel his feet swing. He had let any chance for happiness escape. He had sacrificed it to the gods of perfection. Hope was lost, and like Tantalus in the underworld, he would spend the remainder of his life longing for what he could never have.

"I will leave you to your privacy, then." The moisture in his eyes blurred his vision, and he stumbled from the room, closing the door behind him. His fascination with Esmie Fortune had begun in his sanctuary, and there it must end. Fitting. But the neat tying of loose ends offered little comfort to his bruised and battered heart. With heavy steps, he turned down the hallway, heavy with the knowledge that he had lost the one person who mattered most to him.

Three days after accepting Mr. Lambton's proposal, Esmie was drowning in misery. She'd hoped to console herself with thoughts of the creature comforts life as Mrs. Lambton would bring, but even Mr. Lambton's promise of her own library at his palatial London residence had brought no joy. The finest library she enjoyed in isolation would never replace the dream of her modest school, and Mr. Lambton would never be Julian.

Today, though, she had resolved to set aside her

wounded heart and concentrate on the children's well-being. They were to present their tableau after luncheon. She had so far managed to persuade Mr. Lambton he need not hurry to London for the special license, but he planned to leave on the morrow and return within the week. Miss Lambton would go with him. The immediate necessity of wedding clothes dictated extensive consultations with her modiste. With a pang of longing, Esmie thought of all the books the money spent on Miss Lambton's trousseau might buy.

"Miss Esmie, is it time yet?" Caroline had asked the same question every five minutes for the past hour.

Phillip's head snapped round. "She told you, when the long hand reaches the twelve and the small hand is on the two, Caro. Can't you let her alone?" He had become very protective of Esmie over the last several days.

"Time?" Esmie asked, as if she'd not heard the question before. She reached out to smooth Caroline's cheek with her hand. "Almost, dear. Let's get you into your costume."

Sophie fussed over the drape of Phoebe's Grecian gown as James fashioned the last crown of laurel leaves. The children had not slept well the night before. They so wanted to meet with their father's approval. If he did not applaud at the end of the tableau as if it were the finest performance ever witnessed, Esmie would strangle him. Not that she needed much provocation to do so, not after his high-handed behavior the night he'd found her with Mr. Lambton.

"They're coming," Sophie hissed, as Esmie heard the confirming footfalls in the hallway.

"Places, everyone. Places." She clapped her hands, and the children ran behind the makeshift curtain to take up their positions. Esmie sent up a brief prayer—not for herself, but for the children. *Please let him be proud.*

The schoolroom door opened, and Esmie stepped forward to greet their guests. Mr. Lambton came in first. He smiled with pleasure and lifted her hand to his lips. Sophie, who peeked out from behind the curtain, giggled in the usual way of ten-year-old girls. Miss Lambton swept past Esmie without a proper greeting, and the earl hovered in the doorway, looking as if he were about to hurl himself into Hades.

"My lord." Esmie dropped the faintest of curtsies. She refused to show the wounds he had inflicted. "The children are very excited."

"Indeed." His noncommittal reply did nothing to quiet the flutters in her stomach. Fortunately, Mr. Lambton drew her attention away by asking where they were to be seated. Miss Lambton had not waited for any such direction and settled herself into the most comfortable chair. Heart in her throat, Esmie slipped behind the curtain to ready the children. She found them already in place and Caroline close to tears.

"I shan't remember my lines. I know I shan't."

"You will, darling. You'll be splendid." Esmie hugged her, and then set her back upon the small ottoman that was her designated perch. James handed Esmie a script so she could prompt anyone who stumbled.

"Very well, then." She took in the sight of the children who had become so dear to her. Caroline on her stool, the living embodiment of Persephone, with her golden curls and a basket of pomegranates in her lap. Phillip and Phoebe stood behind her, side by side, representing those famous immortal twins, Apollo and Artemis. Sophie, in keeping with her romantic nature, had chosen Aphrodite. And then James, tall and strong for his twelve years. With his dark good looks, he might have been Hades, but somehow the role of Zeus the others had thrust upon him suited him to the ground. Esmie's heart tightened within her chest. She wondered that the earl could look at him and doubt the child's paternity.

With a nod and a wink of encouragement, she pulled the rope that opened the curtain. Mr. Lambton had the good grace to lead an initial round of applause and Esmie, who could see him from her vantage point in the wings, experienced a small stirring of hope. Surely one could be happy if one were willing to put effort into the enterprise. Miss Lambton's hands hardly touched as she clapped and the earl banged his palms together in a determined fashion.

James began, enunciating each word with precision.

"The gods have gathered, O mortals, to tell you the story of their birth, to recount their famous deeds, and to give you a glimpse of immortality. . . ."

Esmie barely heard the words, and yet she registered each one. Tears sprung to her eyes, and she brushed them away before the children could see. Mr. Lambton leaned forward in his chair, an eager audience, and Miss Lambton looked about the room as if taking inventory for future refurbishment. The earl's face might as well have been carved of stone. Esmie could only hope the children would not look at him too often, lest they lose their courage and stumble.

Caroline proceeded through her first speech without a mistake and visibly relaxed onto the ottoman when she finished. She relaxed so thoroughly, in fact, that the basket of pomegranates tumbled to the floor with a thud. James broke off in the midst of his recitation of Zeus's challenge to the Titans. All eyes went to Caroline, who turned bright red. Phillip reached out a hand to touch her shoulder in a brotherly gesture of encouragement, but the damage was done. Caroline wailed and the tableau broke apart.

Esmie took a step toward the girl and caught her toe on the hem of her gown. She tumbled, hard, onto the ottoman. Phillip tried to catch her, and the three of them ended up in a crumpled heap. Sophie made a dive for the curtain pull to screen the disaster from the audience, but she jerked too hard and the entire thing came down on top of the little troupe. Esmie, entwined in the old linens, could not right the catastrophe.

Caroline wailed in even greater earnest. James barked orders no one heeded. Phoebe had somehow twisted herself so tightly in her costume she couldn't free herself. Sophie screamed in frustration and the others shouted her down.

Suddenly, the sheet was snatched away and Esmie could see once more, though she would rather have remained blind to the disaster. What had moments before been a presentable tableau was now an impossible tangle of linens and children. Her hair tumbled as stray hairpins slipped down the neck of her gown.

"Silence!" The earl's roar quieted the room as easily

as Poseidon stilling a storm at sea. Everyone obeyed, except Miss Lambton.

"For this I was kept from my packing!" She half rose from her chair, but her father laid a hand on her arm.

Esmie braced herself for the scold that would follow. Once again, she had failed. The children looked up at their father with renewed dread, and he frowned down upon them as if they were a pack of urchins he had encountered in the East End of London.

"First we shall free Miss Fortune," the earl commanded. "Then we'll see about the rest of you." And then his warm hands were on her upper arms. With brisk efficiency, he stripped away the makeshift curtains. He lifted her to her feet and brought her close against him to steady her. Esmie's breath caught in her chest and her knees gave way.

"Steady." The earl drew her even closer, and Esmie knew if he continued to help her in such a fashion he would soon be lifting her into his arms to bear her weight entirely. Miss Lambton made a snort of protest.

Esmie stiffened her knees and her resolve as she pushed away from the earl. "I am sorry, my lord. This was never meant to happen."

Was that a twinkle in his eye? It vanished too quickly for her to be certain. His stern demeanor slipped into place.

"I should hope not, Miss Fortune." He looked at the remaining tangle of his offspring. "Sadly, 'tis hard to distinguish between the costumes and the curtains. Perhaps you might give me some guidance?"

Esmie looked at the mess she'd made, and swallowed hard. The children needed her strength at this moment, not her pity. They had so hoped to show to good advantage.

"I believe we might free Sophie if we begin here." She stepped toward the sobbing girl and grasped one end of the linen. Mr. Lambton freed James, and the two of them stepped around the disaster to disentangle the twins. It did not take so long as Esmie might have imagined, and the children, once free, regained their composure. Caroline scrambled through the linens in search of the lost pomegranates.

The earl faced them all and opened his mouth as if to say something, but then must have thought the better of it. Mr. Lambton leapt into the breach.

"Well, children, it appears you have single-handedly brought down the gods from Mount Olympus. An impressive showing, I must say."

Caroline giggled first. Sophie and Phoebe joined in next, and the sound of girlish laughter triggered an equal response in the boys. Esmie, able to see the ridiculousness of the moment now that she was freed from her linen prison, did not hold back the laughter that rose in her own throat. Mr. Lambton added his hearty baritone and then, miracle of miracles, the earl began to laugh as well. The sound had a rusty quality to it. Esmie could not help but look at him, and the sight of the laugh lines around his eyes and mouth touched her heart as only a particularly dear imperfection in one's beloved can. This was the real man, the man who he was in his depths, where the molding influence of the earls of Ashforth had not fully reached. This was the man who might prove a father to children who were not of his body but who had staked their claim upon his heart.

Her eyes met his, and she saw Julian there, the Julian she had seen in the dark hours of the night and the Julian she had seen behave so tenderly toward Caroline at Cortland Manor. Esmie shivered. The feelings that leapt between them must be visible to everyone in the room. Esmie felt them in every part of her being, and from the intensity of his gaze, she knew he felt the same.

Miss Lambton erupted to her feet in a flurry of livid muslin. "There is no excuse for such foolery." She turned on Esmie like a lioness on its prey. "For *this* the earl pays you wages?" She snapped her fingers in front of Esmie's nose. "When I am mistress here, you will be dismissed immediately." She turned to Julian, and Esmie feared the worst. Never mind the wager or the money, the *Corinna* or her feelings for the perfect Earl of Ashforth. The children should not suffer because the adults in their world were self-centered and ridiculous.

Miss Lambton looked at Julian with uncharacteristic fierceness. "This must end, my lord."

The looks on the children's faces showed that they,

too, feared the worst. What's more, their expressions showed they believed that this very adult conversation concerned them and their behavior, not the inappropriate attraction experienced by an aristocrat and his paid servant.

"You are correct, madam," Esmie acknowledged with a small bow of her head. She stepped forward to intercede. The children would have enough to be frightened of when Miss Lambton became their *mama*. "This must end. I am clearly not up to the task of being the governess in this household." She turned to Julian. "I will tender my resignation, my lord. If perhaps the coachman could convey me to the village, I will be gone by nightfall."

"No, Miss Esmie!" Caroline shrieked. James frowned as forebodingly as the earl and the twins threw themselves forward into Esmie's arms. Even Sophie looked distressed.

"Yes, dear." She stroked Caroline's hair. "Miss Lambton is right. It will be best if I leave."

"But *she's* leaving," protested Phoebe. "Going to London. You can stay."

Miss Lambton went a deeper shade of red as her indignation increased.

"No, dear." The words choked Esmie, but she said them anyway. The weight of her failure settled like a stone in her midsection. She looked up at Julian. Severe, forbidding crevices had replaced the laugh lines around his mouth and eyes.

"Miss Fortune is correct. She will need to go." He looked at Mr. Lambton. "Besides, Miss Fortune is to be a married woman of some consequence very soon. She has been kindness itself to stay with us for these last few days."

He said the words with no emotion whatsoever. She had failed in the most thorough manner. No *Corinna,* no prize, no Athena Hall—but even more painful, no father for the children she had come to love, and no future with the man who had thoroughly claimed her heart.

"Miss Fortune," Mr. Lambton intervened. "I would be delighted for you to make use of one of my properties in London until I can procure a special license. You will want to have bridal clothes as well, and though I have not as fine an eye as Maria, it would be my pleasure to escort you to the modiste. And let us have no more talk of the coachman conveying you into the village. You will leave on the morrow with Maria and me."

Esmie thought steam might escape from Miss Lambton's ears at her father's offer. Then she saw the exact moment when Miss Lambton realized the wisdom of conveying away the threat to her betrothal.

"That is a fine suggestion, sir." Esmie dropped a faint curtsy to Mr. Lambton. He looked at her kindly, but a niggling distrust wormed its way into her brain. Mr. Lambton was no fool, and not for the first time Esmie wondered if he meant to carry through with his proposal of marriage. Suppose they reached London and he turned her off? Truth to tell, she would be no worse off than if she left on her own aboard the mail coach when it passed through the village. "I shall be ready to depart in the morning."

"No!" A chorus of protest went up.

"Miss Esmie!"

"Ahh!" Caroline tossed the remaining pomegranates into the air. " 'Tis not fair!"

Esmie could not have agreed more. Tears threatened, and so she bent and scooped up the battered linens from the floor. "Come, dears. We'd best tidy this mess."

The children stood stiffly for a long moment, and Esmie feared a general revolt. But then, slowly, James joined her. One by one, the children followed suit.

Miss Lambton turned to the earl and all but forced him to offer her his arm. "Good day, Miss Fortune," the young woman hissed. Mr. Lambton cast her a sympathetic glance and followed the couple from the room. The earl said nothing, and Esmie fought the temptation to watch his broad shoulders as they left the room. She did sneak one quick glance. Any hope he might return her last look died as the door closed behind them.

Esmie bit her lip to keep back the sobs. A small, warm hand slipped into hers, and she looked down to see Sophie gazing up at her with sympathy.

" 'Twas bound to happen, Miss Esmie. 'Tis not your fault. No one is perfect."

The words were meant to comfort, but they sliced through Esmie like a knife.

"Very well. Let us dispense with the mess, shall we?"

Phoebe burst into tears. Phillip's lower lip trembled, and suddenly the children piled into her arms. Sophie, Caroline, the twins, even stalwart James. The combination of their weight sent Esmie toppling to the floor, but she didn't care. She hugged them close, feeling the awkwardness of their growing limbs as she inhaled the mixed scents of grass, ink, and jam.

"Don't go, Miss Esmie," Phillip whispered, and then all was tears.

"I must, Phillip. I must."

Esmie wept, too. Because though she had never truly believed the earl might fall in love with her, she had at least hoped to make him fall in love with his children.

Chapter Eighteen

$\mathcal{T}$he next morning, the Lambtons' sleek, well-sprung carriage stood ready in the drive. Esmie's boots tapped a rhythmic good-bye as she descended the steps of Ashforth Abbey. So much had happened in such a short period of time. She was a different person from the woman who had arrived on the earl's doorstep a few short weeks ago. Love had changed her. Love for the earl, love for the children. Her redemption might be incomplete, her dream dead, but in her heart of hearts she could not be sorry. She would not have missed knowing Julian or his children.

The children had, in fact, been forbidden by their father from seeing her off. There had been such a storm of tears after dinner the night before that further goodbyes had been prohibited.

Footmen were loading luggage into a second, more careworn equipage. Though Miss Lambton had not yet appeared, her numerous trunks had. Esmie watched as the servants hoisted her own lone, battered trunk aboard. Its worn leather trim and dented surface told of hard use, and looked shabbier than ever next to Maria Lambton's gilt trimmed cases.

Esmie was about to climb into the carriage unassisted when she heard footfalls on the steps behind her. She looked back. Julian descended at a leisurely pace. The moment he realized she was alone, he faltered. Then, with a lift of his chin, he came toward her and planted himself in front of her.

"I regret much of what has happened, madam." His

clenched teeth almost prevented him from speaking the words. "My actions have affected you adversely, and yet marriage to Mr. Lambton would seem to atone for any distress I have caused you."

He was angry. Angry she was to marry Lambton. Esmie tightened her grip on her reticule. What right had he to be livid with her? He had initiated a betrothal of his own, long before she had acquiesced to hers.

"In future," he continued, "we shall see one another on numerous occasions. It would be best if we agreed not to speak of the past few weeks. Let us allow bygones to be bygones."

So he would not allow her to retain even one shred of dignity. The feelings that had passed between them were to be dismissed, denied, refuted as if they had never occurred. Just when she believed she had placed herself out of his power to hurt her, he struck another blow.

"You may be sure, my lord, that I think on recent events with as little pleasure as you do. I should be happy to erase the last few weeks from mind. Except for the children, of course. I should not like to forget them. But, you . . ." She let the words trail off, and her silence spoke all she needed to say.

"Yes, madam. You wish you had never met me. It is ungallant, but I would be less than honest if I did not say I wished the same. But what's done cannot be undone."

"Only denied." She wanted to smack him until her hand was raw and sore from connecting with his cheek. She wanted to shake him until she forced some sense into him. Of all the ignorant, stubborn-headed fools . . .

The letter she had written him the night before almost burned a hole in her reticule. For a moment, she thought of not withdrawing it, not handing it to him with instructions that he read it when he was alone. It would serve him right never to know the truth about James. He deserved the unhappiness he had created for himself with his obsessive pursuit of perfection. But James did not deserve to be kept at arm's length by his father for the rest of his life. Esmie only regretted she could not do for the other four what she might do for the eldest— give their father a reason to love them.

"You will do me the kindness, my lord," she said, as she withdrew the paper from her reticule, "of reading these few lines I have penned. There is also another letter enclosed that you may find of interest."

The earl arched a skeptical brow. "A love note, is it?"

"You flatter yourself, my lord," she snapped.

"Very well, then." He slipped the letter into his coat pocket just as the Lambtons emerged through the wide double doors at the top of the steps.

At the sight of Esmie tête-à-tête with the earl, Mr. Lambton hurried to her side. "I am sorry, my dear, for the delay."

"It is of no account, sir. I was merely bidding the earl good-bye. It will be some time before we all meet again."

"Not so very long," Miss Lambton interposed with a feline smile. "You and Papa will not miss the wedding, I am sure. In fact," she eyed Esmie's worn traveling costume, "I must introduce you to my modiste so you will have something suitable for the occasion. She can do wonders with even the worst of figures."

Mr. Lambton made a move to protest his daughter's rudeness, but Esmie waved it away. "I will contrive not to embarrass you, madam. I am capable of that much, I am sure."

Miss Lambton turned away from Esmie with a flounce, and engaged the earl's attention. Mr. Lambton took advantage of the opportunity to hand Esmie into the carriage. Before she knew it, the other two were seated, and the coachman had whipped the horses into motion. She should have no opportunity to say good-bye. The Lambtons were determined on that score. She sat facing the front, and could not even turn back for one last look at Julian.

Her hands trembled, but the rattle of the carriage disguised the tremors. Mr. Lambton patted her arm as they rolled past the stone gates of Ashforth Abbey and turned into the lane.

"There's no need not to settle this immediately," Miss Lambton said to her father, and Esmie frowned. *Settle what?*

Mr. Lambton reached for her fingers and took her

hand in his. "My dear, now that the Abbey is behind us, let us come to terms. Shall we not?"

"To terms, sir?"

Even she was surprised at the alacrity with which he flung off his pretense of being enamored.

"Yes, my dear. Terms. You are intelligent enough to know I would rather provide for you than marry you." He smiled at her with the same pleasantness he'd exhibited the day he first kissed her.

"Provide for me?"

"Yes, Miss Fortune. A generous settlement. Shall we say ten thousand pounds?"

Esmie gasped, and Maria Lambton did, too.

"Ten thousand pounds?" Esmie echoed. Was she so odious that a man would pay such a sum to escape her bed? Her stomach rolled in the same swaying motion as the carriage.

"Of course I am serious, my dear. 'Tis worth such a sum to avoid a marriage. Come, Miss Fortune, do not frown at me so. Good business is good business."

"Indeed." It was enough to repay the earl for the loss of the *Corinna* and make a significant start on her school as well. Esmie could hardly breathe. She had thought all was lost, and though Mr. Lambton could not retrieve her heart from Ashforth Abbey, he could certainly salvage her dream of Athena Hall.

"You might be independent anywhere in the world on such a sum," Mr. Lambton went on. "Say you agree, and we will have the papers drawn up when we arrive in London. My solicitor will be happy to see you settled somewhere, should you need his assistance in procuring a cottage."

"Papa," Miss Lambton scolded. "You need not be so generous. She may be had for less than half the sum."

"Maria!" He frowned at his only child, and then sent an apologetic glance to Esmie. "What say you, Miss Fortune? It is not marriage, but perhaps in your eyes it may be better."

Was it? Esmie wondered for the first time why she had never taken into account the loneliness of her dream. Yes, she might have her own school, but with whom would she share her joy in her students? Who would advise her, console her, encourage her? And why must the Earl of Ashforth's face leap into her mind's eye when she asked herself such things?

"I cannot take your money, Mr. Lambton." The words fell from her lips without a conscious decision to speak them, but the moment she heard them, she knew she had done right. "Such a fortune would be meanly gained. I am no schemer to wring guineas from men who would escape my clutches. No, you may set me down in Oxford."

Miss Lambton glowed with triumph at her refusal of the money and her stupidity in turning it down. Mr. Lambton's face creased with troubled lines. "Set you down in Oxford? With no place to go, no one to turn to? I will not, Miss Fortune. I may have been born to the shop, but I am not insensible to what you face without fortune or connections in this world. At least let me return you to your family."

"They would not receive me, sir. And I have a position waiting for me. As a lady's companion. I had not yet written Lady Crabbe to inform her of my change in plans, and so she still expects me."

"You will not take the money?" Mr. Lambton looked more troubled by her refusal of his offer than by her vulnerability as a single woman alone in the world. "You would reject such a sum categorically?"

"Yes, sir. Categorically." She was a fool, she knew. Mr. Lambton had offered for her of his own free will; why should she allow him to escape his own machinations with no penalty?

Esmie sighed and twisted the strings of her reticule. She had known all along, in her heart of hearts, he only wooed her to come between her and Julian. He had been right to do it. She should thank him for his intervention, not use it to extort such an extravagant sum, even if it was freely offered.

"You are sure the position still waits for you?"

"For heaven's sake, Papa, she has said so."

Hot words flew to Esmie's lips, but she held her tongue. Maria Lambton would gain all she desired. She would spend the rest of her life married to a man who would see only blemishes and flaws in his wife. She would live in a cold, sterile, perfect world and never know joy. Esmie might be a fool. She might dream dreams that would never be. But for a brief time, in the earl's arms and with his children, she had known joy. And that was a greater possession than any Maria Lambton would ever own.

Julian stood at the bottom of the front steps until the Lambtons' carriage disappeared from sight. Hollow as a drum, he continued to stare down the drive. The emptiness threatened to consume him, so he spun on his heel and marched into the house. He mounted the stairs with fixed determination. The way to forget her? By the same means he used to forget his children, his late wife, and how much he hated the life that had been chosen for him. He'd found his escape in books and in brandy. Both awaited him in his library.

He did not hesitate this time when he passed the schoolroom door. The children had been livid when he'd banned them from Esmie's departure. He'd done it not to be cruel, but to save himself, for if he'd been forced to witness another torturous round of good-byes such as the one he'd endured after dinner the night before, he would have refused to let her go.

How long, by Jove, had it been since he'd hurt so much on behalf of his children? Perhaps not since the day he'd discovered his wife's perfidity. He'd isolated himself for so many years, and yet in a few short weeks, Esmie Fortune had cracked open the ice that surrounded his heart. Exposure, raw and painful, washed over him as he entered his library and shut the door firmly behind him.

The *Corinna* was gone. A month ago, he would have turned to its pages for comfort. Now, his only idea of comfort was the kind to be had in Esmie Fortune's embrace. No! He must stop such thoughts. He reached for the enormous volume of Thucydides and plunked it down upon the long table. He settled himself into a chair and tried to clear his mind of anything but the ancient Greeks.

He'd not scratched more than a few words upon his page when a soft knock came at the door.

"Go away, Mrs. Robbins. You are not wanted."

Despite his rebuff, the door opened. Julian sighed and put his head in his hand. Was he never to have any peace?

" 'Tis not Mrs. Robbins, sir." James's dark head appeared around the door. The boy stepped into the room, followed by Sophie and the twins. Caroline slipped in around them and stood by her elder brother. They presented a heart-wrenching tableau, far more pitiful even than the tangle of sheets, arms, and legs they'd been the day before.

"Yes?" He kept his voice gruff to hide his vulnerability. Esmie's letter lay heavy in his pocket.

"Please, sir," James began, and then faltered.

"Papa, we would like to ask . . ." Sophie made a good start, but then fell silent.

Phillip squared his shoulders and stepped forward. "We should like to know, sir, whether now that Miss Esmie is gone, whether we shall be . . ." His voice failed him as well.

"What Phillip means to say, my lord," Phoebe said, moving to stand shoulder to shoulder with her twin, "or, rather, what he means to ask is whether—"

"Whether we shall all be sent away to school!" Caroline's wail finished the garbled question.

"To school?" Julian frowned. He considered lying to them. But perhaps there had been enough deception practiced at Ashforth Abbey for one summer. "I suppose you shall. After Miss Lambton and I are wed."

"Even me?" Caroline bit a trembling lip.

"In time, poppet."

Their faces, so different except for the similarities in the twins, crumpled in identical grief.

James cleared his throat. "I see, my lord. Very well. We thank you for the honesty of your answer." The boy wavered between holding his ground and turning to flee. The waves of hurt and disappointment that washed over his children struck Julian like a physical blow. God, what was he doing? What was he doing to himself? And what was he doing to them?

"But Papa," Caroline whispered, moving forward until

she stood close enough to lay a hand upon his sleeve, "we don't want to leave you."

Her touch was as light as a feather, but never had Julian known a greater weight. A buzzing began in his ears, and suddenly he felt quite light-headed. Good thing he was seated, because at that moment he felt as if he might crumple. The children, sensing something amiss, moved forward en masse and surrounded him. God, he would suffocate. Their concern pressed against his lungs like a giant hand squeezing out what little air remained.

"Oh, Papa," Phoebe moaned, and then to his surprise, she fell into his lap and buried her face in his neck cloth. Sophie fell against his other shoulder and burst into sobs. Caroline scrambled for any contact she might have with him, and even the boys moved closer. He could feel James against his sleeve.

"Don't you love her?" Phoebe whispered. "Just a little?"

Pain ripped through Julian and he reached out, enveloping his children and wrapping his hands around their arms and shoulders, wherever he might reach them. It was like being wrapped in a blanket of love. By the gods, *they* were comforting *him,* as if they were the adults and he the child.

And in that moment, he was a child. Or at least, he remembered what he had felt at their age. The loneliness. The desperation to be perfect so he might please his father. The emptiness and the longing for any scrap of affection. His father had withheld it all, but he, Julian, did not have to do the same. The thought took his breath away.

In that moment, Julian Armstrong, Earl of Ashforth, comprehended what an utterly imperfect fool he had been.

"Yes," he gasped, his throat raw. The honesty of his response both thrilled and shocked him. "Of course I love her."

"But you sent her away," Sophie whispered.

"I am an engaged man. I could not offer for her."

The words fell like bricks, and all was silent for a moment except for Caroline's gentle weeping.

Phillip pressed against his shoulder. "Do you love *us*, my lord?" His voice was little more than a breath. "Do you think you might love us as well?"

He could defend his heart no more. The dam broke and the river poured through, drenching him. The flood should have damaged him in some way, but he was caught up in its power and lifted above the swirling depths. "Yes, Phillip. I do love you. By the gods, I do."

The children lifted their heads in unison and stared at him with their mouths agape at the fierceness of his response. Their common looks of astonishment forced a chuckle from his throat. And then, on the swift turn of a moment, bedlam broke out. Like a dying man in a desert, Julian drank in every drop of it. He cuddled and comforted and pounded the boys' backs. The children took turns upon his lap, and the girls pressed kisses to his cheeks. In a matter of a very few minutes, he was tousled, damp, and thoroughly beyond repair.

He had never felt so wonderful in his life. Or so crushed. Esmie Fortune had worked this wonder. He felt the loss of her presence as keenly as he embraced the joy of becoming a true father to his children. Brick by brick, the façade of perfection crumbled, and Julian could only revel in the devastating crash as his prison tumbled to the ground.

Chapter Nineteen

*B*edtime that night in the nursery took on a new character, one with which Julian was as unfamiliar as he was satisfied. If his candlelight appearance shocked the old nurse, she gave no sign. The door to the governess's room remained closed, a reproach to Julian and a silent reminder of what he had lost. The children piled onto James's bed, and Julian soon found himself in their midst, a child's book of Greek mythology pressed into his hands amid fervent demands that he read to them.

Soon enough, the children were tucked tight beneath their covers—in all likelihood far too snugly, but it had been difficult to restrain his solicitude. He blew out the last candle, left the nurse snoring in a chair by the schoolroom fire, and retreated to his library.

Even the prospect of his books, though, did not calm the restlessness that had been born within him earlier in the day. By accepting his children, he had opened the rest of his life to assessment and alteration. One unhappiness, confronted and conquered, gave the other discontents permission to rise and demand recognition.

What made him most restless, though, was the letter that lay tucked in his pocket. With a sigh, he poured a brandy and sank into the familiar comfort of his wing chair. A single lantern lit the room, reminding him of the night he had first found Esmie Fortune here, and of another night, when he had overheard Mr. Lambton's proposal to her. When Mr. Lambton declared himself, Esmie had stood on the very spot where Julian had first embraced her. His fingers tightened around the brandy snifter. Esmie and the Lambtons were no doubt sharing a late supper at an inn between Oxford and London. Mr. Lambton had been an astute businessman, so deftly snatching temptation from beneath Julian's nose. She would be married to Lambton erelong, and irretrievably beyond Julian's reach. He downed the brandy in one gulp.

It was time to read the letter. He withdrew it from his pocket and picked up an opener from the table. With a sense of foreboding, he slit the seal and drew forth the pages.

The top page was a brief letter in Esmie's hand.

Lord Ashforth,
   I have wronged you, in withholding from you information you had every right to receive. I found the enclosed letter in your late wife's trunks the night we searched the attics. Its contents should ease some of your pain, but I beg you not to let it prejudice you against your other children. When I came to the Abbey, I had no thought to the five persons who would be under my charge. I cared only for finding the Corinna. *Now, I would give a thousand* Corinna*s if you would but love your children as they love you.*
   What has passed between us has been nothing more than an ague, a summer fever that is best forgotten.
   I remain your servant,
   Esmerelda Fortune

Pain and pleasure warred within him and brought mist to his eyes. The first part of her letter puzzled him, though not as much as the closing sentences pained him. With trembling hands, Julian placed Esmie's letter in his lap and turned to the next sheet of paper. He recognized his late wife's hand. Phrases jumped out at him in a disconnected jumble.

   . . . I have told Julian the child is not his, merely to have the satisfaction of distressing him. . . .
   . . . If he complies with my wishes, I will tell him the truth. . . . James is his child.

All breathing stopped. He read the words again, and then a third time, before his lungs began to function again.

By the gods, James was his true heir.

He waited for the anger to come. He prepared for fury. He expected vindication and the warm glow of righteousness to descend. He expected to feel a new fondness for his son and heir.

Only he did not. The words wounded him, but to his surprise, they did not affect his feelings toward his son or his other children. The expected anger only made it as far as an odd sense of relief.

James was his son. Once upon a time, those words would have meant the world to him. He would have done anything to make them true. Now they were genuine, handed to him on a platter by Miss Esmerelda Fortune. His jaw clenched. She had kept this information from him. She had known and had not told him. Why?

He pulled her letter atop that of his late wife. *I beg you not to let it prejudice you against your other four children.*

Julian snorted. She had made out his character very well in the short time she had been at the Abbey. A few weeks ago, he would have let this news have its most disastrous effect, and singled out his eldest son for love and privilege. Now, though, he found the very idea repugnant. Thanks to Miss Fortune, he loved them all, and this news—this admittedly welcome news—would not change his feelings.

Julian dropped the pages into his lap. When had she wrought such a change in him? He had not been aware of her working in his heart, but she had. As he'd confessed to the children, he did love her. It was too late, though. Too late for love, for imperfection, for striking out on his own in defiance of the heritage he safeguarded. Esmerelda would be Lambton's wife, and even if she were not, he was an engaged man who could not jilt his bride and retain any sense of honor. He had made his bed, and now he must lie upon it with Maria Lambton.

His hands no longer trembled as he folded the letters and returned them to his pocket. *An ague. A summer fever.* One from which he should never recover. She had given him the gift of his children, but she had taken his heart in payment.

A fortnight later, Esmie slipped away from the home of her employer and made her way to the Sheldonian Theatre. The Classics Society would announce the winner of the prize today, and though she had little hope of being awarded the honor, she could not stay away.

Cortland Manor was to be auctioned. The solicitor she'd approached to handle the matter had informed her she should not expect much, given the state of the house. Even her consolation of a small cottage in an obscure village lay in doubt. After she repaid Julian for the *Corinna,* she would have almost nothing left.

A large crowd had gathered in the theater for the announcement of the award. Esmie recognized a number of faces from Julian's lecture. She had not prepared herself, however, to come face to face with Julian himself. She turned to search for a chair in a forgotten corner and found herself nose-to-neck cloth with her perfect earl.

James stood by his side, and though it was a breach of etiquette, she greeted the boy first. James bowed and took her hand in his like a young gentleman. "Miss Esmie." The sadness in his eyes brought tears to her own.

The earl frowned down at her. "Miss Fortune."

Esmie searched his face for some sign he'd read the letter she'd given him. "My lord." The awkward silence stretched like eternity. Why did he not move away?

The earl cleared his throat. "I am surprised Lambton has brought you here, madam."

Esmie drew herself up to her full height, though even under the best of circumstances the earl loomed above her. "Mr. Lambton did not bring me. I came on my own."

James plucked at her sleeve. "Will you sit with us, Miss Esmie? I should like it if you did."

James might like it, but the earl looked as if he would have preferred to eat ground glass. Irritation stirred within her. What right had he to be angry? If there was to be nothing between them, it was because he chose for it to be so. "That would be pleasant, James. You may tell me how the other children are getting along with their lessons."

James led her to a chair, and, to her surprise, the earl took the seat on the other side of her, so she sat tucked between father and son.

"We have no lessons, Miss Esmie. We're all to go away to school at Michaelmas, so the earl . . ." He broke off and looked at his father. "Papa says we may enjoy ourselves for the remainder of the summer."

"Away to school? All of you?" Esmie had thought before that her heart had been broken in as many bits as possible, but . . . Had her letter meant nothing to him? "Even Caroline?"

The earl pokered up, his spine ramrod straight. "Caroline will remain at home for another year. Then she will join Sophie and Phoebe at a seminary for young ladies in Bristol."

Esmie longed to flee. If she'd not been so tightly wedged between the earl and James, she might have leapt to her feet and made for the door. Instead she remained, trying not to let her shoulder brush the earl's. The slightest contact brought an agony of longing to her midsection. Desire and anger intermingled until she could hardly tell one from the other.

The president of the Classics Society called the assembly to order, interrupting any further discussion of the children's futures. Esmie's eyes burned with tears of fury. Had she accomplished nothing?

The opening speeches rambled on at great length. Finally, the speaker turned to the subject at hand. "The winner of this year's prize for outstanding scholarship is . . ."

The audience leaned forward in their seats, eager to be the first to hear the news.

". . . Viscount Stanleigh."

For a moment, the name meant nothing to Esmie beyond the fact it was not her own. And then James rose to his feet from his seat next to her. She looked at him, and their eyes met. Understanding dawned.

"James?" She looked at him questioningly.

Instead of looking happy, the boy appeared to be misery personified. "I'm sorry, Miss Esmie. I'm so sorry. I just wanted him to notice me."

Esmie suddenly remembered the parcel James had sent his godmother the day she'd mailed her own package to the Classics Society. It had not been a gift for an elderly godparent at all, but his own entry in the competition.

"It was wrong to take it, but don't be sorry you've done your best, James. Never be sorry for that." They clasped hands and exchanged a look of perfect understanding.

Julian looked at both of them in bewildered confusion. The president of the Classics Society beamed proudly. "We see Viscount Stanleigh follows in his father's footsteps. The work he submitted is a flawless translation of the legendary manuscript, the *Life of Corinna*."

The crowd gasped in awe and approval, and a round of applause went around the theater. Esmie swallowed hard. It had been beneath their noses all the while, pilfered in a childish attempt to win his father's approval.

The president tapped his gavel to regain their attention. "But beyond the excellence of the translation, Viscount Stanleigh receives this award for the quality of his refutation of the *Corinna*'s authenticity. He has made the case that the manuscript is of medieval construction, and so puts to rest one of the great scholarly mysteries of our time."

By this time, James had reached the podium. The president shook his hand and hung the medal around James's neck. The crowd continued to clap heartily, and Esmie, tears in her eyes, lifted her gloved hands to join in.

Julian sat still as death next to her for the longest moment, and then, as if recollecting where he was and how many eyes were upon him, he began to applaud heartily, as if having his son translate the manuscript had been at his own instigation. Esmie saw his chest swell with pride. Curiously, the earl's approbation deflated Esmie's momentary happiness. Here would be another reason for the earl to single James out above the other children.

"Excuse me." She rose to her feet and stumbled past

the earl. The heat of the assembled crowd pressed in on her until she thought she might suffocate. Not caring about the stir she caused, she reached the end of the row and bolted up the aisle. The doors of the theater sprung open at her touch, and she was out in the street, drinking in deep breaths of air. Too distressed to return to her employer's house, she headed toward the river without lifting her eyes from the cobblestones beneath her feet.

"Miss Esmie!" James's cry stopped her in her tracks, but she hesitated, for she did not want him to see and misunderstand the grief written on her face.

"Miss Esmie." James scrambled to a stop beside her. "I can explain. Please don't be angry."

"Oh, James." She spun and grasped the boy in her arms. "I'm not angry. Not with you."

James pushed back and looked up in her face. "But you're crying. I know you entered the competition, and I'm sorry I won. I'm sorry I took the *Corinna*."

"No, no." Esmie dashed away tears with the back of her hand. "I will not allow you to be sorry. You are an excellent scholar."

James looked at her, bewilderment in his dark eyes so identical to his father's. The earl had been a fool not to see the resemblance.

"Don't leave. Papa is taking me to dine at an inn. You could join us."

"Oh, James, it wouldn't be at all the thing." She hugged him again, and they clung tightly for a long moment. "But never doubt I am proud of you. So very proud."

James hugged her in return and then stepped back with his head high and his shoulders thrown back, doing his best to look like a young man instead of a boy. "I have something for you, Miss Esmie." He fumbled in his pocket and withdrew a cheque. "I want you to have this. For your school. My father told me about your house and your plans for the school."

"Your father told you?"

"He says you will marry Mr. Lambton since you don't have the money for your school. But now you can jilt Mr. Lambton. I don't want you to marry him either."

"Either?"

"We took a vote, the five of us, and it was unanimous. Mr. Lambton is not the proper husband for you. You don't look at him like a new bonnet."

More tears threatened. "Tell your brothers and sisters they needn't worry. I have jilted Mr. Lambton already."

Heavy footsteps sounded behind them, and Esmie looked up to see the Earl of Ashforth only a few feet away. "Jilted Lambton? Miss Fortune, what manner of madness are you engaged in now?"

"The self-sufficient kind, my lord." She turned to James, ignoring the earl. "I cannot take your prize money. 'Tis a generous offer, but one I must refuse."

Hurt showed in the boy's brown eyes. "But I will be the first patron of your school. A founding patron. You can name a classroom or a playing field for me." He grinned. "Assuming girls will have playing fields. Perhaps you should buy them some supplies for trimming bonnets instead."

Esmie laughed and reached out as if to box his ears. James dodged away, but not before he managed to press his cheque into her hand. The gesture twisted her heart until she thought it might collapse in upon itself.

"James—"

"I will add to that, Miss Fortune." Julian's stiff air of formality had returned. Esmie pushed a wayward curl behind her ear and looked at him. In his eyes, she saw the truth, that he had indeed read her letter. "Since the *Corinna* is inauthentic, and since I have no doubt my son will restore the book to me, it is of little value. You need not repay me, for I have lost nothing." He paused for a long moment and cleared his throat. He reached into his coat pocket and withdrew a slip of paper very like the one James had just given her. "Here is a bank draft for the amount we agreed upon for your services."

Esmie stepped back. Her hands went up in a gesture of denial. "I did not fulfill my part of the bargain, my lord. I left too soon."

"You may have made an early departure, but you accomplished another task that more than met the terms of our agreement. Here." He pressed the bank draft into her other hand. Confusion and longing jumbled her thoughts.

"I cannot, my lord. Nor can I accept your money, James. It is too much."

"We are not merely giving it to you, madam." The earl frowned so deeply lines etched his forehead and mouth. "We expect a return on our generosity. Between these two amounts, there is enough for the establishment of a school."

"But . . ."

It was everything she had wanted when she arrived at Ashforth Abbey, but now what she wanted was so different that the enormous amount of money pressed into her hands seemed of little consequence.

"We insist." The earl's gaze met hers, and she saw all the things she felt in her own heart reflected in their brown depths. Longing, impossibility, resignation. "Please." He lowered his voice. "You have done a great thing for me. Allow me to do this for you." He stepped back, cleared his throat and looked at her again, this time with all trace of emotion wiped from his expression. "Allow *us* to do this."

It had been a very long time since Esmie Fortune had been the recipient of a gift. She had not had much practice in that particular exercise.

"You are sure?" Her damp palms curled around the cheques. "Perhaps I am not trustworthy. Perhaps I shall abscond with the funds to live a life of debauchery in Paris."

Even as she said the words, a smile rose to her lips. James laughed. "Debauchery? Miss Esmie, what could you know of debauchery?"

The earl said nothing, but now his eyes reflected his remembrance of just how well acquainted she was with the term, thanks to him.

The earl put his hands behind his back in his schoolmaster pose. "I believe, Miss Fortune, you will do what is right with this money. That is all James or I could ask."

And it was all he would ever ask. Even as one dream came true, another died.

"Your wedding, my lord? It will be soon?"

"As soon as Miss Lambton fixes the date. Though you have broken off with Lambton, you will still receive an invitation."

"I shall not be there." How could he even suggest it?

"No. I suppose not."

James looked back and forth between the adults, but held his silence. Esmie was the first to find her voice.

"I must return to my employer. Lady Crabbe will need my assistance."

Julian's shoulders drooped the merest part of an inch. "You cannot join us at the inn for a celebration?"

"No, my lord. I must keep my word to Lady Crabbe. I told her I would return in time for supper." She could not endure another moment in his company.

"Very well, then, Miss Fortune. I believe, then, this would be good-bye."

James opened his mouth as if to protest, but his father shot him a look that silenced him.

"Yes, my lord. Our ways part here."

Julian shifted from one booted foot to the other. "I cannot escort you to your employer's house?"

"There is no need, my lord. I will make my own way. I have always known I would need to do so." There were no words for the good-bye her heart longed to say, not in front of James. But even if the boy had not been present, what language could possibly have expressed her grief? Her love, their love—to be offered as a sacrifice on the altar of perfection. A terrible tragedy. A terrible waste.

"Lambton is a fool." The earl's low, ferocious words nearly tore her heart from her chest. Esmie whirled away and forced her feet to move in the direction of Lady Crabbe's house. James sputtered a protest, but she kept moving as she placed one foot in front of the other until she reached the corner. As she turned down a side street, she broke into a run. The cobblestones jabbed at her feet, and she could hardly breathe for the sobs that choked her throat.

Chapter Twenty

*J*ulian stood in the middle of the grand salon and turned about as if entering the elegant room for the first time. Once, the Hepplewhite furniture, Carrara marble mantelpiece, and Adams ceiling would have filled him with remarkable pride of possession. Now the pretentiousness of the room depressed him. Was this all the sacrifice of his heart had preserved?

He'd not even finished dressing today before he'd come downstairs to breakfast. His valet's alarm at seeing him stride from his rooms in his shirtsleeves proved most comical. The servant had not been allowed the use of a razor on his lordship's cheeks, either. All in all, Julian thought, he was a rather frightening creature when he was not perfect.

Julian recognized Mrs. Robbins's knock and turned to see her standing in the doorway. She bobbed a curtsy and cleared her throat. "A visitor, my lord. Mr. Lambton."

"Lambton?" He'd been expecting a letter any day informing him of the date of his confinement to the matrimonial state. "What the devil is he doing here?"

Mrs. Robbins pulled a face. "I'm sure I do not know, my lord."

Before Julian could reply, Lambton himself entered the room. "Good God, Ashforth, is something amiss? You look the very devil."

The other man's assessment of his present state did nothing to soothe the turmoil that had brewed in Julian since he'd watched Esmie Fortune flee across the cobbled streets of Oxford.

"Perhaps I am distraught with love." He kept the sneer of self-derision from his voice, his words merely cold.

"Distraught with love? I doubt it." Lambton glanced around the room. "You are alone, my lord?"

"Yes." A perfect assessment of his present condition.

"Then we may speak of private matters."

So, the blow would be delivered in person. Julian braced himself. "I assume you have come to inform me of my wedding date. Miss Lambton must have made headway with her trousseau."

Antagonism had crept into his voice. Like a dam crumbling in the face of the pressure that had built up behind its walls, Julian feared he might come apart.

"I have a letter for you. From Maria." He reached into his pocket and pulled out the folded paper. "You may wish to read it in private."

Julian took it from him. "My wedding date will be public enough, once the announcement is placed in the *Times*." He opened the seal with his finger.

> *Ashforth,*
> *I have decided we should not suit. Papa will manage the details.*
> *Regards,*
> *Maria Lambton*

Julian's breath froze in his chest. It could not be true. Half hope, half despair, he refused to give in to the wave of relief that set his nerve endings on fire. Maria's note contained what he both desired and dreaded.

"She has jilted me." Julian folded the letter and looked up at Lambton. "You knew she meant to do so?"

"Yes." Mr. Lambton nodded toward the arrangement of settees at the end of the room. "Perhaps we should sit."

Julian didn't want to sit. He wanted to jump up and down as Caroline did when she received a new doll. Though the consequences for his future were disastrous, he wanted to swoon like a maiden or screech like a banshee. Maria Lambton had sprung him from parson's mousetrap. His knees weak but his dignity intact, Julian followed Lambton and sat down across from him.

Mr. Lambton cleared his throat. "I'm not sorry that Maria has broken off with you. In fact, she did so at my urging."

Julian frowned. "I thought you approved the match."

"I did. But I desire my daughter's happiness more than I do her acquiring a title."

Julian blinked. Lambton hardly sounded like a ruthless businessman now. "What brought on this change of heart?"

The other man smiled. "Miss Fortune."

"Your former fiancée?" The word stuck in Julian's throat.

"I offered her the sum of ten thousands pounds to jilt me, but she did it for nothing."

Julian's head snapped up. Anger flooded his chest and pressed against his lungs. Esmie, of all people, did not deserve such shabby treatment. But the sharp retort that sprang to Julian's lips halted unspoken. Ten thousand pounds would have been more than enough to realize her dream of a school. What had happened?

"She would have no part of it," Lambton continued. "Foolish chit."

"And she asked to be set down in Oxford." Julian could see the entire exchange in his mind's eye. Proud, stubborn, willful girl. She had more courage than all of them put together. "She chose instead to take employment as a lady's companion."

"Yes." Lambton leaned back and laid his arm along the top of the settee. "It was her choice, and an honorable one, if not very practical."

"And how did Esmie's refusal of your ungentlemanlike offer turn you onto the course of Maria's happiness?" Like witnessing a carriage accident, he found he could not turn away.

" 'Twas not easily done, I assure you, to turn Maria's thoughts from marriage to you. A great deal of crockery was shattered in the process. My favorite brandy snifters as well."

He cleared his throat. "But in my short acquaintance

with Miss Fortune, I have been vividly reminded of what
love does to women. Makes them fools. Turns them
down difficult paths." He paused and rubbed his hands
together. "But it is in a woman's nature to attach herself,
Ashforth, and she won't be satisfied without it. Maria
doesn't love you, though she loves what you possess. It
would not suffice, in the end—all this elegance and
perfection."

"No," Julian agreed as he rubbed his temple. "I have
it on the best authority it would not."

"This will, of course," Lambton said, "complicate matters related to the settlement of your debts. The vouch-
ers I hold against the Abbey must be resolved. I am not
averse to giving you time to scrape together the blunt,
provided this matter does not drag out. Shall we say
a fortnight?"

A fortnight. Julian barked a laugh. "Ten years, sir,
would not suffice for me to arrange the repayment of
the debt."

"Still, they must be satisfied." The implacable businessman had replaced the doting father.

"They shall be satisfied." Julian had thought he would
be the sacrifice, but as with so many things, he had been
too blind to see what must happen. "I will make arrangements to sell the Abbey, for it is unentailed, and it is
mine to dispose of as I wish. I have been approached
any number of times by gentlemen of means. If you will
allow my solicitor time to conduct the transaction, the
debt will be satisfied."

Lambton raised his eyebrows. "You say that so
calmly, my lord. This has been your family seat for
three generations."

Julian smiled, the first genuine smile he'd experienced
since Esmie had left the house. "It has also been my
prison, sir, but you are a benevolent jailer and have
opened the gates."

Mr. Lambton rose to his feet. "You may regret such
a hasty course, my lord. You will have your solicitor
contact mine?"

"Indeed." Sharp and bittersweet, the deed was done.
"Then I bid you good day."

Lambton made his bow and strode from the room.

Julian dropped onto the settee once more. He was free. Esmie was free. Ashforth Abbey and the perfection of the earls of Ashforth were to be thrown to the winds of fate and fortune.

Julian's shoulders were lighter than they had been in years. Like a condemned man given a pardon, he knew relief and bewilderment in equal measure. What was he to do now? And more importantly, where was Esmie Fortune? Would she have him if he groveled sufficiently?

He was Perseus lost in the labyrinth with no Ariadne proffering a thread to help him find his way out. Or maybe he did have an Ariadne after all. With frizzy hair and the most intriguing gray eyes he'd ever seen. She'd dangled the means of his salvation in front of him, only he'd been too stupid to take hold and follow her lead.

Julian ran a hand over his chin, his stomach a mass of insecurities. First he would shave. Then he would ride to Oxford. Soon, he would make the necessary arrangements to pay his debts and rid himself of all ties to the Ashforth perfection. Except for the title. That he could not sell and it would follow him all his life. For now, he would pay a visit to Cortland Manor. An imperfect, imploring visit. And if he were very, very lucky, his plans would culminate with Esmie Fortune stepping into his arms. For now that he no longer bore the burden of perfection, there was room for her there.

"Are you sure, Mr. Bruton, you will not consider serving as a master at Athena Hall? I offer inducements you may not receive at any of the colleges."

The young man barked with laughter, and then grimaced. "Miss Fortune, if I were to accept a position at a school for young ladies, I should end my academic career before it began." He wiped his mouth and placed the napkin on the table. "You are mad to think you may find men of any standing here in Oxford who will serve upon your faculty. Anyone desperate enough to take the position would not be worth the having."

Esmie rolled her eyes. She knew as much already from sitting across the table from a succession of starving young academics who wolfed down bread and sausages at her expense and laughed at her offers.

"I will settle the bill then, and leave you to finish your meal in peace." She stood and hung her reticule over her arm. "Good day, sir."

Mr. Bruton only grunted in acknowledgement as he continued to shovel food into his mouth. Esmie turned away in disgust, glad to escape the tavern's stuffy confines. She had been hopeful that Bruton would accept her offer. He was not the best of scholars, but even one faculty member might turn the tide of rejection she battled. He had been the last candidate.

It had not occurred to her that finding scholars to share her dream would prove more difficult than acquiring the funds to renovate the house. She had posted notices throughout Oxford and had received several replies. But when the young men found they were to teach young ladies, their interest turned entirely to their bread and ale. She needed just one scholar of repute, one man with standing in the academic world to lend her school credence. But where was such a man to be found?

The necessary renovations had begun on her house. She parceled out shillings as if they were golden guineas, but little by little the damp had begun to recede from the vigorous assault of two young housemaids. Stout men from the village had patched the worst bits of the roof. Esmie herself had begun the reclamation of the kitchen garden. But all would be for naught if no masters could be found.

And always, the sad weight of regret caused her step to drag. At night, alone in her chamber, she imagined Julian with his children, happy and involved in one another's lives. She deliberately omitted any thought of Maria Lambton or of boarding schools.

Discouraged, she turned her steps from the center of town and toward the river. The hedgerows and grassy meadows grew so green it almost hurt to look at them. Summer scents drifted over her, and when she reached the river, she paused to watch two young men pole along in their flat-bottomed punt. Perhaps she had been wrong, after all. Perhaps even an abundance of money could not ensure the school she dreamed of. If even the life of the legendary *Corinna* could not be remembered, if her work could not survive beyond the merest fragments, what hope had she, Esmie Fortune, of making a mark on the world? Worst of all, perhaps she had been wrong even to try to follow her dream. For if she'd not dreamed, then she might still be under his roof, might still see him upon occasion. Might torment herself with her feelings for the rest of her life. But she would do that anyway, wouldn't she?

Esmie shuddered. Such thoughts must not be allowed to take root and flourish. Julian had made his choice based upon his position, his breeding, his title. Esmie Fortune had no place in his world, and the sooner she accepted that fact, the better. But as she made for the bridge, she wondered how the right decision could feel so utterly wrong.

The journey to Oxford had never seemed so lengthy. He had meant to depart immediately, but a crisis with the sheep, and then the complaints of a tenant had kept him from springing into the saddle. Finally, though, he had made his escape. Now, Julian turned his horse toward the little bridge that crossed the river near Christ Church Meadow. He paid little heed to the canal boats that maneuvered through the water, as his thoughts dwelt more on the papers in his saddlebags than on his surroundings.

He would soon be free. Frighteningly free. He would have no Abbey to bind him to the Ashforth perfection, but neither would he have a feather to fly with. If she turned him away, then he and his brood would load up what few belongings remained to seek out some modest lodgings in Bath or Tunbridge Wells or wherever penniless aristocrats went to set up housekeeping. At times, the reality stung. No dowries were left for the girls. James's school fees would be a burden, but Julian was determined to send him to Eton. The servants, even his valet, would remain with the Abbey and its new owners. A shiver coursed through him. If Esmie turned him away, if she rejected his proposal, then the consequences would be dire indeed. The thought, though, rather than deepening his distress caused Julian to laugh out loud.

He, the Earl of Ashforth, would be marrying Esmie Fortune for her worldly wealth. Lo, how the mighty had fallen.

The path wound through the meadow just as he remembered from his previous visit. As he approached the house from the rear, he noticed the tumbledown garden wall had been repaired. Several large drays stood nearby, and the sound of hammering drew his attention to the roof, where three men labored.

The workmen paid him little notice as he tethered his horse and found the gate. The kitchen garden had been cleared and signs of new growth abounded. A hissing sound to his right made Julian turn, and there crouched the foul cat Esmie had inflicted on the Abbey. What was his name? Plutarch. Trouble more like it. The sight of the mangy creature sent a pain of regret through Julian. He'd not been anything like a gentleman the night he'd dragged Esmie onto the bed in the Abbey's guest chamber. That night, only some cat dander had stood between himself and his honor as a gentleman. No, he'd not been nearly perfect that night.

Or perhaps he had. Perhaps he had been perfectly himself. The man he'd been longing to be, flaws and all.

The kitchen door stood open, and he entered without pausing to knock. Two young women looked up from their duties. One was up to her elbows in flour. The other stirred a large iron pot over the fire.

"Your mistress? Is she about?"

Both girls, noting his aristocratic manner, bobbed curtsies. "She's above stairs, sir. With the children."

"The children?" Surely Esmie could not have found pupils so quickly.

He turned and found his way to the main part of the house. The oaken banister of the staircase had been polished until it shone. Gone were the patches of damp and mold from the walls, and the floor was neatly swept and polished. Esmie and the maids had been hard at work.

Voices drifted down the stairs, and so he followed them. Ariadne's thread, indeed. He could hear Esmie, but could not make out the words. He reached the top of the stairs and made his way down the corridor.

The closed door was no impediment. Without knock-

ing, he opened it. He stopped in the doorway, frozen by
the sight that greeted him.

Esmie sat propped against the headboard of the massive bed with a book open in her hands. Around her, a
tumble of children clustered like grapes on a vine. Not
just any children. *His* children, who had told him they
meant to closet themselves in the nursery and attend to
their lessons today. No doubt they had wheedled horses
for the carriage from his bailiff for this clandestine visit.

"Papa!" Caroline clambered from the bed and ran to
him. He scooped her up in his arms, thankful for the
feel of her and her willingness to forgive him all the
years of inattention.

"This is a surprise, my lord." Esmie flushed. The children looked sheepish, but not terrified. That fact alone
made him disinclined to scold.

The sight of Esmie on the bed caused his resolve to
falter, his will to fail. She had no need of him. All her
dreams were coming true while his life had fallen into
the dustbin. She could rub along perfectly well without
him. The only thing he had to offer her was his children.
Would she think they were worth the price of taking
him on as a husband?

"I came for the children," he lied as his resolve wavered. If she rejected him, not only would he be without
any claim to perfection, he would be without any claim
to pride.

"We're going to have a picnic by the river when Miss
Esmie finishes reading the story," Phoebe pleaded. No
doubt the children had failed to inform Esmie they had
come without his permission.

Julian could not suppress the envy that rose within
him. He wanted to share that space with Esmie in the
midst of the big bed, with the children gathered around
them like bees around honey. But such a treasure would
not be gained without risk. How strange. He'd once
thought the Abbey the one thing he could not afford
to lose.

Gathering his courage, he addressed his next remark
to Esmie. "Perhaps I might join you, then? A fine day
such as this deserves a picnic."

Esmie scrambled from the bed, her face still red. "If

you wish, my lord, though 'twill not be anything like what you are accustomed to."

No, but he imagined it constituted far more than he would soon be used to eating. "I am sure it will be perfect."

She flinched at the word, and Julian swore under his breath. He had no chance to offer an apology, however. The children were transported with delight at the thought of having their father and Esmie to themselves. Not more than a quarter hour passed before the entire band was traipsing toward the river. James and Julian were both weighed down with baskets, and Esmie and Sophie carried a blanket apiece.

They made short work of the food, and soon the children had busied themselves constructing boats from leaves and twigs to race in the river. Julian cautioned them, but otherwise left them to their own devices. Esmie busied herself repacking the hampers and avoiding his gaze.

The time could not have been more perfect, but he found himself unable to broach the subject he most wished to address. They sat on the same blanket and watched the children, calling occasional encouragements, but between the two of them, only strained silence and forced smiles existed.

"You are happy, then?" His tentative question hung in the warm summer air. "You have what you wanted?"

He expected an immediate, affirmative answer, but Esmie shrugged her shoulders instead. "Happiness is a tricky business, my lord. No, I shouldn't say I've achieved that state quite yet."

"The house is much improved." He was so obviously fishing, he might as well have equipped himself with a rod and tackle.

"Hmm."

Her spine was as straight as he'd ever seen it, which meant she was not as complacent as her noncommittal responses implied.

"You've hired masters, I'm sure, and the other staff necessary."

The silence grew so lengthy he thought perhaps she'd not heard him. A fine tremor went through her, and her spine curved. She looked away to where the children played on the bank.

"Esmie?" Her name tasted so sweet upon his lips.

When she turned back to him, tears glistened in her eyes. "It seems that no man cares to sully himself by associating with a school for young ladies. I have fed half the starving scholars of Oxford, but none are desperate enough to take my bread more than once."

Julian's heart tightened at her words. She had accomplished so much, clung so tenaciously to her dream, and now it would be denied by prejudices far beyond her control.

"Not even one hungry scholar would condescend?"

Her silence answered his question.

"So, you have openings to fill, then?"

More silence.

"Then I should like to apply, Miss Fortune."

Her head whipped around. "Your jest is poorly timed, my lord."

Julian swallowed and steeled himself. The moment for revelation had come. "I do not jest, Esmie. I am seeking employment."

Hot color flooded her cheeks, and her eyes snapped with fire in the manner he'd come to adore. "Have you not tormented me enough? I have paid for my presumption in loving you five times over. You've treated me abominably and still I cannot order you from my home." She climbed to her knees, and then stood on shaky legs. "I have made a perfect fool of myself over you, and who in Oxfordshire does not know it? So you may cease with your jokes. You have humiliated me completely. No, I have humiliated myself completely. What more is there to accomplish?" She wiped the tears from her cheeks with the back of her hand, and Julian scrambled to his feet. She backed away, but he followed.

"Fool? I am the fool, Esmie. For I have had the greatest treasure a man could possess under my very nose, but have been too blind to see it."

She inhaled sharply and her face turned ashen. "You will persist, then, in mocking me?"

"No, madam." He put his hands on her shoulders and used all his force of will not to crush her against him.

"I would never mock you, but you may mock me all you choose." On instinct, he let go of her shoulders and reached for her hands. He dropped to one knee in the grass, and Esmie gasped.

"I have nothing to offer, madam, except a brood of unruly children, a rather good library of classical works, and my highly imperfect self, but I will make this offer nonetheless."

Out of the corner of his eye, he saw the children had stopped their play and were fascinated by the sight of him down on one knee. Fine, let them watch. Perhaps it would influence her answer.

"Esmie Fortune, will you be my wife?"

He didn't see the blow coming, and when her hand connected with his cheek, his head snapped back. She had a strong arm, and the force of the blow knocked him from his precarious position. He tumbled to the grass amid a chorus of protest from the children.

"Miss Esmie! Stop!"

Phoebe loomed over him, and then small, dirty hands helped to right him and bring him to his feet. James glared at Esmie, but Julian laid a hand on his shoulder. "I deserved that, son. That and much more."

Esmie stood with one hand over her mouth, aghast at what she'd done. He moved toward her again, this time more cautiously.

"Is that to be your answer, then?"

By Jove, he was a glutton for punishment.

"I fail to see the humor, my lord, in such a mockery of a proposal. What of Miss Lambton?"

"She has jilted me, much to my great relief."

"Jilted you? I don't believe it."

"Yes, well, when Lambton realized he could have the Abbey without sacrificing his daughter to me, he chose the more prudent course."

"Have the Abbey?"

"Debts, my dear. Perfection has been quite an expensive endeavor."

"Are you saying you are poor?" Disbelief sharpened her features.

"As a church mouse. I'm afraid the offer I make you is rather a meager one. I have no fortune, no home. My only asset is my heart, Esmie, but if you will have it, it is yours."

"Well?" James stood with his hands on his hips. "What say you, Miss Esmie? Will you have him?"

Julian swallowed a small laugh at the myriad of expressions that flashed across her face. Surprise, incredulity, disbelief. But then the one he hoped for appeared. A shy smile traced her lips and spread its light to her eyes.

"It is a most imperfect offer, my lord."

"Indeed." He took the liberty of reclaiming her hands. "I am a bad bargain, Esmie Fortune, but to my credit, I am a scholar of some note and will lend credence to your school."

She had not looked up at him yet. "Your children are a great inducement as well, my lord."

He was surprised by how that statement wounded his pride. Esmie might indeed agree to marry him so she could be mother to his children. But it would not be enough. Nothing less than her heart would be enough, for she held his in her keeping.

Her chin rose and her gaze met his. "All the scholarship and all the *Corinna*s and all the perfection in the world could not induce me to marry where I did not love."

Her words alone could have ripped his heart from his chest. But the look in her eyes gave him hope.

"What say you, then, Esmie Fortune? Will you have a poor scholar with five unruly children for your husband?"

She smiled, and he wondered he'd ever thought her anything but beautiful. "No, my lord. But I will have my perfect earl, if he will have me."

Now Julian reached for her and crushed her against him. His lips found hers, and he kissed her with all the longing he'd suppressed, all the regret he'd endured. The children danced around them with gleeful shouts. All would be well. He believed it with all his heart, until he heard a loud splash.

"Papa!"

Caroline's head bobbed up and down in the river. "Help!" she shrieked, and Julian sighed.

"Caroline, 'tis not necessary. Miss Fortune has said

yes." He waited for his youngest daughter to turn on her stomach and swim for the bank.

"Yes, Caroline, do come out," Esmie called.

The child, though, thrashed about in the water. Julian's heart went still. Dear God. . . .

Before he knew what was happening, he had launched himself into the river. The splash next to him told him that Esmie had followed. It took only a moment to reach Caroline. She grasped at him, clawing his face in the process, and choking on water. Julian turned her in his arms, and then Esmie was there. She grasped the girl's hands as they all three struggled toward the reeds at the water's edge.

"Are you sure, Esmie?" He sputtered the words as he shoved his daughter onto the bank. "We're a bad bargain."

Esmie laughed. "I will not change my mind, my lord." She wiped a wet strand of hair from her cheek. "Because the lot of you are perfect for me."

Chapter Twenty-One

*B*y the time the banns had been read three weeks later, the Abbey was ready to transfer into the buyer's hands. Julian would not allow Esmie to help with the chore of readying the Abbey for its new occupants, though he did permit a brief visit to select the few pieces of furniture to be conveyed to Athena Hall. Between the two of them, they had scraped together enough beds, tables, and chairs to furnish the ramshackle house.

She had been permitted to help the children pack their trunks, and had dried their tears, for the nursery was the only home they'd known. Finally, Julian had asked her to assist him in packing his library for the move. It was the one thing of value he'd salvaged. Soon, the library at Athena Hall would have one of the finest collections of classical works in England.

The wedding had been planned for the parish church near their new home, and the kindly vicar had expressed great pleasure in performing the office. Julian seemed almost relieved at the loss of his fortune, and smiled more than Esmie had ever seen him smile. But something was still amiss. She was happy, the children were delighted, Julian was loving and attentive. Yet Esmie could not be easy within herself.

Truth be told, she dreaded her wedding night.

The worry had started innocently enough, sparked by some veiled comments made by Mrs. Robbins. Her own insecurities had seized the opportunity to grow a great crop of doubt, and the harvest disquieted her indeed.

Julian said he loved her. She believed it to be true.

On an intellectual plane, she might meet him as an equal. But once the bedroom door shut behind them. . . .

Esmie carried her dread through the wedding preparations and indeed through the ceremony itself. Julian had refused to make of their nuptials anything grander than a private party. The children served as attendants on the hot August morning, and the vicar's wife signed the register as witness.

The wedding feast at Athena Hall proved simple but joyful. But as evening drew near, Esmie's anxiety increased. Anxiety turned to dread and dread turned to stark terror when they completed supper and Julian led her upstairs. The old nurse had come to Athena Hall with them—one of the few retainers in the household—and she shooed the children to their rooms.

Esmie jumped when the door shut behind them, leaving her alone with Julian in the twilight. He lit a candle beside the bed, though the summer sun lingered far into the evening.

"Esmie." He said her name softly, but his gentleness did nothing to ease her fears. "Esmie, look at me."

She turned toward him, and would have given anything to transform her thin face, wispy hair, and bony figure into a wedding-night bride fit for the man she loved.

A frown marred Julian's face, his forehead lined with concern. "You are frightened?"

"Yes." Her whispered assent was the truth, but not in the manner he thought. Intimacy with her husband did not scare her. No, unknown and mysterious as that might be, what truly scared her was that her husband might find her lacking. She did not want only a marriage of the minds. She wanted one of the body as well. For even as imperfect a body as hers cried out for love, for admiration, for recognition of its value.

"Turn around," Julian instructed, and she did as bidden, presenting him with her back. Far better to do so than to continue to watch his face for signs of distaste.

His fingers unhooked her gown, and the material slid from her shoulders. She vibrated with awareness. He mistook her tremors and wrapped his arms around her, pressing her spine to his chest.

"Are you cold?"

"No." She couldn't form words, not when her mind was fixed on the feel of his body against hers.

"You needn't fear me, Esmie. I will do nothing without your consent."

"I know." Where was her wit now? Had marriage sapped her once formidable intellect? She swallowed. "I'm not afraid of you, Julian."

"Then what is it?" He turned her in his arms and one hand tilted her chin up so she looked into his eyes.

"I am so . . ." She couldn't tell him, couldn't invite his pity. She'd rather he turn away from her in disgust than pity her.

"You are what?" His mouth turned up at one corner. The glint of amusement in his eyes disquieted her. Did he not appreciate the gravity of the business?

"I am so imperfect," she bit out. Her spine straightened, and she drew back her shoulders. Indignation pushed back the fear. "Is it not obvious? No, don't humor me." She raised a hand to stop him from speaking. "I am keenly aware of my inadequacies, my lord. My mother has cataloged them for me all my life. Just remember . . ." She paused to jab his breastbone with her forefinger. "Remember you chose this alliance freely, and however disappointed you may be in my . . . my physical form, I shall not tolerate any deviation from our marriage vows."

"Deviation from our marriage vows?" Julian's eyebrow arched with incredulity. "By the gods, Esmie, we've not even had a wedding night yet and you accuse me of looking elsewhere for pleasure?" He frowned down at her, suddenly quite intimidating. "Do not forget, my dear, I have extensive experience with the unfaithfulness of a spouse. Do you truly think I would subject you to such humiliation?"

Esmie suddenly felt very small. "No. Of course not."

"Do you think I am still so shallow that I would turn away from you at the first sign of imperfection?"

Esmie swallowed past the lump in her throat. "No," she answered meekly.

His hands gripped her shoulders, much as they had when he'd proposed by the river. "I would think I have much more to worry about from you, Lady Ashforth, than you do from me. You were the last one to enter into an engagement with someone else."

"Only after you did!" Esmie shot back, but then she saw by his self-satisfied smile he'd intended to set her back up.

"Much better."

Before she could say anything else, he bent toward her, taking her lips with his. She sputtered a brief protest, but the movement of his mouth decimated any further objections. Esmie melted against him.

"I'm not perfect, Esmie," he whispered against her cheek as his hands roamed her body, trailing delight in their wake. "Yet you love me. Do you not?"

She answered by pressing her lips against his, seeking more of that vital contact. "Yes, Julian." Her words barely escaped from between their lips. "I love you."

He drew back, and the loss of his mouth against hers pained her. "You love me," he whispered as he threaded his fingers in her hair and massaged her scalp. "If I have any claim to perfection, Esmie, it is because of your love." He scooped her off her feet and deposited her on the bed.

"This time," he went on, as he covered her body with his own, "there will be no cat and no children. This time, you will be mine and mine alone."

"Yes, my lord." Meekness seemed an attractive alternative for once.

"Alone, we are a disaster." Julian's hands caressed her until she thought she might shatter. "But together . . . Ah, Esmie. Together, my dear, we are perfection itself."

"Caroline! Come down!" James hissed, as he hung out the window and looked up toward the roof. Caroline sat comfortably in the twilight on a bundle of slate the laborers had left for the next day's work.

"No. Not until you apologize."

"I'm sorry, then. Please, come back inside."

"I want Miss Esmie. I mean . . . Mama. I want Mama."

"I told you, they're on their honeymoon. You shall see her in the morning."

Caroline crossed her arms, and her heels beat a tattoo against the tiles. "I shan't come inside. Not until I see my new mama."

Sophie appeared beside James at the window. "Won't she come inside?"

James threw up his hands in disgust and slipped back into the room. "She can kill herself, for all I care. I'm sick to death of retrieving her from roofs and rivers."

"James." Sophie's dark eyes flashed disapproval. She reached down to scoop up the cat that wound itself around her legs. "Here, offer her Plutarch. If he cannot lure her inside, nothing can."

James heaved a great sigh and took the cat, sticking his head out the window once more. "Caroline! Plutarch is waiting for you."

The lure of the forbidden gave his sister pause. She twirled a blond curl, bit her lip, and then let out a huge sigh. "Very well. I shouldn't trust the lot of you to care for him properly."

James swallowed an indignant protest. Girls. A great lot of trouble, and not worth half the bother.

Caroline climbed down from the pile of slate and moved with catlike grace of her own across the roof. James wouldn't let her take Plutarch until she scrambled over the sill and was safely in the room. He closed the window with a firm hand. He would speak with his father first thing at breakfast about more secure latches for the windows. He refused to spend the next decade luring his sister down from the roof.

When he turned back toward the room, he was struck by the picture his brothers and sisters presented. Sophie had curled up in a chair with a book. Phoebe and Phillip had fashioned paper pirate hats, made swords from sticks, and were engaged in a duel for control of the Aegean. Caroline teased Plutarch with a small felt bag filled with catnip.

James sighed. He would miss them when he left for Eton within the month. He'd first refused when his father had informed him of his acceptance, for he knew the financial implications of the loss of Ashforth Abbey. But his father had been firm, and Esmie had reassured him they could very well afford to send him to school,

since the girls would be educated at Athena Hall. He'd
reluctantly agreed, even as he'd been secretly relieved.
For all James wanted, really, was to be like his father,
the most perfect man in the world. It was a great deal
to live up to, to be sure, but now that the Abbey was
no longer part of the legacy of the earls of Ashforth, he
thought he might manage it. As a scholar, he was quite
sure of his abilities. As a gentleman, though . . . Well,
he had his father now to teach him what he needed to
know. James would always thank Esmie for that. And
perhaps the younger ones would not remember, as he
always would, how very gray life had been before Miss
Esmerelda Fortune came to Ashforth Abbey.

"Come on. Bedtime." His brother and sisters groaned
at the reminder, but for once they proved biddable. Sophie laid aside her book, and with a soft *good night,*
ushered Phoebe and Caroline toward the room the
three shared.

Phillip shoved the swords and pirate hats beneath his
bed and climbed between the sheets. James reached to
extinguish the candle, but stopped when his brother
spoke.

"We were right about the cakes and sweets, weren't
we, James? And the new bonnets. Is this a happy ending,
then? Like the ones in the books?"

James blew out the candle and settled back against
the pillows, drawing the coverlet up to his chin.

"Yes, Phillip. Yes, I believe it is. A very happy ending, indeed."